Praise for Gwendolyn Zepeda's Novels

Lone Star Legend

"In her fresh and smart second novel, Zepeda explores how share-everything online culture affects real-life relationships. Readers will relate to Sandy's quest to achieve professional success without sacrificing herself."   —*Booklist*

"Zepeda gives readers a funny and smart heroine that [they] will easily pull for."   —*Publishers Weekly*

"A book filled with rich descriptions of action, emotions, and people—all combined with her storytelling to give a really good page-turner read."   —Examiner.com

"A timely tale...an interesting look at modern media with a Latin spin."   —*RT Book Reviews*

Houston, We Have a Problema

"Zepeda...presents a debut about the everyday struggle to find one's way but adds unusual and alluring touches, namely the vibrant Houston setting and the novel's emphasis on Tex-Mex culture, art, and folklore."   —*Booklist*

"Jessica's evolution from self-uncertainty to self-empowerment is amusingly charted, and Zepeda's take on the popular fascination with good luck charms, horoscopes, psychics, and unreliable predictions is laced with rueful zeal."

—*Publishers Weekly*

"Reading Gwen's book was like going to a family BBQ—full of drama, juicy gossip, and lots of laughs."

—Mary Castillo, author of *Switchcraft*

"An entertaining lighthearted Latina chick-lit romp focusing on the metamorphosis of a young woman...Fans will enjoy this fascinating coming-of-age tale."

—*Midwest Book Review*

"The premise is quite cute and flows nicely, casually integrating Latin culture into the fold. Madame Hortensia, the entrepreneurial psychic, is a great comedic stand-out character."

—*RT Book Reviews*

"Zepeda is great at both voice and dialogue; the dialogue is clever and powers the story forward."

—SadieMagazine.com

"[A] funny and heartwarming tale that follows the life of Jessica Luna through love, tears, and plenty of laughs."

—BookPleasures.com

Better With You Here

Also by Gwendolyn Zepeda

Better With You Here

GWENDOLYN ZEPEDA

FREE PUBLIC LIBRARY, SUMMIT, N.J.

GRAND CENTRAL
PUBLISHING

NEW YORK   BOSTON

This book is a work of fiction. Names, characters, places, and incidents are the product of the author's imagination or are used fictitiously. Any resemblance to actual events, locales, or persons, living or dead, is coincidental.

Copyright © 2012 by Gwendolyn Zepeda

All rights reserved. In accordance with the U.S. Copyright Act of 1976, the scanning, uploading, and electronic sharing of any part of this book without the permission of the publisher is unlawful piracy and theft of the author's intellectual property. If you would like to use material from the book (other than for review purposes), prior written permission must be obtained by contacting the publisher at permissions@hbgusa.com. Thank you for your support of the author's rights.

Grand Central Publishing
Hachette Book Group
237 Park Avenue
New York, NY 10017
www.HachetteBookGroup.com

Printed in the United States of America

RRD-C

First Edition: July 2012
10 9 8 7 6 5 4 3 2 1

Grand Central Publishing is a division of Hachette Book Group, Inc.
The Grand Central Publishing name and logo is a trademark of Hachette Book Group, Inc.

The Hachette Speakers Bureau provides a wide range of authors for speaking events. To find out more, go to www.hachettespeakersbureau.com or call (866) 376-6591.

The publisher is not responsible for websites (or their content) that are not owned by the publisher.

Library of Congress Cataloging-in-Publication Data
Zepeda, Gwendolyn.
 Better with you here / Gwendolyn Zepeda. — 1st ed.
    p. cm.
 ISBN 978-0-446-56403-8
1. Divorced mothers—Fiction. 2. Children of divorced parents—Fiction. 3. Custody of children—Fiction. I. Title.
 PS3626.E46B48 2012
 813'.6—dc23

                              2011035213

3 9547 00371 8462

For Dat, with love and gratitude

Natasha

MISSY MAKES US *real* cupcakes."

This is what my own son says to me, at 7:05 in the morning—five minutes before we have to get out the door—referring to his father's new girlfriend as he glares at the whole-grain minimuffin I just served him.

I'm standing at our too-shallow kitchen sink, rubbing a bloodstain with dish soap. The stain is on the yellow LYNX SPIRIT! T-shirt that my daughter just told me all kindergartners were required to wear to school today. It's fresh from the pile of clothing in the corner of the bedroom that she shares with her brother. That corner smells like mildew. So before I could even start working on her T-shirt, I had to find the source of the smell. It turned out to be a pair of slightly damp Spider-Man underwear, and now I know that Alex sneaked a soda last night before bed. But his sheets aren't wet, thank God. Regardless, we're running late now, and I'm scrubbing as fast as I can, because Lucia's front tooth finally fell out, just ten minutes ago, and of course her first instinct was to wipe the gum hole with her freshly Febrezed T-shirt and get blood right smack in the middle of it.

Fifty percent of my job as a mother is cleaning up bodily fluids. That's what it feels like. And then the other fifty percent is worrying.

Lucia's waiting in her camisole, sitting with her brother in the breakfast nook—or the breakfast square yard, as I like to think of it—at the table I put together with an Allen wrench a month ago, which barely seats the three of us. She's picking at her own whole-grain minimuffin, which is not, as Alex has noted, a real cupcake. She's looking back and forth between her brother and me, watching to find out who's going to win the fight and which way, therefore, her loyalties should lie.

I pause midscrub to regard my son, Alex. Or Venom, which is the only name he'll answer to this morning, since he's wearing his Venom mask. Venom, the black Spider-Man. The first time Alex explained it to me, I thought he meant African-American. Maybe my son's comic books were finally getting a little diversity, I thought. But no, Venom is actually black—Spidey's literal dark side, the result of one of those scientific accidents he has a habit of getting into. This one was so bad it affected not only his personality but the color of his costume fabric, too. Serious stuff.

Never mind that this mask was a gift from me, Alex's loving mother, for his birthday three weeks ago. Never mind that I'd spent two lunch hours trudging down Jefferson, looking into all those flea-markety little shops in search of something I could afford that was still cool enough for my beloved child.

I'd gone looking specifically for a luchador mask—the headgear of a Mexican wrestler. Not because I wanted to honor our Hispanic heritage or anything noble like that, but because Alex was temporarily obsessed with a Saturday-morning cartoon about luchadores. I searched the faces of skeletons, dudes made of gold, and what looked like robotic roosters, but none of them were good enough for my boy. Then I found him: Venom. Or at least the Coahuila knockoff version of him. The Mexican black Spider-Man, you could say. The perfect gift.

Alex loved the mask more than the Venom comics and action figure I'd also bought him. More than the cake and the ice cream. Not to be catty, but he liked it way more than the single present his father bought him—a video game for the wrong gaming system, featuring the wrong Spider-Man.

So now I find it a little ironic that Alex uses my gift to explore his own dark side and then aims the results at me. Missy makes them real cupcakes, he says.

If this kid is trying to hurt me, he's going to have to try harder.

If he'd said, "Missy has way less cellulite than you, even though you're the same age," it might have stung a *little*.

If he'd said, "Missy has a happier, healthier relationship with Dad than you did, even though at first she seemed like a rebound," it might have broken my skin. But my son, with stubbornness and smart-assery that are strangely familiar, isn't trying to sting or scratch. No, he's going in for the kill.

He says, "I want to go live with Missy and Daddy. I'm tired of living with you." Then, to make sure I'm listening, he picks up his minimuffin and throws it at the wall.

Lucia immediately commits a copycat crime, pushing her own muffin off its plate so that it rolls in slow motion to the floor. Then she lets out a quiet noise, a cross between wicked glee and immediate regret.

I look Alex right in the face. Right in the eyeholes, so I can make sure he's not crying and hasn't lost his mind. No—his eyes are blazing. He's glaring at me, *daring* me to lose it. And right now I think I might.

Right now I see his father in those eyes, and I feel like hitting him. Like maybe I can slap Alex hard enough to make Mike feel it, right through their shared DNA.

But instead I smile. "Well, sweetie, I'm sorry to hear you say that. Sometimes I wish I could stay home from work and make you cupcakes every day."

His eyes are locked on mine. He's listening.

"And sometimes I wish *you* could stay home from school and make *me* cupcakes. But, unfortunately, we all have to do things we don't like, or else our lives would fall apart. Right? Like, right now I have to go to work so I can buy you healthy food, even though I know you're going to complain about it. But I have to do it, because I love you and I don't want you to get fat and have all your teeth fall out. You know what I mean?" He looks down. I wait for him to look back up at me. "And right now you have to clean up the mess you made and then go to school."

He climbs out of his chair and picks up the muffin. I can see that he's a little embarrassed, but also still angry with me. And that's just the way it has to be for now.

Lucia sniffles and picks up her own muffin without being asked. Poor kid—a rebel without a cause, nipped in the bud.

For the rest of the hour, we move like soldiers, swift and silent. I wring and blow-dry the lynx shirt and pull it over my daughter's head, then quickly repair her ponytail. The kids put on their shoes and the sweaters they don't want to wear, the ones they won't appreciate until they get out to the bus stop and feel that, hello, it's October. Then we shoulder backpacks and purse and march out of the too-small apartment, past the broken elevator, down the nappy carpeted hallway, out the complex's front doors, through the rocky parking lot and chipped front gate. As we wait on the sidewalk with the other kids, I hum and chat to Lucia until the bus materializes at the corner. Alex stays quiet but lets me squeeze his arm good-bye.

And then they're gone. Not for long, but long enough to worry about, no matter how many times they go and come back again. Because half my job as a mother, I swear, is being worried. At least fifty percent of my life is mentally preparing for every single thing that might possibly happen when I'm not there to protect them.

I take a step back and draw a deep breath. Something's poking me. Jabbing me in the chest, it feels like.

I feel it now, that thing my son said. And it hurts like hell after all.

Natasha

CHICK-N-BIX is always the same, no matter what neighborhood you live in. The one I used to take the kids to, on the northern edge of Dallas, had a kids' area filled by a two-story maze of red and yellow tunnels and slides and ball pits, which were all undoubtedly filled with bacteria. And so does the one here, adjacent to Oak Cliff, on the opposite side of town. The Chick-N-Bix up north, in the cute new suburb where we used to live, was filled with bored moms eating their kids' leftover chicken biscuits and watching them navigate the germy tunnels. And so here we are, myself and my friend and former neighbor Kate, eating and watching in the very same way we used to, in this completely different neighborhood where I now have an apartment.

"Zach," she says. "Zach! Zach. Zach!" Every time she says his name, Kate pops out of her red plastic seat, as if to run and save him from a fall, then slowly sits back down. With her yoga pants and stretchy T-shirt, it looks like she's doing squats. Maybe that's how she stays so thin. And the yoga pants must help. They fit tight around her butt, like a string around her finger, reminding her that she's not supposed to eat more than two of the waffle fries. Meanwhile I've eaten all of mine and half of Lucia's. I can't resist waffle fries, and that's why I wear really loose-fitting jeans.

Kate's son scrambles through the lowest levels of the maze, rolling and tumbling along, never losing his determination to keep up with Alex and Lucia. And I remember when Alex was that young, so very long ago, when I still had only him to worry about and I lived in fear of everything. At least I lived in fear of totally different things than I do now.

"Do his legs look a little bowed to you?" Kate asks me.

"I don't think it's worth trying to judge until he's totally out of training pants," I say.

"Was Lucia that clumsy when she was three?" Kate asks me.

I say, "I don't think she could do the slide as well as Zach's doing now until she was four." It's a lie. Honestly, I don't even remember how old Lucia was when she first success-fully made it through the Chick-N-Bix playroom, because I'm now experienced enough to know that it doesn't matter. My kids are healthy, thankfully, and now I understand that all those little charts and records I used to keep about their first steps and first teeth were nothing but exercises in OCD.

But I don't mind slandering my own child if it'll get Kate to calm down. And it does. She finally stops calling her son's name and turns back to our conversation. "So," she says, "Terry thinks therapy's a waste of time, and Joe's still sleeping on the couch."

"What is she going to do?" I say. This story is very interest-ing to me, because if Joe and Terry get divorced, Mike and I will no longer be the only divorced couple in the neighbor-hood gang. Not that I'd wish divorce on anybody for such a petty reason. But I'm interested.

"She doesn't know. They're going to try a different thera-pist, I guess," says Kate. "They didn't even talk to anybody at the block party. They were too busy arguing."

The block party. God. I don't want to ask, but here it comes out of my mouth before I can stop myself. "Was he there?"

"Yes." Kate knows who I mean—Mike—without having to ask. She's a good friend, not just because she still drives way over here to hang out with me but because she gives up the gossip on my ex-husband without judging me for asking. "He was there, and he brought her with him. She was way over-dressed. We were all like, 'Why is she even here?' I mean, it's one thing for Mike to show, so he can see all the guys at the same time. But she should've stayed home."

This is gratifying. I'm not going to ask for any more. I'll just use my imagination. I'm good at that. Despite the fact that I'm in the middle of a fast-food restaurant, surrounded by children's screeches and the smell of their shoes, I can clearly imagine Mike and Missy at the block party in our old neigh-borhood. Missy is wearing one of her ridiculously low-cut, flowered sundresses and high-heeled sandals, even though it's October. And too much makeup, of course. The guys are ogling her on the sly, except for Rick, who's openly staring, which pisses off Tammy and causes her to open another bot-tle of beer. And Tammy and the other women are ignoring Missy. They're saying, "God, I wish Natasha was here. I miss her. Mike's an idiot for letting her go." They add, "Mike ruined everything. Now there's no one to make good potato salad, and our block parties suck."

Unless Missy brought potato salad. That bitch—she better not have. I should ask Kate. No, don't ask. Don't say anything else about them.

I take a sip of my diet soda. "How's Shannon doing?" I say, cool as a freaking cucumber.

"Good," says Kate. "Can you believe she's due next month already? I need to hurry up and get her—" She stops talking. She looks away. Under her green eyes, her cheeks turn pink.

"Get her what?" I say.

Lucia lets out a particularly loud shriek then. Her shrieks are very distinctive. I stand and pinpoint her location in the maze. She's at the top right corner, and the reason for her scream was that her foot got caught in the rope ladder. The fastest way for me to get to her is to climb up these stairs and then stand on this plaster clown's head. I take the first step. But now Alex has pulled her foot from the hole and she's laughing again and moving forward, out of my sight. I sit back down. Kate looks stricken.

"They're fine," I say. "Zach's right there in the ball pit, next to the girl in pink."

"No," she says. "It's not that. Natasha, I feel terrible, but..."

"What?" I say. What is it? Missy made the potato salad, didn't she? And it was better than mine, and no one missed me at all.

"Shannon's baby shower is next week," she says.

"It is?" I don't remember getting the invitation. "Did she do those stupid e-mail invitations? Those always go straight to my junk mail."

"No. Natasha, this is so lame, and I'm so sorry to be the one telling you, but she didn't invite you. She had to invite Mike instead."

"What?"

"I know. It's so stupid. I'm sorry. But she and Rajeem wanted a coed shower, with the guys playing poker in the garage, and Rajeem really wanted Mike to be there. So..."

Now I'm the one turning red, most likely. I feel as if someone slapped my face. Neither of us says anything for a moment, and suddenly I'm eating those stupid waffle fries left on Lucia's plate. Just pushing them into my mouth, one after another, the way my mother would chain-smoke unfiltereds.

I don't want to ask, but I can't stop myself. "Is she invited?"

Kate shakes her head. "I don't think so. I mean, I don't know. Probably not personally. It probably just says 'Mike Davila and guest' or something. Right?"

"Right. That would be the polite way to do it." Which is a stupid thing to say, but so is her question. How could I know what the invitation would say? How could I know what these people would do, if they would treat me like this? When they're my friends and neighbors? Used to be my neighbors. Supposed to be my friends.

Zach is crying now, in such a way that Kate really does have to run and get him.

I never cry. I haven't cried in almost a year, and I'm not about to start again now.

Kate comes back with Zach in her arms, his thumb in his mouth. She arranges him on her lap and brings up a new topic of conversion. "Listen. Natasha. Forget all that. What about what we were talking about the other day? My friend? My friend Valerie's friend?"

She means some divorced guy she's trying to hook me up with. "What about him?" I say, more tersely than I mean to.

"Well, has he called you?" She won't make eye contact with me anymore. She feels complicit in the baby-shower conspiracy, simply by virtue of being one of the invited. Who knows? Maybe she feels guilty for being happily married, too.

How long before Terry and Joe give it up and become the second failed marriage in our group? How long before the others are forced to start choosing between them? If Terry keeps the house, she'll be the one at the block parties and the baby showers. But if she and Joe both leave the neighborhood, the way Mike and I had to do because we were only renting, she'll probably have to move to a cheaper place, like an apartment. She won't be a neighbor anymore. And all the remaining husbands might decide that Joe plays pool too well to be kicked off the guest list.

I'm not mad at Kate for being part of this group that's forgotten about me. It's been a year since the divorce, and she's the only one who comes to hang out with me, on these occasional weeknights when her husband's working late.

I'm not mad at the other women either. Most of them have kids starting kindergarten or day care this year. They don't have time to drive over here to visit someone who used to live in their neighborhood.

I'm not even mad at Shannon for not inviting me to her shower. Mike's been friends with her husband since high school, and eleven years of living with Mike taught me that his friends are the core of that social group. Girlfriends come and go. Apparently wives do, too, now. I don't blame Shannon for doing what she has to do in order to keep the peace. I wouldn't have invited me either, if I were her.

I'm not upset at all. And I'm not going to cry. Not here or now at least.

"Natasha. Did he?" says Kate.

"What's that?"

"My friend Valerie's friend Hector. Did he call you?"

"Oh," I say. "Yeah. He asked me to lunch. We're supposed to go tomorrow."

Her face lights up, and now she can look at me again.

"Really? Well, that's exciting, isn't it? Do you know what you're going to wear?"

"I don't know." I want to go home now. I'm suddenly exhausted. "Actually, I'm probably going to cancel on him."

"What? *Why?*" she says, sounding like a teenager, despite the toddler in her arms.

"I don't know," I say again. "Maybe I'm not ready for dating yet."

She says, "What? Don't say that." She shakes her head, but not very enthusiastically.

Inspired by Zach's example, Lucia exits the maze and runs to me, holds out her arms, and makes noises like a baby. I wouldn't normally carry her, because she's too old for that now. But I relent, just this once. I lift her onto my hip and call Alex to my side. I say good-bye to my friend.

"See you soon," I tell her as we gather our children's paraphernalia. Even though I know that "soon" probably isn't the most accurate word.

Natasha

My MOTHER IS so unreliable.

"Why didn't you tell me before?" she whines into the phone at me. "You never give me any notice."

I'm sitting at my desk, trying to look like I'm having a work-related conversation and not an annoying personal one. "I told you two weeks ago," I say. Two weeks and one day ago, I asked her to baby-sit the kids for Parent-Teacher Conference Night. She said she would, and now she's forgotten. She's made other plans. "Can't you go to AA another night?" I say.

"Natasha. You know they only have it once a month. If I miss this one, I can't go until November. And then what about Thanksgiving?"

Because I'm at work, I'm not going to get into it with her. If I were having this conversation at home, at night, but someplace where the kids couldn't hear me either—locked in the bathroom, say—then I'd remind my mother that she'd missed the AA meeting in September and also the one in August. I'd inform her that simply from the sound of her voice I can tell she's halfway through her second glass of white zin. I'd tell her that admitting you have the problem doesn't count as the first step if you never intend to take another step. Then I'd conclude by pointing out that she doesn't need the whole month of November to plan a burned turkey and a box of cornbread dressing.

Instead I say, "So you're not going to baby-sit for me?"

She says, "If you'd told me a week ago, I would have. But this Thursday? I just can't." And now I can't go to Parent-Teacher Conference Night.

She's still talking. "See, Natasha, this is what I've been trying to tell you. This thing with you divorcing Mike—you should've thought about how it would end up. You're making it hard on all of us. Ever since you left him, I've been—"

"Mom, I have to go. Good-bye."

The rule is, don't get emotional on the phone at work. That's why I hang up on my mother when her voice sounds like cheap white wine. And that's why I never call Mike from here either.

And now my phone rings, and it's a number I don't recognize.

Which reminds me that I forgot to call that guy Hector and cancel our lunch date. Our blind date. No, I did meet him once, a long time ago, before he was divorced. So make that our *legally* blind date.

Because that's what my good friend Kate thought my life was missing: one more thing on my plate. One more straw on the stressed camel's back. Lately it feels like I'm eating stress for breakfast. There were no arguments this morning— if anything, Alex was completely penitent about yesterday's outburst—but Lucia's teddy bear's arm ripped at the seam again, and she bawled all the way out the door. And then, on the way here, the Blazer was acting up again. I need to schedule that oil change. I need to find someone to watch the kids on Thursday. I can't miss the Parent-Teacher Conference.

Alex's teacher has been such a witch to him lately, and I need to get that straightened out. I need to hurry up and make that appointment with the dentist, before the deductible starts up again . . . I'm going to tackle that—everything on that list—as soon as I finish this phone conversation.

"Waterson Price Merman O'Connell. This is Natasha."

"Hello. I'm calling for Natasha?" he says.

Great. Good listening skills, guy. "Speaking."

"Natasha, sorry." He laughs a little. "I didn't hear your name at first, with all the others. It's me, Hector."

He tells me he's two minutes away. It's too late to cancel on him now. There's nothing to do but grab my purse, tell the others I'm leaving, and get this stupid thing over with.

HECTOR IS SHORTER than I remembered. Shorter and a little heavier. He still has black hair, and the same amount of it. Slight mustache. He's wearing a sport coat, no tie—his uniform for client meetings, he says. He looks like a nice enough guy. Nothing wrong with him.

Now I'm trying to remember if I was thinner than this back when he first met me. No, don't think about that. What does it matter?

If I did gain weight—if he's disappointed—he's too much of a gentleman to show it. He says, "Is the chicken salad good?" He's worried because neither of us has ever been to this café. He found it online by looking at a map of restaurants near my work.

"It's pretty good," I say. It isn't. The dressing's too sweet. And I don't like the café itself either. The tables are too small and close together. But there's no need to be rude, so I don't complain. "How's the burger?"

He says, "It's pretty good." After a moment he adds, "Maybe a little dry."

That's how the conversation has gone so far: stops and starts of meaningless comments. You can almost hear our thoughts between the words, and we're both thinking, *Why did I agree to do this?*

What the heck...? I say, "Are you wondering why you agreed to do this?"

He laughs. "No. Are you?"

I laugh, too, and I hear how nervous it sounds. "Kind of. No offense—you seem like a nice guy. But I'm starting to realize that I'm not ready to start dating again. Since the divorce, I mean."

He shrugs. "Let's not call it a date, then. Maybe we're just two people who are looking to make new friends."

I can't argue with that. "Sure. I could always use another friend." It's a funny thing to say. Is it really true?

Sometimes, since the divorce, I feel like a rocket. Not one of the space shuttles they use now, but one of those old-fashioned rockets we studied in school, the kind that breaks into pieces as it gets higher in the sky. First I had to break away from Mike. He was too heavy, dragging me down, and I needed to drop him if I wanted to go any higher. Then I lost our house—another section falling away. Slowly, my old friends are dropping away, one by one, whether I like it or not. What's left? My mother? Maybe I'll jettison her on purpose. All that's left, eventually, will be Alex, Lucia, and me, flying alone through space. After everything that's happened in the past year, they're the only part of my life that I can't stand to lose.

The question is, do I really need new friends right now? I'm kind of busy here, trying to hold my rocket ship together.

Hector's staring at his dry burger, thinking about something serious. He looks up at me and says, "You know, when Maribel and I first split up, I kind of lost touch with a lot of people. Friends, family. For a long time, I felt like, if I don't need her, maybe I don't need anybody."

I nod. Yes, I know exactly what you're saying, Near Stranger.

He goes on. "But lately I've been thinking that was all wrong, like some trick my mind was playing on me. See, the easy thing to do would be to stay by myself and not worry about anybody new letting me down, the way Maribel did." He looks at me like he's asking for my understanding, my compassion. "But it's not supposed to be easy, right?"

I drop my fork. My hand loosens up somehow, and the fork just slips out, onto my skirt, then onto the floor. Immediately, Hector swoops down to pick it up. I look down and see the back of his head, all covered with thick black hair, there near my lap. I can smell his cologne. It's like woods, smoke, crisp air. I feel a jolt in my thighs, like a sudden fear that he's going to reach out and touch me.

But it isn't fear. No, I recognize this feeling now. I *want* him to reach out and touch me. And I'm only afraid that he'll look up at me and know.

Something is wrong with me.

He does look up—sits up with the fork in his hand, sets it on the edge of the table. Takes his own fork, unused, and offers it to me with a friendly smile. And I wonder, fleetingly, what the expression on my face is conveying to him, because he stops smiling and just stares.

I reach out and touch him. I put my hand on his and say, "Can we go somewhere else?"

Something is so very wrong with me. What am I doing?

He says, "You mean for coffee?"

I shake my head no.

He says, "You mean...for...somewhere...alone?"

I say, "Yes."

If he's shocked, he rallies quickly and says in a discreet tone, "A motel?"

I nod.

I know exactly what I'm doing. It's stupid and crazy, and I don't care. I just don't. It's my turn to do something irresponsible for once. Everyone else gets to do whatever they want—make messes, throw tantrums, move in with women they've just met. And I'm the one who's left cleaning up the results. But now it's my turn to be bad.

BEFORE TODAY I WAS worried that Mike would be the last man I ever had sex with. And when was the very last time with him? In his mother's house, last Thanksgiving, fast and full of shame.

No, it was in our bedroom, while the kids slept. Fast and dry and resentful.

No. It was a couple of weeks after I moved out, in a last-ditch effort to save our marriage. And it was slow and desperate and sad. So I don't want to remember it now. It never happened.

I'm only thirty-two and probably—knock on wood—won't die anytime soon. But still, I worried that Mike would be my last. Until right now, because here I am in the Blazer, following a Chrysler to a motel. A silver Chrysler Sebring, driven by a man I barely know.

I used to be so proud that Mike was only the third guy

I'd ever slept with. Third and a half, if I count that guy Federico, which I don't, because that only happened once, and then he didn't even come, and then he cried and confessed that he was gay...So embarrassing. I would never tell that story to anyone. But back when I was first married to Mike, eight years—no, almost nine years ago now—my relative inexperience was something he valued in me, and therefore I valued it, too. The way brides in Third World countries must feel when they bring their new husbands a goat or a cow.

And now I look back on the twenty-three-year-old pregnant bride I was and feel sorry for her, for being such a dummy. What a sad waste. What was the point of giving myself—my young, chubby but still-firm body—to one man for what I thought was supposed to be the rest of our lives? At the time I had no idea that our marriage would eventually become years of once-a-month sex between two people who shared a mutual dislike and slept together only because they had no other options. Although I *still* think Mike tried to seduce that coworker of his and *would* have cheated on me if he'd found someone willing to help him.

Why *didn't* I know better, though? Look at my parents— they lasted longer than Mike and me, had two kids like we did, but hated each other. They would've gone on forever, making each other miserable—Dad turning into more of a bitter hermit and Mom more of a screeching nag—if my brother and I hadn't sat them down and begged them, emotionally blackmailed them, into getting the divorce. Twenty-five years of needless hell there. Why did I think my own marriage would magically end up better, with an example like that?

I remember Dad's jokes that one day, if I kept making

chicken and rice as well as I did, a rich man would be happy to marry me. Maybe I'd even score the quarterback for the Houston Oilers if I kept on frying pork chops like that. Presumably, in Dad's mind, these millionaires wouldn't mind that I'd never finished community college, that I worked in the grocery-store deli. They'd appreciate my cooking more than he appreciated my mother's, more than he appreciated that she managed to stay thin after two pregnancies and all that chicken and rice.

Then there was Mom, the devil on my shoulder across from Dad's angel. She had no qualms about telling me that I was lucky to land someone like Mike. In her mind his full-time job and half-white good looks made him eligible for something much better than my diet-resistant body and "god-awful" frizzy hair. Who knows what kind of man she thought I deserved, with my smart mouth and thunder thighs. Maybe none at all, since I was already twenty-three and didn't have any kids, and her sister's daughters—all petite beauties with long, stick-straight hair—each had several kids with several men by the time they were twenty-two.

Mom should have divorced Dad earlier and married Mike herself. That would've been a better match, because they both have that need to suck the happiness out of everyone around them. So if they got together, they'd deplete happiness until it created a disturbance in the space-time continuum, just like in one of Dad's sci-fi books. And then maybe that would've fixed them both. Or at least kept them too busy to suck on the rest of us.

I spent so many years trying to fix my parents' problems, then trying to fix my own marriage, before I finally stopped caring and gave up. Bailed on it. Put the oxygen mask on my own face before assisting the kids with theirs, then pulling up on our flotation devices and getting the hell off the burning plane.

Now that I'm free and clear of my delusions, I wonder why *anyone* gets married.

WHY IS THIS CRAP streaming through my head like a sad movie right now, of all times? Stop thinking about it. Get back to the mood that made me fire up the Blazer and follow this man. The impulse I'm already second-guessing.

Why am I doing this? Is it a pheromone thing? A chicken-salad roofie, maybe.

It's *not* because Mike's already dating again and I'm trying to compete. Is it? No. Say it: He's *been* dating Missy for six months. From what the kids say, they'll be moving in together any day now. And Mike and I have barely been divorced a year. Jesus, *is* that why?

No. I don't care about that. I don't care about anything right now. Specifically, I don't care about what's going to happen when I undress and undo all the straps and the elastics and then . . . Expose the lumps. The pouches. The dimples, the stretch marks, the *flaps*. There's no hiding them in the daytime. But who cares? I barely know this guy. If he doesn't like it, he never has to see me again. But I have the feeling he won't mind. He's been around the block a few times, this Hector. From what I remember, his ex was no closer to a su-permodel than I am.

It's so strange, not to care. Strange and exhilarating.

Now we're here. Now I'm out of the Blazer and walking next to him.

He's talking to the front desk, and I can't hear. I don't care what they're saying. His white work shirt is stretching across his chest a little, across his stomach, and I'm having this hallucination that I can smell his shirt and his chest and his stomach, and it smells like salt and that one cologne I dislike and something else. But the smell doesn't bother me.

Now we're in the room. The yellowed walls and the scratchy-looking flowered bedspread should fill me with disgust but don't. All I see is what's about to happen, as if it's a haze surrounding us. We're not talking at all, and that's fine, too. He locks us in, and I lay my purse down; he does something with the room key, car keys, wallet... And now we're standing next to the bed, stripping as fast as we can. We're in a movie, and someone has hit fast-forward.

I didn't notice until right this second how strangely sexy Hector is. His body is short and kind of blunt. His chest is covered with wiry black hairs, just like the ones he needs to trim from his sideburns, but on the whiter chest skin with the blue veins. They're swirling around his brown nipples that face slightly downward, like two eyes that are shy, and that's a turn-on, too, for some reason. His little beer belly—I can see it now. It's round and smooth, and I want to reach out and touch it, put my hand over the black hairs that look like an ant trail coming out of his belly button and heading down, down to what I see now is a patch of blacker hair hiding under his pleated pants, which he's pulling down now, uncovering the blackest hairs that lead the way into faded blue boxer briefs. Which also come down. And then there it is. Shorter than I expected, but thicker, too. With that nice lighter color—not the red, thank gosh—and even bluer veins than the ones on his chest. And it's curved.

It's cute. I reach for it.

He must be looking at me in the same way as I reveal my body bit by bit, blouse by skirt, and he must like what he sees, or not mind it, because he only gets thicker. He tries to get longer, too, I think, but it's as if the curve won't let it. So I help him by pulling. I pull it in the right direction.

I'm going crazy, and I'm going to hell, but right now I don't care.

I must be hallucinating, because I don't feel my body anymore. If I did, I'd certainly feel my stomach, and I'd be trying to curl myself in a way that would hide it. I'd be trying to create some optical illusion on my stomach, my thighs, certain angles of my butt, maybe the insides of my upper arms . . . but I'm not doing any of that. I can only feel my hands as I use them to pull him toward me. I feel them stroking, then sort of pinching and scratching. It's like they don't belong to me anymore.

And then I can only feel my mouth, so I kiss whatever's near it.

And then I feel another part of myself, stronger than anything else, and I reach out to pull him into it. We're lying on the bed, kind of, somehow, and I grab him and manage to pull him on top, between my thighs, and into me at the exact right angle.

And then I feel my voice. It says, "Fuck the hell out of me, Hector."

And Hector listens.

Alex

I'M A SUPERHERO, and my superpowers are flying, super strength, and mind control.

Whenever Devonique opens her mouth to tattle on me, I can use my mind rays to make her be quiet. Or I can fly in the air and kick her in the head.

Whenever Ms. Hubacek gets mad at me, I can use my mind rays to make her forget. Or I can fly away from school. Or I could go back in time, because I also have time-travel powers. Like when Melinda kept talking to me and I told her to shut up. I'd go back in time and make it so I whispered "Shut up" instead of saying it too loud. Then Ms. Hubacek wouldn't hear me saying it, and she couldn't get mad and tell my mom that I always speak out in class and then argue with her about it.

Also, I can stop time. I can make the world stop. Everybody around me freezes, and then I can get up and do whatever I want. I can get my favorite eraser back from Ms. Hubacek's desk. I can draw a funny picture on Michael's binder. I can go to the bathroom real fast, then be back at my desk when time starts up again.

Also, I can hold my pee for as long as I want. I can hold it until recess, or until I get home, or forever.

Alex

I PEED MY PANTS. I didn't ask Ms. Hubacek for permission to go to the restroom because I already knew what she'd say. "You were supposed to go right after lunch. Only kindergartners don't know when they're supposed to go to the bathroom, Alex." That's what she said last time, and everybody laughed.

This time we're in Resource Room, and I really couldn't hold it. So it's not just a little bit of pee, and there's no table to hide it. Devonique sees and raises her hand. "Ms. Hubacek, Alex had a accident over here." I don't like Devonique.

Ms. Hubacek gets mad. I hate it when that happens. She breathes real loud and says, "Alex." She gets up and comes over to my carpet square and sees how it's dark and wet all around me. She grabs my arm, and her sharp orange nails pinch through my shirt. Everybody's staring at me. She drags me to her desk and writes the paper for me to go to the nurse. My legs are starting to itch inside my jeans. Ms. Hubacek slams her pen on the desk and hands me the note. I go out the door and down the hall.

The nurse looks like my grandma, but nice. She's not dressed like a nurse or a teacher. She just looks like a regular lady. She doesn't get mad. She just reads Ms. Hubacek's note and then gets up to check her cubbies. There's no extra clothes with my name on them. She says, "I guess your mama never sent any."

She sits back at her desk and looks at her computer. Then she calls somebody on her phone. She says, "Mrs. Davila? I'm calling to tell you that Alex has had an accident and he needs some clean clothes to be brought to the school." Then she hangs up and says, "She didn't answer. I guess we should call your daddy."

She calls on the phone again. She says, "Mr. Davila? I'm calling to tell you that Alex has had an accident. . . . Mm-hmm. . . . No, I mean a bladder accident." She tells him I don't have any clothes in the cubby and then says "Mm-hmm" a bunch more times. Then she hangs up and says, "I guess your daddy's friend is coming to bring you a change of clothing." I think she means Missy, my dad's girlfriend.

The nurse tells me I can go sit in the other room, the one with the orange plastic chair and the cot where kids sleep when they're sick. So I go in there. I don't know if I'm supposed to sit down with my pants wet, so I stay standing up and just wait. I hear the nurse typing on her computer for a long time.

The nap-room door is open a little bit, so I can see when Missy comes in. She's wearing her sunglasses and carrying a bag from Target. The nurse stares at her, probably because Missy has long legs and long blond hair. That's what my dad said he first noticed about her, and he couldn't stop looking. I heard him tell his friend that. He said Missy actually works at keeping herself in shape, unlike some other women he could mention. That means she's good at sports. My dad likes sports a lot.

Mom used to be good at sports, but she stopped playing

when she got out of school. She doesn't keep herself in shape, Dad says. So she just looks normal, like all the other moms.

Missy talks to the nurse and makes her laugh. Then they call me out of the nap room and give me the Target bag and tell me to change and use the wipes on myself. So I go back in the nap room and close the door. I open the bag and see jeans and Transformers underwear.

I don't wear Transformers anymore. I only wear Spider-Man now.

I take off my peed pants and underwear. I don't know where I'm supposed to put them, so I leave them on the floor, in the corner, under the cot. After I put on my clean clothes, I see the wipes that they were talking about on the counter. I get one and use it to wipe my hands.

When I come out of the room, Missy and the nurse are talking. Missy says, "...missing his dad." The nurse is nodding. They stop talking when they see me.

"Where are your dirty clothes, tiger?" Missy says.

I point behind me, to the floor in the little room. I wish Missy wasn't here. I wish I hadn't peed my pants, or I had the superpower to go back in time. Or to make Ms. Hubacek let us go to the restroom whenever we want.

The door to the nurse's office opens. It's Mom. She's here. She looks mad. When she gets all the way inside and sees Missy standing there, she looks even madder.

Ms. Garcia, the school secretary, comes in behind her. I've never seen Ms. Garcia come out of the main office before.

Mom says, "And I'm trying to find out why exactly I wasn't called."

Ms. Garcia looks at the nurse. The nurse says, "Well,

we called your work, Ms. Davila, but we couldn't reach you, and that's why we called Mr. Davila, and he sent over Ms. . . . um . . . He sent over his friend."

My mom looks the way she did that one time when we went to Grandma's and Grandma gave Lucia that pink dress and it didn't fit her, and Grandma said she'd have to return it and get a bigger one. And Lucia asked if Grandma could get her a black dress instead. And Grandma said that Lucia ate too much and that she wasn't very ladylike. When Grandma said that, Mom stood up real straight and crossed her arms, like she's doing right now. Her eyebrows went down, and her mouth got skinny, just like right now. She told Grandma, "I'm not going to let you give her a freaking complex. If you're so worried about the kids' weight, quit giving Alex so much candy."

But I don't think Mom's going to say that Ms. Garcia and the nurse are giving me a freaking complex. I think she's mad because they didn't tell her what happened. Mom hates it when she doesn't know what's going on.

She tells Ms. Garcia, "So now anyone off the street is allowed to come into the school and undress my son?" She means Missy, except Missy didn't undress me. But I guess Mom thinks she did. Now Missy looks mad, but she doesn't say anything.

"Well, no, Ms. Davila," says Ms. Garcia. "But your husband's—your ex-husband's—friend is an authorized contact for Alex. Mr. Davila added her name to the list two weeks ago." She means Dad. Mom hates it when people forget that Dad's her ex-husband and call him her husband instead. She always calls him "my kids' dad."

Mom's voice gets loud now. "Why didn't anyone call my

cell? I didn't get the message until I got back to work, and then I had to drive like a maniac to get Alex's clothes and get over here. And now that I'm here, you're telling me that instead of calling my mother or my cousin or someone else that I put on the emergency contact list, you called a woman I barely know to come here and take my son's clothes off?" She's yelling at them now. Everybody in the office looks scared.

Missy says, "I didn't take his clothes off." She's looking at the floor, not at Mom. "I was just trying to help. But I'll be leaving now." She walks behind Mom and goes out the door. My mom is looking at her like she has laser rays in her eyes and wants to burn Missy with them.

Mrs. Garcia says, "Well, we're sorry, Ms. Davila. We thought your ex-husband or his girlfriend would tell you. Or . . . well, that Alex would tell you what happened when he got home."

Mom turns around and sees me watching everything through the door. How did she know I was watching? Oh, no. She's going to yell at me next.

But no, she's smiling now. Not like she's happy to see me, but like she's telling the secretary and the nurse that they've gotten on her nerves so bad that she's not going to waste her time talking to them anymore. She tells me, "Hi, sweetie. Let's get you cleaned up, okay?"

She comes into the nap room and closes the door behind us and looks at my dirty clothes on the floor. Then she looks at the jeans I'm wearing and shakes her head. "Missy didn't help you change?" she says.

I shake my head no.

She opens the door again and tells the nurse, "There's no sink in here."

I hear the nurse saying something, and then Mom says,

"Well, how about a towel and a bucket of water, then? *Some*thing. And I need real soap." Then she says "Jesus" real quiet, like she does when she's driving or talking on the phone to my dad.

She opens the black bag she brought with her and takes out jeans, my underwear, some socks, and a new pair of tennis shoes. They're the same as my regular shoes, the ones from Payless that have Venom on the sides. She says, "So what happened?"

"I don't know. I just had an accident."

"But why, sweetie?" She's not mad anymore. She's just frustrated. "Didn't you tell Ms. Hubacek you had to go to the bathroom?"

"No," I say.

"Why not?"

"Because she doesn't let us. It's a rule."

"But her class is right after lunch," my mom says.

I tell her, "I know. But we're only supposed to go at after-lunch break, and if we have to go after that, we're supposed to hold it until recess. Last time I asked her, Ms. Hubacek said that only kindergartners can't hold it until recess. And then that stupid Devonique laughed and started calling me 'Kinderbaby.'"

Mom says, "She did, huh? Well, it sounds like I need to have a talk with Ms. Hubacek."

I can tell she's thinking about what she's going to do next. I bet she's going to go talk to Ms. Hubacek right now. Or, if they don't let her, she'll write a long e-mail to the principal and get Ms. Hubacek in trouble, like that time before we came to this school, when she got the day-care lady in trouble for calling Lucia "a little beaner girl."

The nurse sticks her hands in the door and gives Mom some little blue towels like the ones the cafeteria ladies use, one of the soaps from the restroom, and a bottle of water from the Coke machine in the teachers' lounge. Mom takes all the stuff from her and closes the door again. She wets one of the towels with the water bottle and rubs soap on it. "Okay, mister," she tells me. "Strip."

The diaper wipes are still on the counter in the corner. I wonder if I should tell Mom that Missy and the nurse only made me use the wipes.

Mom looks at me and says "Hurry, sweetie." The towel's all soapy, and she has the same face like when she gets down on the kitchen floor to scrub it with the brush.

I decide to keep quiet, and I take off the clothes I just put on. I'm glad that I'm not Ms. Hubacek right now, because I know she's going to get in trouble after this.

Natasha

I ALWAYS FEEL guilty. About everything.

Every workday I leave the office at four-thirty while everyone else stays until five-thirty or six, and that makes me feel bad. Even though I come in at seven-thirty every morning and the others don't roll in until nine or nine-thirty. Even though many of them come in even later than that, now that I've started working here and they know I'm taking care of everything early in the morning.

No one really expected me to stay late today, to make up the time I lost dealing with Alex's problem at school. But I would've felt like a bad employee if I hadn't. Like I was letting my bosses down.

And now it's raining and traffic is keeping me from getting home. It doesn't matter that we live only five minutes away, because someone's stopped on the side of the road with a flat tire and all the rest of us have to slow down and stare and say to ourselves, *I'm glad I'm not stuck on the side of the road in the rain.*

By now the school bus has ferried Alex and Lucia home, and Alex has had to use his emergency key to get into the apartment. This is the third time he's had to do that since we've been living here. It makes me feel like the world's worst mother. I need to call them to make sure they're safe.

"Hello?"

"Lucia." Why is she answering the phone instead of Alex? "Hi, baby. How was school today?"

"Good," she says. I hear the TV in the background.

"That's great. I'm almost home. I'll see you in a few minutes. Give the phone to your brother, baby, okay?"

Alex says hello, and I immediately lay into him. "Alex, what have I told you about letting your sister answer the phone when I'm not there?"

"I saw your name on the screen. We knew it was you," he says.

It's my turn to pass the poor sap on the side of the road, finally. I don't even look at him. Let the guy suffer with one less person in the audience. Now the traffic's speeding up a little, thank gosh. But I still have to ask Alex certain questions. "Is the door locked?"

"Yes."

"Go double-check, please."

"It's locked."

"What do you do if someone knocks on the door?"

"Don't answer it."

"What do you do if someone calls and it's not me?"

"Don't answer the phone." He sounds like he's reciting multiplication tables, and I wonder if he understands the importance of his answers. How can he possibly imagine the things that I worry about when he and his sister are home alone?

I'm almost there now. But I don't want to hang up. As if keeping him on the phone will keep him safe, I hold on. For instance, if Alex had actually left the door unlocked and a criminal who'd escaped from the county jail came barreling through the door, I would know about it, because I'd hear the whole thing on the phone. And then I could keep the kids safe by ... asking Alex to hand the phone to the criminal, right? And nagging the guy to death. Sure.

"Are you guys eating anything?" I ask.

"I made ham and cheese for me and peanut butter for Lucia," he says. "With one bread only, and the new strawberry jelly."

"Good," I say. "Remember ..."

"Don't use the stove," he says. "I know. And we're not putting forks in the microwave either."

"Okay," I say. "How was school this afternoon, baby?"

There's a pause. I hear him tell Lucia, "Throw away your trash." Then he says, "I don't know. I stayed in Resource Room, when fifth grade was there, to make up my work." He sounds upset about that. "Dad called, too."

"Just now?" I say.

"Yeah. He said for you to call him when you get home."

Damn it. Of course Mike would call right now. He *never* calls the kids right after school, but the one time he does is the time that I'm not there. Great. He probably wants to curse me out for what happened at school today. But what's he going to say? "Natasha, how dare you complain that a stranger was pretending to be Alex's mom?"

I'm not going to get upset about future conversations with Mike right now, though. Not while I'm on the phone with my son. Alex has had a rough enough day.

No matter how hard I try, I can't keep Alex from knowing that his dad and I don't get along. Lucia is young enough that most of it goes over her head. But Alex is too smart for that. I hate that he has to feel the slightest bit stressed, carrying messages between his dad and me. So I make my voice extra breezy and casual and say, "Okay, baby. I'll call him when I get there. I'm real close to the apartment now."

I HAVEN'T EVEN begun to feel guilty over what I did during my lunch hour. What I did with Hector, I see now, in retrospect, was like those days when I say "Screw this diet" and eat a bunch of doughnuts. A bowl of ice cream. A big, fat slab of red velvet cake to celebrate someone's birthday at the office. At that moment of indulgence, and for several glorious, sugar-high moments after, I feel fabulous. And then the guilt kicks in and I end up hating myself. Always. Hector was a dozen doughnuts, and the sugar crash is hitting me right now.

Was Alex's accident my punishment? Instant karma, boomeranging right in my face?

No. That wasn't punishment for me—it was a humiliating experience for Alex, and it's my job to help him deal with it.

I can't sit here reflecting on what happened with Hector. Not right now. Maybe tonight, when I'm alone in bed and the kids are fast asleep, I'll replay it all in my mind and feel guilty as hell.

At least sleeping with Hector didn't make me gain weight.

WHEN I GET INSIDE, Lucia is sitting on the couch, holding Mr. Beary's torn arm against his chest while they both watch television. Alex is standing in the middle of our tiny living room, back in his Venom mask, looking as unhappy as I feel. He stands perfectly still and wrings his little hands.

"What's wrong?" I ask him.

He doesn't answer.

"Alex." I set my bags on the coffee table and go to him, put my hands on his shoulders. "Talk to me, baby."

He sighs. With a glance at Lucia, he says very quietly, "What if I have to go to the restroom tomorrow and Ms. Hubacek says no?"

Jesus. If I could make his teacher appear here right now and give her *another* piece of my mind, for putting my son through this... "Come in here with me." I walk him into my bedroom, where we can talk in private. We sit on the edge of my bed. "Would you please take off your mask, so I can see your face?"

He hesitates for a moment, then pulls it off.

I say, "I already talked to Ms. Hubacek about that. If you ask, she'll let you go."

"But what if she's just lying? What if I ask her and she still says no?"

I sigh. I don't think that'll happen, after our conversation today, but I can see how Alex might have a hard time believing that. "If she says no... well, you just get up and go anyway."

Now he's looking at me. He sniffles. "You mean without permission?"

"If you have to, yes. If she doesn't understand that it's an emergency."

He takes a minute to absorb this. Then he says, "I don't want to go to school tomorrow. Everybody's going to make fun of me."

I can't think of an easy answer to that one. I remember how elementary-school kids can be. I know damned well they'll make fun of him.

Can I keep him home? No, not unless I call in sick myself. Which I can't afford to do right now.

It's my turn to sigh. "You're just going to have to ignore them if they make fun of you."

Stony silence. He goes back to staring at the wall. And I don't blame him. It's a crappy answer. It didn't help me to ignore the kids who used to call me "Fatty," or "Fat-tasha," or "Jerry Curls." And yet that's the only advice my mother ever had for me.

"Did I ever tell you," I say, "about the time these girls in my class were making fun of me?"

Alex sniffles. "For what?"

"For being fat," I say. I know he's familiar with this concept. In our old neighborhood, there was a pretty chunky kid who lived down the street. More than once I had to point out to Alex and his friends that it wasn't nice to call that kid names.

"What did you do?" Alex asks me.

"I ignored them," I say. "Well, mostly. Sometimes I told them to shut up. Or sometimes I'd think of funny names to call them."

"Like what?"

What were they? There was that one girl who tortured me all year. She came back from spring break with lice, and I called her "Bugs Bunny." That made the other kids laugh and actually made me popular, kind of, through the end of fourth grade. But instead of telling Alex that, I say, "It doesn't matter. The point is, I never let them see that it bothered me when they called me fat. Because if they'd known it was hurting my feelings, they never would've stopped."

He thinks about this for a while, then says, "But this is

different. Having an accident at school is way worse than being fat."

"I know," I say. "But you have to go back to school tomorrow and act like it was no big deal. If the other kids say anything about it, you have to laugh or make a joke or say, 'Yeah, whatever.'"

He remains unconvinced. No one can do a face of skepticism as skeptically as my eight-year-old son. "Look," I say. "Let's practice it now. Pretend I peed my pants, and make fun of me about it."

"Really?" says Alex.

I nod, and that's all he needs to sink into the role. His face transforms to that of a sneering second-grade bully, and he says, "Hey, Kinderbaby. You peed your pants! You stink like piss!"

That's a little harsher than I was expecting. But I compose myself and ignore the bully he's portraying.

He stands up and taunts more loudly, closer to my face. "Hey, Piss Baby! You got stains on your underwear?"

I give him a look of studied, casual disdain. And, unable to resist the opportunity for a comeback, I say, "Why are you so worried about my underwear?"

He's taken aback but stays in character. "You'd better go to the bathroom, Piss Baby."

It's really bringing me back, this fake bullying. I remember the faces of the little brats who called me Fatty every day at lunch. I feel a shrill retort welling up within me. I feel, all over again, the swelling of elementary-school rage. But I'm older now, and it's so much easier to figure out what the best response would've been to kids like that. Kids who grow up to be adults like that. There are so, so many of them. All I want, right now, is to impart my grown-up understanding to my son. I look his bully character directly in the eye and say, in just the right dismissive tone, "You're right. I'd better go to the bathroom, before I throw up from looking at your face."

He laughs, and now he's my son again.

I say, "Now I'm going to be the bully. Are you ready?" He nods. I say, "Hey, Pee-Pee Baby. Are you going to pee on yourself today?"

He looks back at me, perfectly mirroring my expression of disdain—it's almost like we're related—and says, "Why are you so in love with pee? That's all you ever talk about."

I act surprised and sputter, "No, you are! You're the one who peed!"

Alex executes a perfect fake chuckle and says, "Then why are you the one who smells?" Then he mimes going back to his schoolwork.

"That's really good. I think you've got it," I say.

He smiles. It's good to see him smiling again.

"And now I think you should probably take a shower."

Natasha

I WILL CALL MIKE, but not until later. Right now I have too much to do, and just hearing his voice puts me in a bad mood. So I'll save it until after I do laundry.

That's what I miss most about being married—my washer and dryer. And I miss our old neighborhood, of course. To this day it annoys me that Mike didn't want to buy the house we were living in. They gave us the option to rent instead, and that's what he convinced me to do. He wanted to see if they'd drop the price after a few years. That was Mike: always holding out for something better. Never making decisions until I forced him to.

Sears sells little washer-and-dryer sets that stack one on top of the other. I could fit one in the corner of my bedroom if it had the right kind of connections on the wall. But it doesn't, of course, and the likelihood of convincing the property manager to install them seems pretty nonexistent. We need to move to a better place. Or else I need to save my money and try to buy my own house. But I can't do either yet. I've only been working full-time for the past year, and the kids just got settled in this new school. So now *I'm* the one who can't make decisions—who has to sit back and wait. I hate it.

Time to quit thinking whiny thoughts and haul this basket to the laundry room. Lucia wants to go with me so she can beg me for quarters for the candy machine, but I'm going to make her stay in the apartment.

This complex isn't too bad. The paint in the hall could use retouching, sure. But our doors are nice and strong. It's pretty difficult to get into the parking garage without a security card, which is a good thing.

But some of the people living here are a different story. There's the one guy who haunts the laundry room like a perverted ghost, looking into the windows and then creeping around the dryers that people leave filled with clothing. I know he's probably looking to steal some college girl's underwear. I don't put anything in the dryers unless I have time to monitor them religiously. Which is annoying, because it means standing around the stuffy laundry room for half an hour instead of doing something useful upstairs.

I should have brought my paralegal study guide with me, so I could read while I waited. Too late now.

And, speak of the devil, here he is. The Laundry Pervert himself, approaching a gently spinning load. I walk into the room and set my basket on one of the washers, avoiding eye contact with him. Very slowly, he turns and oozes over to the soda machine. Stands there like he's trying to decide between orange and lemon-lime. He's older. He wears a greenish jacket and cap that look like they came from an army-surplus store. I pretend not to notice him as I push my dollar bills into the change machine. And he pretends to ignore me. But there's a sickly web of tension between us. I wish he'd leave.

I pretend to read the notices on the bulletin board next to the detergent vending machine. Oh, look—there's an advertisement for computer repairs. And here's a lost Chihuahua. Wait . . . here's something of interest: a baby-sitter.

EXPEREINCED GRANDMOTHER. HOME
COOKED MEALS. CALL GERONIMA.

I'm tempted to pull one of the sign's hanging tabs, painstakingly imprinted with the woman's phone number. I can't help but notice the misspellings, her strange name. Maybe she's from Mexico and English isn't her first language. Would I leave the kids with an old woman who doesn't speak English? Would that be safe?

Who am I kidding? I can't leave them with a stranger.

I'm getting a headache from holding my face in this rigidly neutral position. Holding my arms crossed in front of me defensively while Laundry Pervert slowwwly shuffles around the room. God, I wish he'd leave.

Someone else comes in. A short woman with long hair. She hauls two plastic laundry baskets, pink and yellow with broken mesh that makes holes for her dirty clothes to puff out of. I've seen this woman around the complex before—she lives on our floor, I know—and she always looks familiar to me. Probably because she reminds me of my cousins on my mom's side—the ones with all the kids and no husbands. This woman has a little girl following her now, like a shadow with wildly curly hair. I think she has one or two more children, in addition to this girl. I've seen them in the parking garage, getting into an old brown sedan.

I pass the time by watching this woman load her washer with what seems like hundreds of little dresses and T-shirts and tiny socks in every color of the rainbow. And so does Laundry Pervert. And now I hate him with renewed passion. Alex and Lucia are waiting for me. I want to get back to them. But I can't leave, because I'm afraid this guy will mess with my clothes. Maybe it'll be safe to leave now, though, now that this other woman is here.

"Can I help you?"

She's speaking to him. Out of the corner of my eye, I see her looking directly at Laundry Pervert, addressing him in a wrathful voice. He's just as surprised as I am and can't seem to think of a reply.

She says, "Hey, I'm talking to you. What are you doing here?"

In a voice like a cough, he says, "I'm...uh, washing my clothes."

"No you aren't." She's shorter than this guy by a good six inches, but the way she's leaning into him now, you'd think she was two feet taller. "You don't have any clothes. You're always in here, and I never see you wash anything. What the hell are you doing, old man?"

He just stares at her. He's as shocked as I am.

"Boy," this woman says, and she takes a deep breath like she's winding up to punch him. "If I ever find out you're in here messing with my clothes..." She points to me now. "Or *her* clothes, or anybody else's, I will *beat* your ass *down*. You hear me?"

He says, "Now, hold on. I'm not trying to do nothing." His words come out all garbled. From alcohol or fear, I don't know.

"I don't want to hear it," this woman says. "Just get the hell out of here, before I call security."

As he shuffles out of the laundry room and down the covered walk, she calls out the door, "And don't let me see you in here no more!"

This whole time her daughter's been standing directly behind her, twirling like a ballerina. She's not even afraid, this little girl. She's used to her mom going off on strangers, apparently.

Her mother turns to me. "Sorry about that. But that guy's been giving me the creeps for two days now."

"No, don't worry about it," I say. "I'm glad you told him something. He's been creeping me out, too." I smile down at her daughter for good measure. The little girl avoids making eye contact and runs over to the candy machine.

The woman goes back to sorting through her children's laundry but keeps talking. "Sometimes you just have to tell these dudes, you know? Guys like that see a single mom and think they're gonna take advantage, you know?"

I do know. I'm starting to know, now that I live here. Watching this woman, listening to her, makes me realize that I need to dust off the skills I learned in high school, which was full of girls like her and my mother's cousins. Skills that kept me from getting my butt kicked.

High school . . .

"You went to Lincoln, didn't you?" I say.

She glances up at me with a black eyebrow lifting into an arch. "Yeah. You just figured that out? We had gym together. Natasha, right?"

I nod. What is her name? I do recognize her now. She's older, and her hair is black instead of purplish red, but I remember her sitting in the back of my health class, fast asleep in a flannel shirt. Now she's standing here in shorts and a Tweety Bird T-shirt. She could pass for a high-school student still, if you didn't see her face. Her face is hard, angry. Or maybe just . . . wary. As if she's always expecting trouble.

I think back to Coach Romeo calling the roll. Fernando, Jasmine, Edgar . . . "Sara."

"Right." She smiles, and it makes her look like a different person. A friendly, happy young mom in place of the growling mother bear who was just standing here. She says, "Are you thinking about taking your kids to Geronima's?"

What? Who? Oh, the name on the baby-sitting flyer. "Um. I don't know. I was just looking at it. But I don't really..." *I don't really need a baby-sitter*, I'm about to say. But that's not exactly true.

Sara says, "She's good. I've been taking my kids over there for a few months. She cooks them dinner and everything."

I don't say anything. I'm still absorbing all that's just happened: The stress of being here with Laundry Pervert, the shock of watching a tiny woman chew him out and send him packing, then finding out this woman knows me and is recommending a baby-sitter.

Sara says, "You want me to take you to meet her? Let me just get this shit started up." She means her laundry. She fishes her electronic card out of her pocket and inserts it into each of the three washers she's filled. Then she says, "Come on," to me and barks, "Monique!" over her shoulder. Monique is her daughter's name, apparently, because that's the little girl's cue to shuffle reluctantly from the candy machine to Sara's side.

"Okay," I say.

I follow her out the door, back to the covered walk that leads to my building, as opposed to the other building in the complex, where Laundry Pervert apparently lives. Good—this Geronima lives close to me. I feel like I've been away from my own apartment forever, but it's really been only ten minutes. Alex and Lucia won't even notice for another ten or twenty.

Geronima lives on the top floor, two above me. The carpet

up here is a different color: deep red instead of the Astroturf-ish green on my floor. Sara leads me to the door marked 312 and rings the bell. The woman who answers is not the frail little Mexican lady I imagined, but a big, sturdy grandma with wiry copper hair and a bright flowered dress that smells like baby powder and bacon. She's wiping her hands on an apron—a real live apron, with an embroidered rooster—and she greets Sara by saying, "Hi, m'ija." Sara introduces us, and Geronima says, "Natasha? Hi. Well, come on in." Her eyes are crinkly but sharp as she smiles, and I feel like she's taking in everything about me. But in a friendly way. And now she's ushering us into her apartment.

It looks like she's lived here for decades. The living room is crammed full of flowered furniture and doilies, reminiscent of my mother's house, but more old-fashioned and less dusty. There's an old man, thin and well dressed, asleep on the overstuffed couch, snoozing upright as if he just fell under a spell. "That's Oscar," says our hostess, waving at him as she leads us directly to the kitchen. Her apartment has the same floor plan as mine. Two bedrooms over there. Only one bath. But Geronima's somehow made her kitchen look twice as big as mine, and she's filled it with ten times as much stuff. There's no breakfast nook. She's enhanced that space with an additional butcher block, which is loaded down with food. They must eat in the living room, then.

"Are y'all hungry?" Geronima says to us. I see the source of the bacon smell. Two, no three pans on her stove, all siz-zling. There's beans, meat with vegetables, and some kind of sauce.

"No, thank you," I say. I wonder who she's cooking all this food for. It's way too much for her husband and herself.

"Oh, you don't have to be polite," she tells me.

"Gero, we just came by to say hi," Sara says. "Natasha wanted to meet you 'cause she's thinking about getting you to watch her kids."

"How many kids do you have?" Geronima asks me. Meanwhile she's begun warming a tortilla on the stove's last burner, directly on the open flame. She flips it with her fingers once, then picks it up and smears a thin layer of beans on it, folds it into a skinny cylinder of a taco, and hands it to Sara's daughter. The little girl takes it and pops it into her mouth without saying anything. Like a bird or a squirrel.

"I have two kids. A boy and a girl," I say.

"Do they go to Zapata Elementary?" she asks me. I'm wondering if she's going to make me a taco, too. But instead she wipes her hands on her apron and focuses on my face with a smile.

"Yes, they do," I say. "Alex is in second grade, and Lucia's in kindergarten."

"Oh, then Lucia might be in Tiffany's class." Tiffany, I suppose, is one of the other children she baby-sits. Geronima turns to stir the pan of meat. It's beef and yellow and green squash, I see now. I've had that dish before, a long time ago. It's called . . . carne guisada. My mother used to make it, back when we were really young, when she still cooked. And the third pan on Geronima's stove is full of roasted chili peppers simmering in tomato sauce. She's making her own salsa, it looks like. She sees me looking at the food and says, "Why don't you bring them over for dinner?"

"Oh, no. Thank you. I couldn't," I say. Dinner. Jeez. I need to get back to my own apartment and make something for the kids. There are two bags of Chicken Magic left in the freezer.

I'll make the Chicken Magic Alfredo—the flavor Lucia complains about least.

"Are you sure?" Geronima says. "I wish y'all could come over. I made way too much food for just me, Oscar, and Tiffany. Sara's coming over with her kids. Aren't you, Sara?"

"Sure," Sara says. I get the impression that she's a frequent guest here.

I say, "No, I really shouldn't." But I'm starting to wish that I could. The meat and beans smell so good. As if to tempt me further, Geronima lifts the lid on a round container next to the stove, overflowing with orangey-yellow Spanish rice. It really is too much food for just three people. And it looks so much better than a bag of Chicken Magic.

"Well..." I find myself saying. "Are you sure you'll have enough?"

Geronima laughs and says, "Of course." Behind her, Sara nods and gives me the thumbs-up.

Alex

MOM SAYS WE have to go eat dinner at some lady's apartment. I don't want to go. She says some kids from my school will be there and I might like them, but I know that I won't. The only kids at school I like are the ones who don't live at our apartments. I hope it's not Devonique or Jose. But I don't think Mom would make me have dinner with them.

We have to go up the stairs. Mom never lets us ride the elevator. She says it's too rickety. Lucia's happy. She keeps jumping up and down and asking Mom who we're going to meet. Mom says, "A little girl named Monique and a little girl named Tiffany. And maybe one or two other girls." They sound boring. I wish we could stay in our apartment and Mom would let me play my games until bedtime. Or we could just watch TV. Or I could read my comics.

Lucia brought her stupid Mr. Beary. The other kids are going to think she's a baby.

It takes a long time to go up all the stairs. When we get to the top, my mom tells me, "Help me, Alex. We're looking for apartment number 312."

"I'll help you!" Lucia says. But she can't even read the numbers on the doors. They're too high for her to see.

"Here it is," I say. It's an old, scratched-up door, just like ours. But the numbers are gold, and our number 127 is white.

Mom lifts up Lucia so she can ring the bell, and an old lady answers the door. She looks kind of like Mrs. Garcia at school, but fatter and with orange-er hair.

"Hello, hello," the lady says when we get inside. "Who is this?" My mom tells her our names, and the lady says, "Alex, Lucia. I'm so glad y'all came." Maybe she's one of our aunts or my mom's cousin. She acts like she's in our family. She tells me and Lucia, "You can call me Miss Buena, okay?" Then she tells my mom, "That's what all the kids call me. It's easier for them to say." I wonder what her real name is. I bet *I* could say it, if they told me.

Miss Buena's apartment is full of stuff that old ladies always have: clocks and little statues of animals and flowers on everything. There's an old man on the couch. Miss Buena tells us, "This is Mr. Oscar." Like Oscar the Grouch. He has bushy eyebrows like Oscar the Grouch, too. We say hello to him, and Mr. Oscar shakes my hand.

"Tiffany, come out here, m'ija," says Miss Buena. "This is my granddaughter, Tiffany." A little girl comes out of one of the bedrooms. She has ponytails tied up with a bunch of ribbons and beads. She's wearing a dress like one of those dolls on the commercials. She looks at my sister and says, "Lucy."

"Is Tiffany in your class?" my mom asks Lucia. Lucia nods. Miss Buena says, "Why don't y'all go play in Tiffany's room until everybody gets here?" Mom has to push Lucia forward. I know what's wrong. Now she's embarrassed that she brought her teddy bear, because this other girl isn't carrying one.

Mom knows, too. She opens her purse, and Lucia stuffs Mr. Beary inside. Then Tiffany says, "Come on!" and Lucia runs off with her.

They probably only have girl toys in Tiffany's room. Maybe

Mom and them will let me watch TV. Mr. Oscar's watching TV real quiet, but it's the news. But maybe they have another TV in one of the other rooms.

The doorbell rings, and Miss Buena goes to answer it. A lady with blond hair comes in, with a little boy. The lady looks kind of like Ms. Hubacek, but taller and prettier. Her son looks like he's in kinder or pre-K, but I've never seen him riding our bus.

"This is Haley," Miss Buena tells my mom. She tells me, "And this is Jared." I've never heard of anybody named Jared, except that guy on the commercial who used to be fat before he ate a bunch of sandwiches. But this kid's not fat. He's little and has long hair, like a baby.

My mom tells the lady her name, and then Miss Buena says Jared should go play with Tiffany and Lucia until the others get here. How many other people are coming? I guess it's just going to be a bunch of little kids. I guess I'll watch TV with Mr. Oscar, even if he only watches boring shows.

My mom and the Haley lady are talking about their shoes, because my mom used to have some shoes like Haley's but they were a different color. Then Haley has to take Jared into Tiffany's room, because he's too scared to go by himself. Then the doorbell rings again, and Miss Buena says, "That must be Sara and her kids."

She opens the door, and this time it's a lady with long black hair, and she has three kids. One's a baby. I can see his diaper coming out of his pants. Then there's a kindergarten girl. I've seen her on our bus. And then there's another girl. A tall girl, with long, curly hair. I've seen her on the bus, too. She's in third grade. She plays by the trees at recess.

My mom and the other ladies have to say their names to

each other again. Then they call Lucia and them out of the other room, and they say all the kids' names. The baby is named Junior, just like my cousin, and his sister in kindergarten is Monique.

The third-grade girl's name is Angelica. Mom asks if we know each other from school. We both shake our heads. Miss Buena says, "You two can sit together, since you're the oldest."

I look at my hands, and Angelica looks out the window. She's wearing jeans instead of a dress. She doesn't have any ribbons in her hair. Maybe that means she likes good stuff and not just girl stuff.

NOW IT'S TIME to eat, and all the little kids have to sit on the floor around the coffee table. The grown-ups are sitting on the couches and chairs with their plates on their laps. Me and Angelica are big, so we get to sit on these little footstools and hold our plates on our laps, too. Because Miss Buena said she knows we won't spill any food on the carpet. It's kind of like Thanksgiving, except no one's yelling.

Mom keeps laughing. Sometimes she laughs at stuff the other ladies are saying, but also she's just smiling for no reason at all. Back before the divorce, we used to go to parties at our neighbor's house, and Mom would talk to the other ladies in the kitchen. But those ladies didn't make her laugh like this.

I'm listening to them, but I can't understand what's so funny. Haley, the blond lady, tells a story about finding a big roach in her shower and trying to hit it with her shoe. Angelica's mom tells a story about finding a mouse in the swimming pool. Then my mom tells a story about some guy in the laundry room and how Angelica's mom got mad at him. Everybody's laughing at that, except for Mr. Oscar. He's listening to them, but he's watching TV at the same time.

Angelica touches my arm. She says, "Do you want these?" It's all the green pieces, left on her plate.

I don't want them. I didn't eat my green pieces or the red ones. The yellow ones were okay, though. "Do you want these red ones?" I tell her.

She says, "They're spicy," and she eats one off my plate.

I don't like spicy things, but I don't want to be a baby, so I eat one, too. "It's not that spicy," I tell her. She eats another one, so I do, too.

I didn't want the beans and rice, but Mom said I had to take a little, to be polite. Now I wish I had some more, because it was good.

"Alex, are you still hungry, m'ijo?" Miss Buena says. She stands up. "You and Angelica come with me and get some more."

We follow her to the kitchen, and she puts more beans and rice on our plates. Then she says, "Hold on." She turns on the fire and opens a pack of tortillas. She puts the tortillas right on the fire, then flips them with her fingers.

"Doesn't that burn you?" I ask her.

"No," she says. "I don't even feel it." She opens the refrigerator and gets a tub of butter. She puts butter on the tortillas and rolls them up, then gives them to us. I take a bite. She says, "It's good, huh?"

I nod my head, and so does Angelica.

"If you start coming to my house after school, I'll make you quesadillas."

I don't know what that is, but maybe it's good. She said

"house," but I know she means this apartment. Maybe Mom can bring us here again, tomorrow after school.

MOM HAD TO CARRY Lucia down the stairs, because she's sleepy. She always gets sleepy before me. When we get back to our apartment, it's dark outside. The windows are all black, and Mom shuts the miniblinds.

After she puts Lucia in bed, Mom comes out and makes me show her my homework. I only had two worksheets, and I finished them right after school. After she checks them, Mom says, "Did you have fun tonight, at Miss Buena's?"

I say, "Yeah. It was pretty good."

She says, "I was thinking about letting her watch you and your sister sometime. Maybe on Thursday, when I have to go to the Parent-Teacher Conference. What do you think of that?"

I say, "That'd be okay."

Mom hugs me and tells me to go brush my teeth before bed.

When we go back to Miss Buena's, I'll bring some of my comics. Then, if Angelica's there again, I can show them to her.

Natasha

IT'S SUCH A RELIEF to have the kids with someone trustworthy, and in my own apartment complex. If I'd left them with my mother, I'd be a nervous wreck right now, worried about rushing through the conference to get back to her house before she could traumatize them in some way.

I'm not *totally* at ease, though.

I turn to Sara in the passenger seat and say, "Do you think Geronima will be okay with my kids and yours? That's six, counting Tiffany."

She turns from the window. "Huh? Oh, yeah. She'll be fine. She likes to have tons of kids over there so they can play with each other and she can cook a bunch of stuff." She sounds sure of that, but she looks nervous.

"What's wrong?" I say.

"Nothing. I just . . . I never went to this parent-teacher thing."

"You haven't?" I take the turn to the kids' school. "You mean because you didn't have anyone to watch your kids before Geronima?"

She says, "Well, yeah, that. But also . . . I don't know. I always felt weird about it, you know? I mean, I didn't even finish school myself. What am I gonna say to a bunch of teachers?"

I glance in her direction and see that she's really eaten up about this. And now I wonder if I was being pushy earlier, asking if she wanted to ride to the school with me. She wasn't even planning on going, I now realize, and only agreed to it for my sake.

"You know, Sara," I say, "I've been to a ton of these things, and it's really not a big deal. You go in and listen to what the teacher has to say about your kids, and then you can leave. You don't have to talk at all if you don't want to."

She says "Oh, yeah?" but sounds unconvinced.

I say, "A lot of times I go and there are parents who don't even speak English."

She looks out the window at the school as I pull in to its parking lot and find us a space. It's not as crowded as I expected. Not half as crowded as it would've been at the kids' old school. I guess Sara's not the only parent around here who avoids events like this.

Before we get out of the car, Sara turns to me and says, "Just give me a hint, real quick. What should I ask?"

"What do you mean?"

"Well, I don't want to look like some asshole who doesn't care about her kids. What are you gonna ask Alex and Lucia's teachers?"

She's serious. She's really at a loss and sees this as something she could fail. Poor Sara. I say, "First I'll listen to what they have to tell me. They'll have something prepared to say about each student. Then, for Alex, I might ask his teacher if she thinks he needs extra help with spelling, because I've been reviewing his homework every night and he always needs to redo his vocabulary lists."

Sara nods, and I wonder if she ever reviews Angelica's homework.

I add, "Since Lucia and Monique are in kinder, there's not a lot to say about their schoolwork. I'll probably ask if Lucia gets along well with the other kids."

Sara nods again. She's frozen in her seat. We've been sitting in the parking lot for a while now. I reach out and pat her on the shoulder. "Hey, it's going to be fine. Just remember, these teachers are here for our kids, and they're going to be glad we showed up. If anything, they're the ones who should be nervous, having to talk to so many people in one night. Right?"

She smiles weakly and says, "Yeah. You're right. Let's do this."

MIKE IS STANDING at Ms. Hubacek's desk. What is he doing here? I can't believe this.

Ms. Hubacek sees me in the window and waves me inside. When I open her door, I see that Missy's there, too, standing behind Mike with her son in a stroller. I feel sick and wish I hadn't come in.

"Is it okay if we do this all together?" Ms. Hubacek is saying. "Or we could have separate sessions. But since you're both here . . ."

"It's fine," I say, more stiffly than I mean to.

Ms. Hubacek leads us to a table set up in front of her desk. I take the seat nearest hers, and there's a delay while Mike drags over an extra chair for Missy.

I can't even look at them, so I focus on the folder in Ms. Hubacek's hand with Alex's name on its label. Meanwhile Mike takes the seat across from me, on Ms. Hubacek's other side.

What is he doing here? Mike's never attended parent-teacher conference night in his life. And why did he bring his girlfriend along? Does he think that spending a few nights a week with him gives her some kind of co-parent rights? I look along the table and see that she's messing with her baby, who's asleep in his stroller. She won't look up. I guess she's as uncomfortable around me as I am around her.

Mike says, "Okay, let's start," as if he's the one running the show. He's smiling at Ms. Hubacek like he would at any other young woman, practically flexing his muscles at her. She's the youngest person in the room, not counting Missy's baby, and she smiles right back at Mike. This is already intolerable. God, why did he come here?

I notice that his face has gotten a little fatter. Probably from too many cupcakes.

Ms. Hubacek is reading from a list that describes Alex as good, good, average, above average, and on and on through every possible aspect of his academics and conduct. But Mike is radiating palpable waves of annoyingness in my direction and drowning out her words. Everything he does makes me want to kick him. The way he's nodding his head knowingly, saying, "Uh-huh, right," as if he knows the slightest thing about what Alex does in school. This is the man who sends Alex back to me every other Monday with his homework untouched, and he's sitting here now acting as if *he's* the one who helps the kids with their math and reads to them every night.

"So do you guys have any questions?" Ms. Hubacek asks.

Mike opens his mouth to say something, but I cut him off. "Yes. Do you think Alex should start staying after school for extra help with language arts? I noticed that he's been having some trouble with his spelling."

Ms. Hubacek considers this, then says, "Well, if you think it's an issue—"

But Mike cuts her off and says, "No, it's fine. I'll work with Alex on his spelling this weekend. It'll be good."

You've got to be kidding me. I look directly at him for the first time this evening and say, "Oh, really? *You'll* help him with that?" He should be able to hear the sarcasm in my voice. I've known Mike for longer than anyone else in this room, and I know that he can't spell for crap.

He gives Ms. Hubacek a big grin. "Sure. I'll work with him for a few hours, and we'll get it all straightened out."

Oh, my God. I have never wanted to throw something at someone as badly as I do right now. How good would it feel to hit Mike with an eraser—to watch that smug grin fall off his face?

Okay. I have to focus now. I'm here for Alex, not to get into it with Mike. "Ms. Hubacek, I wanted to make sure there hasn't been any negative fallout since Alex's accident the other day. The other kids haven't been making fun of him, have they?"

She shakes her head. "No, not that I've seen. Everyone seems to have forgotten about it."

"Okay. That's good. I know we talked the other day about you allowing Alex to use the restroom more often, but I want to let you know that I've given him permission to go whenever he needs to, with or without asking."

She nods and is about to reply, but Mike interrupts. "That's not going to be a problem. I've talked to Alex about it, and he won't be having any more accidents."

I say, "Oh, he won't? And how can you be sure about that?"

Mike is still smiling at Ms. Hubacek, not facing me, as

if we're two students competing for her attention. He says, "Easy. I told him he needs to hold it. Or go in the morning, before school. He said okay, and he's not going to pee on himself anymore."

This is too much for me. It's time for me to point out how full of crap he is. "Really, Mike? You told him not to pee on himself anymore, and now he won't? You think he didn't try to hold it the other day? Are you the first person who ever thought of him holding it?"

"Apparently I am the first one who thought of it," he says. "And apparently you never talked to him about going before school or before lunch."

I knew he was going to do that—try to blame me. I say, "Why should I talk to him about when he should go to the bathroom? Why wouldn't he be able to go whenever he needs to?" My voice is louder than I wanted it to be, but I don't really care. I see Missy put her hand on Mike's arm, but I can't tell if it's to calm him down or to protect him from his big, bad ex-wife.

Mike pats Missy's hand, then turns to appeal to Alex's teacher again. "No one's saying he can't go, but Ms. Huba-sek here"—he can't even pronounce her name right—"can't have the kids getting up and taking off whenever they feel like it. She has a schedule to stay on. Right?"

I *knew* he was going to do that—try to get Ms. Hubacek on his side. That's what he always does: joins sides with whomever he can, against me. It's like he knows he doesn't have a leg to stand on by himself, so he has to win people over in order to create support for his arguments.

Ms. Hubacek may be young, but she's obviously dealt with arguing parents before. She says, "Mr. and Mrs. Davila, I understand your concerns about Alex. I'm committed to making sure he doesn't have any more accidents in class." She looks at me and adds, "And that no one bullies him." Then she turns to Mike and gives him a big smile that matches the ones he's been giving her. I wonder if she thinks he's good-looking, like I used to, back when I was her age.

The meeting's over now, so we get up and make way for the next parent, a tired-looking black woman wearing a pin-striped skirt suit. I break away from Mike and Missy and turn the corner to the front of the school, where Sara and I agreed to meet. Behind me Mike calls my name. I pretend not to hear him and keep walking. Whatever he has to say to me, I don't want to hear it.

I make it to the front, to the big foyer where lots of parents are milling around talking, and I look for Sara. It won't be easy to see her in this crowd, given that she's pretty short.

Mike and Missy have caught up to me. "Natasha. Would you wait a minute? I wanted to talk to you," he says.

I turn to face him, arms crossed over my chest. This is it. He's going to try to defend Missy's honor because of the other day, and I'm going to have to tell off both of them, right here in front of everyone. God help me.

He says, "I think you should let Alex spend more time with me, so I can help him with his math and his other issues at school."

Is this a joke? Some kind of prank? No, it's Mike trying to show off for his girlfriend, and for everyone around us. He wants to look like a good dad, and he thinks I'm going to play along. But he's not, and I won't. I say, "Look, Mike, I don't know why you're here, pretending you care about the kids' school all of a sudden, but you can give it a rest. I have it under control, all by myself, just like I always did."

Missy stands there with one hand on his arm and her other hand on the stroller, looking at Mike or at the baby—anything other than me. I'm sorry he's dragging her into this, making it awkward for her, but it's not my problem.

He leans close to me and says, "You're being a real witch, you know that? I'm just trying to do what's right for my kids."

I can't help but laugh at that. "Oh, really? Since when?"

He takes a step back, and I take the opportunity to walk away. I have to walk away now, before things get really ugly. I hurry around a group of couples chatting, bolt toward the front doors, and practically run into Sara.

"Natasha. Hey. What's wrong?"

Do I look like something's wrong? Yes. I'm practically trembling, I'm so angry. "Nothing. Except . . . that was my ex I was talking to."

"Just now?" she says.

"Yeah." I lead the way out the doors, into the parking lot, and she follows.

"Was that his girlfriend next to him? The blond chick with the baby?" she says.

"Yes," I answer.

We don't say anything else until we're safe in my Blazer. I grip the steering wheel to force my hands still, to try to get hold of myself. "I can't believe he showed up here. He never comes to the kids' school for anything."

"Did he try to start shit with you?" Sara asks.

"Kind of," I say. "I mean, he was just sitting in there, interrupting everyone and acting like he was in charge of everything. Then he followed me out and started telling me he thinks Alex should spend more time with him, since he's such a good dad and I'm doing such a bad job taking care of the kids."

"What? That's total bullshit," Sara says.

"Yeah."

"Fuck him," she says. She sounds as angry as I feel. She clenches her fist, crumpling the sheaf of colored papers she carried from the school. "You know what? Fuck that noise. He was just trying to show off in front of his girlfriend, to make himself look good."

"Yeah. That's what I was thinking, too," I say.

"What an asshole," she says. "You know what, Natasha? Don't let him bother you. You're a good mom. He's just pissed that you left him and now the best he can get is that skank."

I laugh despite myself. "You think she looks like a skank?"

Sara rolls her eyes. "Big time. I saw all that makeup she was wearing and all that shit in her hair. Plus, the girl has no ass at all. You look way better than her."

Is she serious? No, she's just trying to be nice. Loyal, like a friend would be. "You saw Mike, though. He can do better than me." I don't like saying this, but I don't want to sit here and lie to make myself feel better, either.

"What?" says Sara. "No way. I mean, I didn't see him. I couldn't, because there were people in the way. But fuck him. Natasha, you're pretty, and you're smart as hell, and you're an awesome-ass mom. You take care of your kids better than anybody I know. He was stupid to let you go, and now he's just trying to get back at you for it. Don't let him get to you with that shit."

I know she's just trying to be nice, but it feels good to hear what she's saying. To have someone be so firmly in my corner, instead of a bunch of women who are only my friends because they live nearby and who have to stay diplomatic for the sake of their husbands. Sara reminds me a little of my friends from school. My best friends, before we lost touch.

"You know what? You're right," I say. "Fuck him." The word sounds funny coming out of my mouth, and we both laugh. Suddenly I feel like everything's okay. Forget Mike and his pathetic attempts to look important. He doesn't matter.

I start the engine and pull out of the parking lot. "So how'd your conferences go?"

Sara's smiling now, all her anger purged and forgotten. "They went good. It was just like you said—the teachers gave their little spiel, and all I had to do was listen. Oh, check this out. Angelica's teacher said she was doing real good and I should think about putting her in some special thing. Gifted something."

"Gifted and talented?" I say.

"Yeah. That. What do you think? Is that a good thing? Does it cost money?"

It feels nice to have someone so eager for my opinions, for my advice. I *am* a good mother, I can't help but think as we drive back home. No matter what Mike says.

Alex

MOM AND DAD are fighting again. I can hear them through the door. Dad's saying, "Quit being such a witch, Natasha." But then he's saying the other word, too. The B-word. Mom's screaming at him, and I'm scared. I don't like it when she screams like that. Like she really is a witch. If I open the door, will she be Mom or will she be a monster, with a green face and red eyes? I can't open the door.

We're in the car. It's not Mom screaming, it's Lucia. She's saying, "No, Mommy, don't forget Daddy!" Mom's driving too fast, and I see Dad in the back window. He's getting tinier and tinier, and we're going up the freeway, and it's too high. I stick my hands out the window, but Dad can't reach me. He can't see me anymore.

"Alex," says Lucia. Then she says it again, in my ear. "Alex. Alex."

I wake up.

"Are you having a bad dream?" she says. She's standing on the ladder that goes up to my bed, like Mom always tells her not to. "About Mommy and Daddy?"

"No," I say. "Get down before you fall."

She says, "I'm not going to fall." But she climbs down the ladder and goes back to sleep.

Natasha

ALEX AND LUCIA are in the doctor's office, and he won't let them out. They're locked in. He's going to take them to the hospital, without me.

"It's your fault," Mike says. "You eat too much butter. You're always eating a whole stick of butter."

"I don't eat butter!" I scream at him. "*You* do!"

I'm so mad at him for lying like this. He's lying on purpose, to make me mad. I try to hit him, but I can't reach. I swipe and barely graze him with the tips of my fingers. He doesn't even flinch.

"It's your fault," he says. He points behind him, as if to illustrate. There's Missy, skinny in a pair of cutoff shorts. She's bending over, doing some kind of exercise. Her thighs are impossibly slim, like a child's.

I'm so angry, so frustrated I can't breathe. I'm trying to get the words out, to defend myself. "You lie!" I pant. "You tell lies all the time!"

It doesn't make a difference. The doctor gives me a look of disgust, probably believing that yes, I eat butter by the stick. He isn't going to open the door and let me take the kids home.

I can't take this. I can't freaking breathe.

DAMN IT. THANK GOSH for the too-loud alarm clock. How else would I have gotten out of that? I was about to have a heart attack in my sleep. I sit up and force myself to breathe slowly.

"Mommy! Are you awake?" It's Lucia, resident early bird.

"I'm awake, baby."

"Is it time to get ready?" she asks. I see her silhouetted in my doorway, the night-light in the hall making her a shadow in pajamas.

"It is time, baby," I say. "Good job. Is your brother awake?"

"Yes. I made him wake up."

"Good job. Go wash your face. I'll be out in a minute."

She scampers away, and I rub my eyes, waiting for the violent images to dissipate. This doctor/butter dream is a new one. Usually it's that we're moving into a beautiful new house and then I find out that Mike has to live there with us, because I never actually divorced him. I wake up feeling stupid, like a failure. Or, worse, I dream that I'm having sex with him and that I'm enjoying it. Then I wake up hating myself. I feel betrayed by my subconscious and have to spend several minutes reminding myself why I would never, ever live with Mike again. As if there's any risk of that, outside my dreams.

Why can't I dream about something good, for once? Such as Hector and a replay of Monday at the hotel.

No. That would be even worse. Why am I thinking of that now?

Because it's the opposite of my nightmare. Because I'm lonely. Or maybe just because Monday at the hotel felt so damned good.

Stop thinking about it. I can't do that again. It was stupid. Dangerous. I'm too old to act that way.

You know who's stupid? Missy. Mike has her totally fooled. She thinks he's so fabulous—that he's a great catch who had bad luck on his first marriage. A nice guy done wrong by some crazy woman. But she'll find out. Once they move in together, he'll start showing his true colors, and she'll see why he's divorced. He'll quit paying attention to her and her baby and start spending all his time with his friends. He'll stop listening to her, shush her when he's watching TV. He'll treat her like she's nothing more than his maid, his cook, his nanny, his blow-up doll, and he'll be incredulous when she has the nerve to complain about it. Then she'll realize that there are two sides to every story, and she believed the wrong one.

Unless he really has changed. Is that possible? He did put her on his emergency contact list at school. That's a pretty big commitment for someone like Mike.

What if he really loves this woman, more than he loved me? What if he never really loved me at all?

Maybe she really is more than just a rebound for him, and being with me all those years made him realize what he actually wanted in a wife. And he's happy with her, and that's why he's treating her well and wants to be a good stepfather for her baby.

No. It's not possible. Is it?

No. This is Mike. Selfish, inconsiderate Mike. He'll slip back into his old ways, and then Missy will be heartbroken and have to dump him. I almost feel sorry for her, imagining it. It's not her fault that she was dumb enough to fall for his act.

I was that dumb, too, once. And no one feels sorry for me.

Not even I do. It's time to quit wallowing and get up.

THE OTHER WOMEN at work hate using this old blue IBM typewriter, but I like it. Banging the keys and making them clack so loud is a good way to vent frustrations, and Lord knows I can use that.

I like this job in general and feel lucky to have it, this sweet little gig as assistant at a law firm, in this nice little building with its plush carpet and single-serve coffee machine with all the flavors of the rainbow. We get all the normal holidays and Jewish ones, too. I like the peace and quiet in the mornings, before the lawyers and the lazier assistants coast in. There are two kinds of assistants who work here—the pretty ones and the ones who do the work. I know which category I fall into, and I don't mind. Those other girls can keep giggling and applying lip gloss while I get certified as a paralegal. Prettiness lasts a few years, but certification is forever—assuming you keep up with the continuing-education requirements.

The phone rings, and I have to get up from the typewriter, slip back into my shoes, and hurry over to my normal desk. It's my personal line.

"Waterson Price Merman O'Connell. This is Natasha."

"Natasha, hi. How are you? It's Hector."

Oh, no. Hector. Why is he calling? I blame myself. I willed him to call by thinking about him this morning.

Now that I think about the lunch hour we spent together, here in broad daylight I feel completely ashamed. A little nauseated, actually, remembering the things we did in that nasty hotel room. Worse, the things we *said*. All the sex-related things and then, afterward, all the *sad* things. I think he cried. I don't know. I don't want to remember. Just hearing his voice now fills my mind's eye with a close-up of the hole in his black dress sock. And I feel like I have a wiry black hair rolling on the back of my tongue.

"Hector. Hi. What's going on?"

"Listen, I know it's really late to be calling about the weekend, but I just realized that your kids are probably going to their dad's tonight." He speaks quietly, undoubtedly because he's at work, too. "And I was thinking that maybe we could have dinner?"

"You know, I'm not sure that's such a good idea, actually."

"You're not?" he says.

"No. I'm sorry." I need to do this quickly, like ripping off a bandage. Shoot him down and get it over with. "The other day . . . It's not that I didn't enjoy your company, but I don't normally do things like that."

"I don't either. I don't go around looking for women to . . . I'm not that kind of person, generally, and I know you aren't either." He sounds flustered and sincere. Really sincere. "But I'm glad that things turned out the way they did, because—"

I cut him off. "Hector, I'm not ready to get involved in that kind of relationship right now. Or any kind. But no hard feelings, okay? Nothing personal."

He says, "What if it's just dinner? Nothing else? What if I want to get to know you?"

I say, "No, I think it's best if we just leave it where it is. Otherwise I'd just be leading you on."

He's quiet for a second, then says, "Well, okay. If that's the way you want it."

Mr. Merman walks in, and that's my excuse to cut the conversation short. "I have to go. Thanks for calling. Good-bye."

It's over. I sigh. Maybe that was a mistake, but I doubt it.

Get back to work. Move forward.

Natasha

ACCORDING TO THE *State of Texas Handbook for Divorced Parents*, I'm not supposed to bad-mouth Mike or argue with him in front of the children. It states that even if Mike is a self-centered, insensitive jerk, he's still the kids' dad and therefore I have to keep all my anger to myself while in front of them. That's in chapter 3, I think. That chapter also says that it's not the kids' fault that their dad's a jerk. It's mine.

This is my punishment, until Lucia turns eighteen: Being forced to face the mistake I made—the man I married—every first and third weekend of every month. Being forced to pretend that I can stand the sight of my children's father's face and that I don't fantasize about him disappearing from the face of the earth. It's going to be especially difficult to do this tonight, after last night's episode at the school.

We meet him in the complex's front driveway, where the kids catch the school bus. He hasn't been inside our apartment since we first moved here, when he made that crack about Alex and Lucia sharing a bedroom. I don't want to give him any more ammunition for criticism. Never mind that he lived in a one-bedroom apartment for months after we split, even though he easily could've afforded better, and made the kids use sleeping bags during their weekends with him. There's always a double standard—a whole other set of rules and expectations for Mike. When he had the kids sleeping on the floor, he whined that he was going through a rough period and I needed to cut him some slack. Meanwhile I spent money I didn't really have on a sturdy set of bunk beds. But, according to Mike, the fact that Alex and Lucia sleep in the same room makes me a bad mother. "It's not good for a boy and a girl to share a room," he said.

I hate it when he says that. I don't even understand what he's trying to imply, and it makes me wonder what kinds of things went on between Mike and his own sister when they were growing up. Either that or he seriously believes that sharing a room with a girl might turn Alex gay. That's his number-one secret fear, I know—that Alex will turn out to be homosexual. When I met Mike, he acted as if he was okay with gays—as if he had the same basic political beliefs that I did. But the longer I lived with him and heard him make ridiculous comments—like, "Nat, don't let Alex mess with your lip gloss. We don't want him getting the wrong idea"—the more I realized how many idiotic beliefs he really held in that big head of his. Thinking about it today makes me wonder why I didn't divorce him years ago.

Most annoyingly, he seems to feel especially qualified to judge me, now that he spends half his time in someone else's house—a house paid for by some other woman's child support! It'd be funny—hilarious—if it were happening to someone else. Someone on a stupid sitcom, maybe.

The minute I filed for divorce, Mike switched from a full-time salary to hourly contract pay at his IT job. He did it specifically to fudge on his taxes, I know, so he wouldn't have to pay the full amount of child support he would've owed. If he were paying the full amount the judge calculated when we first divorced, I could easily afford a bigger apartment in a nicer neighborhood. Thinking about that used to make me want to kill him, back then.

But I've stopped caring. Never mind any of that crap, because I don't want his money anymore. I prefer to take care of myself and owe him nothing. The less I have to deal with him, the better, because he's the single most stressful thing in my life.

And right now, if I could just get through these weekend handoffs without losing my temper over his stupid comments, that would be a small victory. Here we are in the front of the complex, in the cold and damp, passing the kids between us again, as if we're taking turns kidnapping them and exchanging them for ransom.

"Hey, Alex! Little man! What's up? You missed your dad, huh?" Mike talks way too loud, and people walking down the sidewalk glance our way to see what this big man in the striped golf shirt and khakis is bellowing about. He's putting on his show again: The Good Dad Show.

Alex smiles weakly and mumbles, "Bye, Mom," as I hug him.

"How's my pretty girl?" Mike practically shouts to Lucia. I feel her hand claw at the back of my jacket as I hug her, and I'm worried. She doesn't want to go. Why? Is it Missy? Missy's son? Are they mean to her? Is it Mike, forgetting her night-light or the channel of her favorite cartoon? There's a problem, and it's too late for me to fix it. They're climbing into his car now, and there's nothing I can do. I feel horrible. Guilty. A failure.

"Can we bring my friend Tiffany?" Lucia asks her father.

"Uh ... not this time, honey," he says. Instead of just no. He never says no to them—that'll be my job, later, when she remembers and asks again.

I look up at Mike and feel a wave of fresh hatred. It's amazing that I can feel so much hate, still, after all this time.

Right before he gets into the car, he says, "Oh, I noticed that Lucia needs better tennis shoes. Maybe you could take care of that with the child support I'm providing. Missy's already bought her three outfits this month, and I don't want her to have to buy any more." He walks away from me as he says this. Can't even face me. Gets into the car before I can reply.

"Go to hell," I whisper. I glance down and see Alex watching me through the window, so I change my glare into a smile. Lucia's staring at Mr. Beary, moving his arms in circles. She's already insulated herself from any unpleasantness.

I wave at both of them anyway. Alex gives a nod, almost formal-looking, as they pull out of the space and drive off. Like a proper little old man. I want to laugh and I want to cry. Maybe this one time I *will* end up crying, but not until I'm alone, later tonight, in safe darkness.

I walk back upstairs, toward the apartment that's already radiating emptiness. It's been—how long since the divorce?— thirteen months since I moved out, last September, and ten months since we signed the final custody order, and I still don't know what to do with myself on these first and third weekends.

What do I usually end up doing? Nothing I can explain or even remember. If people ask, I say I'm taking a well-deserved break from parenting—the breaks I never got during my marriage, when Mike spent weekends hiding out in the garage or at his friends' houses. Or I tell people I've been studying for my certification. Or that I'm busy. Too busy to visit my old friends, with their new babies and new dreams. I can't stand walking into their houses and seeing them look at me like I'm the Ghost of Marriage Past, a reason to say, "But *we'll* never end up like *them*," to each other after I've left.

What do I actually *do* during these weekends without the kids? I sit in our apartment and think, with the TV or radio in the background. Or sit in my car and think, while driving between the bank and the post office and the grocery store.

What do I think about? The sad past. The difficult present. The big, blank, terrifying future.

Do I get sad? Yes, but not for the obvious reasons. It's not Missy or Mike or the loss of the rented house in the pretty little neighborhood up north. It's not because I'm suddenly lonely.

I'm sad because I'm *alone*, and leaving Mike only makes me realize that I've always been alone. Now it's crystal clear to me that if I don't bust my butt to make a good life for these kids, no one will. Mike didn't care when we were together, and now that we're apart, he's already involved with someone new, trying to hurry up and replace the marriage he threw away, the same way he used to replace broken tools or run-over pets.

I feel like I'm raising these kids by myself. My goal is to give them a better life than I had, so it's not as if my mother can help me, sitting there in her dark, depressing, white-zin-scented town house.

It's not as if my old friends can help me, either. They were smarter than I was. Every one of them waited until later to get knocked up, and now they're all immersed in worlds of expensive strollers and homemade baby food. Not that I'd ask them for help anyway.

No, it's not that they were smarter . . . it's that I'm a *pioneer*. Of my small group—Yolanda and Connie from high school, Amanda and Yen from community college, I was the first to get pregnant and get married. Even though I was the one who swore I'd never have kids, who was secretly resigned to never having my dream wedding. They were all so shocked that I went through with it. Connie especially, since she'd had the abortion. But I couldn't do that, and so I got married.

I said it then, and I still think so now—giving birth to Alex was the best thing that ever happened to me. It changed my life, and not just in the ways they warned us about, with the bag-of-flour babies in home economics.

Being a mother gave me focus. Until I had Alex, what was I doing with my life? Not a danged thing. Taking random courses at the community college with no plan for a major or a future career. Working that dead-end job at the grocery store every night. What did I have to look forward to, besides the next time I'd be alone with a piece of chocolate cake or masturbating about guys I'd never have? When Alex came out of me, he handed me a mission: to raise him to be the best, smartest, most functional child possible. Everything my parents had failed to teach me, Alex would know. Every mistake I'd made in life, Alex would never have to make.

I was meant to be a mother. I know that now, even during the sucky parts. Looking back, I can see that it was obvious—I'd already raised so many kittens, hamsters, birds, stuffed animals . . . My friends knew it, too, especially when they finally started getting pregnant themselves and realized that I was a treasure trove of experience and advice, instead of only "Natasha who can't ever meet us for happy hour." For every challenge they'd run into—morning sickness, episiotomies,

breast-milk clogs—I'd already been there, done that, and pur-
chased the souvenir beer stein. When Alex hit elementary
school, I was the one looking to book occasional girls' nights
out and my old school buddies were the ones busy with diaper duty.

And then I became a new kind of pioneer: the first one to
get divorced. Again my friends were shocked—as shocked as
they could express through the occasional e-mail or phone
call. They probably believe that I made a mistake. Again I'm
out of sync with them. I'm "Natasha who can't ever meet us
for couples nights." I'm on my own in a different world again,
figuring it out with no help from anyone.

I felt alone throughout my marriage—emotionally abandoned because Mike couldn't handle the responsibility of it
all and preferred to live in the past. And now I'm really alone,
but without the convenience of an absentee husband's paycheck. The only way I can feel *more* alone is without the
kids. I've been glued to them for so long now that I can't remember how I used to live without them.

What am I going to do this weekend, until they come back?
Run errands and clean my kitchen. Watch crappy movies on
cable, lie on my bed, and mope in the dark. Put a wine cooler
on the kitchen counter and dare myself to become my own
mother? Call someone up, maybe?

I'm having a vision: black hair on pale skin and blue veins.
Hector. It makes me feel either nauseated or faint with sudden desire, and I push the thought from my mind.

I have a vision of Lucia looking unhappy, Alex looking embarrassed. A little hand grasping at the back of my jacket. A
tug in my uterus, a pull at my breast.

I need to get hold of myself. Get inside and start the laundry.

TEN MINUTES LATER I'm a laundry-bot, thinking about nothing but soap and softener as I carry our basket down the hall.

Someone's standing on the stairs. It's Haley, Geronima's friend from Tuesday's dinner. She has her arms wrapped around her body and a set of keys in her hand. She's staring down at nothing, her eyes pink and shiny. Her sad face is the only thing detracting from the perfection of her outfit. Sleeveless silk blouse, linen capri pants, chic espadrilles. I'm guessing she didn't go to work in those clothes—that she simply doesn't work. She must get a lot more child support than I do. I know why she's standing here, though. I can tell.

"Hey," I say. "Kid-free weekend?"

She looks up, startled, but then recognizes me and chuckles. "Hi. Yeah, I just dropped Jared at his father's house."

"I just handed mine off to their dad in the parking lot."

We smile in mutual understanding. Then there's silence. What do we say now, we two women who barely know each other? I shift the basket on my hip, wonder if I should go back to my apartment.

Haley says, "So, would you . . . do you have plans? For dinner tonight?"

We're standing at the lockers in our middle school, and she's asking me to the eighth-grade dance. That's how weird this feels, trying to be friendly with another grown woman.

"No, I don't have plans." I say. "I'm still getting used to the whole freedom-every-other-weekend thing."

She laughs, and the tension's broken. "Well, do you want to get something to eat? There's a new Thai place over by the art galleries. I've been wanting to check it out, but not by myself."

"Um. Okay," I say. "Let's do it. Let me ditch this laundry and...change real quick." I'm wearing the cargo pants and T-shirt I threw on after work. And flip-flops. I must look like a slob.

"Okay," she says. "Should I meet you in the parking garage in a few minutes?"

She's standing there with her keys, already dressed to go somewhere, and she lives upstairs. I say, "Or, do you want to come to my place and wait there? I won't be long."

She follows me to my apartment. And again I have the sensation of middle school. Meeting other girls and arranging sleepovers. But this is better, isn't it? Because we're grown women and we have cars. We can buy cigarettes and alcohol if we feel like it. We're free for the weekend, darn it. It's time to act like it. I feel a lightness come over me. Exhilaration, almost.

This is going to be fun. Or I hope it'll be fun.

No, it will. Anything would be more fun than spending another Friday evening alone, feeling sorry for myself.

HALEY'S VOLVO IS so nice. She has a toddler booster seat in the back. I never had to use those with Alex and Lucia—they were grown before the laws changed. Haley's son, Jared, must be smaller than I remembered. He looked at least three or four to me, but I guess not, if he's still using one of those seats.

I'm glad we're in her car, with its moon roof and leather interior, and not in my beat-up blue Blazer. I try to imagine how Haley would react to the Blazer's hideous fabric seats, the way they're tearing at the corners and encrusted with candy and old sunscreen.

"I love this neighborhood," she says as we circle the galleries and boutiques and cute little cafés crammed into a six-block square. "It's so *diverse*, you know?"

She's right. This part of Oak Cliff is new and hip, like a little piece of San Francisco. Then, less than a mile away, we have our apartment complex, which looks like a little piece of Mexico. But all around us are old houses, two-story bricks and Victorians in various phases of renewal. And the oak trees, which make it beautiful. And all around the houses we have the thrift stores and the taquerias. And my work, and the other new office buildings sprouting up like weeds.

"Is that why you moved here?" I ask. "Because of the diversity?"

"That was part of it," she says. "But also because of Geronima." She steps on the gas then, to snag a space on the street, but not before someone in a rainbow-colored car backs into it. "They need valet here," she mutters.

"So you've known Geronima a long time?" I venture. That much was clear at dinner the other night, but I couldn't figure out how they knew each other, or if they were related, or what.

"Mm-hmm. I've known her since I was a child," says Haley. "Geronima used to take care of me."

So Geronima was her baby-sitter? Or her nanny? If Haley's my age and Geronima's in her sixties, then they knew each other over twenty years ago.

"And you've kept in touch with her all this time?" I say.

Haley shakes her head. "No. I just decided to look her up. Last month, when I...when my husband and I were separated."

I say, "You aren't divorced yet?"

She says, "No, not yet."

I say, "It takes forever, doesn't it? Mike and I got our separation last September, but our divorce wasn't final until January. Is your ex giving you trouble over Jared?"

She shakes her head again. "No. He's not giving me trouble over anything. It's just . . . waiting for the paperwork." I get the impression that it's a sensitive subject for her, so I drop it. I guess I didn't like talking about it much either, when Mike and I were first apart.

We finally score parking a block from the restaurant, and I wish I hadn't succumbed to vanity and put on these stupid wedge sandals, because I'm out of practice walking in heels for long distances. My little toes are threatening to slip out of the straps. But I'll make it. This is supposed to be a fun girls' night out. There's no crying in girls' night out.

We're early enough to get a table without a reservation. Our host, a beautiful young man with golden highlights, leads us through shimmering statues of peacocks and elephants and a cloud of dance music to a rattan table in the middle of the darkened room. We take our seats, and our attention is immediately drawn to the colorful drink menu open on the table between us.

"Do you want to have a drink?" Haley says.

Why the heck not? When's the last time I had a fancy mixed drink at a nice restaurant? At least a year. God, maybe two years ago.

Our waiter is another beautiful young man. I tell him I want a Shanghai Surprise, even though I didn't read its ingredients. But it's a beautiful shade of orange. Haley orders a Thai Tiger, and the waiter spins away.

Even the menus are beautiful here, designed to look like inked papyrus on red silk. But . . . "Oh. This is more expensive than I was expecting." I hate to be a killjoy, but I can't totally forget my responsibilities, just because the kids are gone. "I'm just going to have an appetizer, I think."

"Natasha, please," says Haley. "I invited you here. This is my treat, okay? Order whatever you want. I want to try some of everything."

Normally I'd refuse, but I can tell she'd be disappointed. Like she said, this is a place she's been wanting to try. And I'm pretty sure she can afford it, single mom or not.

We end up ordering calamari, three dishes neither of us can pronounce, and chicken pad thai, just in case the other stuff turns out to be too exotic. Haley's already given up on her Thai Tiger, saying it's too spicy. I trade drinks with her. I've never had a spicy martini before, and this one's delicious.

"So why did you move to Oak Cliff?" Haley asks me after our drinks are settled in their rightful places. "You had a house before, right? In Dallas?"

I nod. "We were renting a house on the north side. I couldn't afford to stay there when we broke up, because I was only working part-time. When we separated, I made a spreadsheet of all my options." Hearing myself say that makes me laugh, and Haley laughs, too. At the time, though, it wasn't funny at all. "I got one of those apartment booklets—the ones they have for free at the grocery stores?" She nods. "I made a list of all the apartments I could afford, which wasn't many. And then I cross-referenced their neighborhoods with the ratings for the schools in those neighborhoods. And when I was done, the best choice for us was Oak Cliff."

Haley says, "Wow. That was smart."

"Yeah. Well, it seemed smart. The first place we picked was a total rathole. Literally, it had mice. And mold. Lucia had allergic reactions from the moment we moved in. We stayed there for a week, and then I had to break our lease and leave. I had to practically threaten the landlord in order to get my deposit back. It was horrible. Really stressful." Haley's eyes are wide. "But then everything finally worked out, and now . . . This complex, where we all live now, was second on my list. It isn't the greatest—you know that. But it's good enough for right now. Until I can get some money saved and move us someplace better."

Haley smiles and raises her drink. "To someplace better," she says. I clink my glass against hers. "Do you want another one?"

"No, not yet. Thanks." It occurs to me our apartment complex is probably a little bit more tolerable for Haley, since she only has Jared. I wonder if they have the same two-bedroom plan I do. I don't imagine her being crammed into a one-bedroom with her son. Actually, it's hard to imagine her living in our complex at all. She looks like she could afford better. Why doesn't she rent one of the houses in the neighborhood?

"It's funny," she says. "I totally understand what you're saying about our apartment, and wanting something better. But for me, for right now . . . Living there is kind of an adventure, isn't it?"

"You know, I never thought about it that way." I raise my glass again. "To adventures." She laughs and repeats the toast.

WE LIKE THE pad thai and the yam neua, which turns out to be salad topped with spicy meat, but not the other dishes, so Haley has the waiter take them away. As she picks the peanuts out of her noodles and I devour the last of the salad, Haley tells me about her plans. "I don't need to work, but I want to. You know? I don't want to be dependent on Dave for the rest of my life."

I nod. I know exactly what she means.

"But I feel like, the whole time I lived with him, it crippled me, in a way. Do you know what I mean? While I was there with Dave, being his wife and taking care of our house and our child, everyone else was out learning to do new things and...how to take care of themselves. And there I was, learning nothing but how Dave wanted the housekeeper to shine his shoes."

"Right." Of course, I never had a housekeeper, and Mike never wore shoes that needed shining. But I totally relate to the feeling of stagnation she's describing. I was lucky I decided to work part-time, near the end of our marriage, and that Mike didn't put up too much of a fight over it. Otherwise I'd probably still be looking for full-time work now. And I definitely wouldn't have learned the few computer skills I have.

"What kind of job are you looking for?" I ask.

"I don't know yet. There's not much I'm qualified to do." She sighs. "If I could get paid to volunteer at fund-raisers, I could probably manage that." She smiles wanly at me, and I smile back, as if I have some idea of what volunteers do at fund-raisers. "But I'll find something," she continues. "It doesn't really matter what it is. I'm sure I can learn to do any basic job. I'm not totally incompetent."

"Of course not," I say. I can totally picture her as a secretary or some kind of analyst. She said she went to college in El Paso for a couple of years, so I say, "You could always go back to school, too."

"That's right." Her face brightens. "I could."

"To possibilities," I say, raising my second Thai Tiger.

Haley lifts her second candy-colored cocktail and says, "To *endless* possibilities."

AFTER DINNER, on the way back to the car, we pass a gallery that was closed when we first drove by but is now apparently open. Its doors are swung wide to the evening's random October balminess and webbed with Christmas lights.

"They're having an opening!" Haley says. "Should we check it out?"

I've never been to a gallery opening before, but I don't say no. I follow Haley through the door and accept the folded piece of paper handed to me by a bearded man who points us to a table covered in glasses of red and white wine. I take red and Haley takes white, and we move into an unoccupied space in front of a painting on the wall. Except it's not a painting. It's a rusted metal box, open to a scene of puppets or dolls in a jumble of wires and gears.

"Hmm," says Haley.

"Interesting," I say.

The next piece is another jumble of wires and household items, this time with half a dirty baby doll poking out of the middle.

"Reminds me of giving birth to Alex," I whisper.

Haley giggles, and we move to the next piece. They're all similar, and none of them are attractive in the least. But it's fun to look at them. We are, as Haley said, having an adventure. I feel like I'm at a costume party. Because here, right now, no one knows that I'm Alex and Lucia's mom. Or Mike's ex-wife. I could be anyone: a woman who's happily married, a woman who never married, a woman who used to be a man. I can be, simply, Natasha.

Alex

COME ON, ALEX!" my dad says. "Your sister's doing better than you, and she's a girl!"

"Mike, that's not nice," says Missy.

I hate when we go to Missy's house and dad makes us play outside with him and Missy and Shepherd. They always want to play catch, and I hate playing catch. I'm good at the Super Bullet Balls video game, but I can't throw real footballs good, and Dad always wants me to throw real footballs. When I try to catch them, they burn my hands.

Missy always has a little blue football that she throws with Shepherd and Lucia. That one's soft and squishy, not hard and scrapey like the brown football Dad uses.

We're in Missy's backyard. Shepherd started hitting Lucia with the blue football, so he lost his privileges, and now all three of them are sitting on the swing set watching Dad throw the ball at me. I miss, and it rolls all the way to the fence. Lucia runs and picks it up and throws it back at my dad. It hits the ground, but my dad says, "Good hustle, Lucy!"

My dad throws the ball at me again, and this time I do catch it, but it burns my fingers, like always, so I drop it. I pick it up real quick and get ready to throw it back to him, lining up my pinkie on the fourth thing like he showed me. But he's not there anymore. He walked over to Missy and started talking to her. I hear him say, "...never takes them outside, even." I know he's talking about Mom, because he always says that about her—that she doesn't take us outside enough and that's why I'm not good at sports.

Missy doesn't say anything, but she looks at me and smiles.

Shepherd runs up and grabs my dad's leg. Dad picks him up and swings him and says, "Hey, tiger!" I hate Shepherd. He's a brat.

Lucia goes, "Alex! Alex! Over here!"

She wants me to throw the football to her. I throw it far away so she has to run.

MISSY MADE CUPCAKES again. But this time I can't have one, because I didn't finish my brussels sprouts. I'm not going to eat them, because they look like they have worms inside. There's a picture in my textbook that shows a caterpillar coming out of a ball of leaves that looks just like a brussels sprout. I guess the ones Dad and Missy and Lucia are eating don't have bugs in them, because they're not saying anything, but what if there're only worms in a few of them and I get one of the ones with a worm?

After the cupcakes Missy takes Shepherd and Lucia to the living room to watch *America's Funniest Home Videos*, and Dad says for me to come with him to the garage.

We go outside. There's a bunch of little bugs flying around the garage light. Some of them touch Dad's hair when he opens the door.

I wait for him to turn on the lights inside the garage before I follow him in there. The garage is really dark at night, even darker than the room we sleep in when we spend the night here.

Dad gets the air pump and starts pumping up the basketball that got popped last time we were here. He asks if I want to help, so I push the pump a few times. It's really hard and hurts my hand, but I keep doing it.

"Alex," my dad says, "how's it been going at your mother's?"

"Good," I say.

"That's good," he says.

We work on the ball some more, until it's almost all the way full. Then Dad puts it down and looks in the corner at some tools, like he's trying to decide about what to work on next. He says, "I've been thinking."

I wait to see if he's going to tell me what he's been thinking about or if he's just talking to himself, like he always used to do in the garage at our old house.

He says, "I've been missing you a lot. And I've been thinking ... How would you like to live with me?"

I don't know what he means. Does he mean all the time and then visiting Mom on some Saturdays and Sundays, like the opposite of what we do now? And does he mean with Lucia or by myself?

Maybe Mom told him what I said about the cupcakes, the other day when I said I wanted to live with Dad and Missy. Would she do that? She hates to talk to my dad on the phone, and they usually just talk about what time they're going to pick us up, or else they argue. But maybe she got mad after I said that and told Dad that I want to go live with him.

I shouldn't have even said that, because they're only going to give me cupcakes if I eat vegetables first, and Missy cooks freaky vegetables sometimes. Mom knows which vegetables I like.

Dad says, "You don't have to tell me now, but I'd like you to think about it, okay?"

I nod my head so he knows that I'm paying attention. He doesn't like it when I don't pay attention. Some of the same bugs from outside came inside with us, and now they're flying around the light that hangs down from the ceiling. The light makes a buzzing noise, and I wonder if that's why the bugs like it, because it sounds like them.

My dad walks around and messes with the tools that are hanging on the tool thing. He says, "What with everything that's been going on with you lately . . ."

And that's all. He doesn't say anything after that. I guess he means when I peed my pants.

Either that or he's talking about me and Lucia sleeping in bunk beds at Mom's, with the night-light on. He always tells Mom stuff about having a boy and a girl in the same room, and about me being too big to be afraid of the dark. We're not allowed to have a night-light in our room here.

Dad gets up and rubs his hand in my hair, the same way he always does with Shepherd. Then he walks to the door, and I have to hurry to catch up with him if I don't want to get left in the dark.

Natasha

THE UNSEASONABLE WARMTH has lasted all weekend, which is good, since I have to stand outside waiting for Mike to get here, and, like always, he arrives ten minutes later than he said he would.

He opens one of the back doors of his car, and both kids scoot out of it. Lucia immediately launches into a story about a squirrel she saw through the window during the ride. I listen and express the appropriate amount of shock and awe at the fact that the squirrel had a white stripe on his back. Meanwhile Mike opens the trunk and pulls out the kids' backpacks. He doesn't listen to Lucia's story at all. I wonder if he's relieved to be giving them back to me, these noisy kids whose stories he never hears.

I hold in the words I want to say, the criticisms I'd like to make. Hold my tongue until he's gone and Lucia's waving good-bye at his taillights. Then I turn to the kids. "Well, let's get upstairs and get cracking on that homework." Alex makes a face, so I add, "And let's talk about Halloween, too. It's coming up, and we need to figure out what you guys are going to be."

This is how we spend every first and third Sunday evening—hurrying to make sure Alex's homework is done, because Mike never even thinks about it. As the kids trudge up the hall behind me, I remember Alex's words from the other day, about wanting to live with his dad.

Of course he wants that sometimes. Who wouldn't want to live in a land of no obligations, where homework doesn't exist and cupcakes are plentiful and free?

Alex says, "I finished all my homework already. Dad showed me a shortcut for the multiplication."

"He did?" I couldn't be more surprised if Alex had told me his dad grew wings and flew away.

"Yeah. Can we play outside?" That's another first. Alex never wants to play outside now that the pool is closed.

"What do you want to play?" I ask him. There isn't much room in the apartment's courtyard. But I could sit in the barbecue area and watch them play tag or hide-and-seek, I guess.

He hikes his backpack higher on his shoulder. "I don't know. Do we have a football?" Behind him Lucia echoes, "Yeah! Football!"

"Where's Mr. Beary?" I ask her as I unlock our door and mentally search our apartment for a football, or any kind of ball.

"In my backpack."

Once we're all inside, I tell Alex, "I don't think we have a football, baby. We'll have to get one this weekend. Do you still want to—"

There's a knock at the door, which I've already closed and locked. I peek through the peephole. It's Sara. With all three of her kids. I open the door and say, "Hey."

"Hey," she says. "I came by to see if y'all want to go to the park. I have to take these brats out and let them run around before they drive me crazy."

I see what she means. Junior and Monique are chasing each other in a circle behind their mother. Angelica, however, is as still and quiet as always. "Umm," I say. It is a convenient coincidence that she came by with that suggestion just now, and the weather's nice, but... "I don't know. You mean the park across the street, right? Is it safe over there?"

Sara scoffs, as if it's a silly question. "Yeah. It's totally safe."

"Okay. Hold on. Let me just... Y'all come in." They all crowd into the doorway and remain near it—Sara doesn't let the kids sit down, citing their dirty feet—and I run to my bedroom to throw on tennis shoes. And... I'll leave my purse here, just in case. Keys in my pocket. And my phone, just in case. What else? Sunscreen for the kids? No, it'll be dark in an hour.

Back in the living room, an idea strikes me. "Hey, should we invite Haley and Jared?" I'm asking because yesterday, when I was finishing up the laundry I never did on Friday night, I ran into Geronima, who apparently heard that Haley and I had dinner together. She went on and on about how nice it was that Haley and I were becoming friends, because Haley was having such a rough time on her own and needed to make friends, et cetera, et cetera. I'm sure she was exaggerating a little, just being a busybody in the way older women like to be, but it stuck in my head. Imagining Haley in her apartment right now, probably just sitting there with Jared, makes me wonder aloud if we should invite her along.

Sara doesn't seem to think it's such a good idea, though. She doesn't say anything at first.

I say, "Unless you don't want to. We don't have to."

She says, "No, go ahead. Invite her."

I pull my phone from my pocket and make the call. Haley

says yes, thanks, so we all go into the hall and wait for them to come down.

THE THING THAT makes me nervous about this park, I admit, is the basketball courts. They're always filled with teenage boys, and teenage boys sometimes make me nervous. Especially big groups of them in less affluent neighborhoods. There, I've said it. I'm a horrible person.

I wonder if Haley feels the same way. I see her glancing at the court as we settle ourselves on the benches near the playground. There's a group of five or six boys playing there now, wearing undershirts and baggy shorts. They yell at each other in English and Spanish. "No way, man! Hey, mamón!"

"I hope we aren't stepping on anybody's turf," I say. It's a lame joke, I know.

Sara says, "What, you mean those guys? No, they're cool. That one in the red is my mom's cousin's boy. They won't mess with us." As if on cue, the boy in red turns and, seeing us there, waves. Sara waves back. "They won't let anybody else mess with us either."

It's settled, then. We have the whole playground to ourselves, plus our own personal bodyguards. I sit back on the bench and relax as Alex and Lucia run to join Sara's kids at the swings.

"Okay, Jared, remember to be careful," Haley's saying. She's produced a spray bottle from the tote bag at her side and is spraying her hands with it, then wiping them on Jared's tiny, pale arms.

"What's that?" Sara asks.

"Mosquito spray," says Haley. "Do you want some?"

Sara shakes her head, looking bemused. Haley finishes her

son's rubdown, then reties the laces on each of his shoes. "I wish I'd brought your hat," she says to him. "Okay, you're set. Stay where I can see you, though. Stay right here on this thing. But don't go up the slide." Obviously reluctant, she lets him go, and I can't help but think, *No adventuring for Jared.*

"How old is he?" Sara asks.

"Three," says Haley.

"Really? I thought he was older than that. Baby Junior's three, and Jared's way bigger than him."

Haley gives a little frown. "He'll be four next month." She sounds like this fact makes her sad, or maybe like she can't believe it.

"How come you don't have him in pre-K?" Sara asks.

Haley frowns harder. "I think he's still too young. And . . . I haven't decided what school he's attending yet."

Sara looks at me and raises her eyebrows.

I should've realized that Sara and Haley might not immediately become friends. But I didn't expect the conversation between them to be this awkward either. I try to change the subject to something they'll have in common. "So did y'all have a good weekend, with your kids at their dads'?"

Sara snorts at this. "My kids never go to their dad's."

"Really?" I say.

"Nope." She turns and yells an order at Angelica to keep her brother away from the mud. Then she says, "Once in a while, Monique and Baby Junior's dad will come get them and take them to the flea market, or to his nephews' birthdays or something. Angelica's dad, I haven't seen since before she was born."

Great. I found an even more awkward subject to introduce. Haley stops monitoring Jared's every move for a moment, turning to ask Sara, "Well, why don't you take them to court? At least take Monique and Baby Junior's father, and make him have regularly scheduled visitations?"

Sara lets out a short, bitter laugh. "Why? So I can have him in my face all the time, telling me what to do? I like it this way. He minds his own business, I mind my own business, everything's fine."

I suspect she's being a little more cavalier than she really feels. But she makes an interesting point. How would I feel if Mike stopped taking his weekends with Alex and Lucia? No more parking-lot handoffs. No more stressful phone calls. I'd never have to speak to him again. I'd have more time to do fun things with the kids, instead of just homework and errands.

And it'd be nice if I could afford to turn down Mike's child support, instead of haggling for it in the courts. You have to admire Sara, at least a little, for being so independent. She obviously makes less money than I do and has more kids, but she's getting the job done, with no complaints.

Except I want more out of life than what Sara has. I don't want to struggle so hard or to live in these apartments forever. Maybe if I hurry up and get my certification . . .

Even if I didn't need Mike's money, there'd be no way to avoid dealing with him. I could never get out of the visitations, because the kids would miss him.

I wonder how Angelica feels about her father disappearing. Does she even understand it?

Jared is trying to climb onto the bottom of the little yellow slide. His coordination isn't the greatest, and he ends up falling on the ground. A long, slow wail emerges from his mouth, like a train whistle. But there are no tears in his eyes. He hasn't yet decided whether the fall's worth crying over.

"Jared!" gasps Haley. She jumps up to get him, but my daughter's first on the scene. Lucia runs right up to Jared and hauls him to his feet. "Come here, baby. Did you hurt yourself? No, you're okay. You're okay." Lucia gives him a hug and presses her cheek to the top of Jared's little blond head. He looks astounded, but then he turns to face Lucia and opens his arms. She grabs him, lifts him off the ground, and sets him on the edge of the slide. I can't help but laugh. Sara and Haley laugh, too.

"Like mother, like daughter," Haley says.

Funny. Is that how I look? Is Lucia mimicking me? I feel a mixture of bashfulness and pride swell in my chest. Lucia stands next to the slide and tries to engage Jared in a game of patty-cake. After a few minutes, Monique abandons her swing and runs over to join the game, leaving Alex and Angelica to push Baby Junior back and forth between them.

I feel like someone's missing. Oh. "Should we have picked up Tiffany from Geronima's apartment?" I ask the others.

Sara shakes her head. "Gero wouldn't let you. She doesn't let that girl out of her sight."

"Really?"

Haley nods. "A couple of weeks ago, I went over and asked if Tiffany could come to Earth Foods with us. I thought she'd enjoy seeing all the different organic pumpkins they have. But Geronima wouldn't let her go. She says she worries too much when Tiffany's gone."

So our Geronima's a control freak. She'll watch everyone else's kids but won't let anyone watch hers. I can relate to that, actually. I'm still surprised that I let her watch my kids without having a panic attack over it.

IT'S NEAR SEVEN now and getting dark, but none of us makes a move to leave. The park's well lit, and there don't seem to be any mosquitoes here, despite Haley's fears. Our kids are winding down, rocking slowly on the swings or digging idly in the gravel with twigs. But our bodyguards have endless energy and keep jumping, shooting, free-throwing away. Sara's just told us something very interesting, and no one wants to stop the conversation at this point.

"Wait, wait," says Haley. "You're going to work *now*? After we leave the park?"

"Mm-hmm," says Sara. "That's why I wanted to bring my brats here and get them good and worn out—so they'll go to sleep as soon as they get to Geronima's and stay asleep till I get home."

"What time do you get home?" Haley asks.

"Two-thirty, usually. I'm scheduled to work nine to two tonight," Sara says.

"Is it one of those twenty-four-hour restaurants?" Haley asks.

"Not exactly," says Sara. There's a pregnant pause, during which it becomes evident that Haley and I are waiting for her to tell more. "I'm a cocktail waitress," she says. Then, mumbling, "At my cousin's strip club."

"What?" Haley gasps. *"Wha-a-a-at,"* is what she actually says, in a long, breathy whisper. You'd think Sara had just said she was a secret agent. Haley sounds more intrigued than put off.

I'm curious, too. I don't want to be nosy, but I'll listen if Sara wants to tell us more.

"You work at a men's club?" Haley has scooted to the edge

of her bench and is leaning as far forward as possible with her eyes open wide in big blue circles.

Sara studies Haley's reaction for a while, then laughs. "It's not like you're thinking—not some super-sexy place. It's just a junky little club by the airport."

"Do you dance?" Haley asks. She's like a child, being so curious. No mental filter that keeps her from blurting out personal questions. But that is a good one. Is Sara a waitress or a dancer? I like her, and I don't want to judge her, but I don't want my kids hanging around with a stripper either.

"No. *Hell* no," says Sara. "I don't dance. I just serve drinks. I wouldn't take my clothes off for those losers if they paid me a million dollars."

Well, that's a relief. I guess.

Haley sighs, though, as if the answer disappoints her. "Well, if it's your cousin's club, do you have any say in who gets picked to dance there? I mean, are there auditions? Do you get to watch them?"

Sara raises an eyebrow at her. "Why do you ask? You looking for a job?"

I can tell by Sara's tone that she's teasing, but Haley blushes red, all over her cheeks. "No. I'm just . . . I've never met anyone who's been to a men's club."

"Really?" I say. "Your ex never went?"

Haley considers the question, then blushes again. "If he did, he never told me." She looks like a little girl, with her red face and her eyes standing out so blue. "Did yours ever go?"

"Once in a while," I say. "For bachelor parties."

"And he told you about them afterward?"

"Sometimes," I say. "The first few times, yes. Then I quit asking."

Sara leans back on our bench. "I don't get to pick the dancers. My cousin owns the place, but that doesn't mean I run anything. I just do my shifts and go home."

"Does he pay you well?" Haley says.

"No. But I get decent tips. Not as much as I want, but it's more than I could make at any other job. I do pretty good, considering how I didn't finish school." She turns and grins at Haley then. Changes the subject. "I'd invite you to come see it, but you'd have to sit in my section and order a lot of drinks."

"They let women go there?" Haley asks.

"Of course. Women go in all the time."

"Really?" Haley says.

"Well, not *all* the time. But they do go. Once in a while. Mostly with their boyfriends."

Haley's back to her rapid-fire questioning. She can't resist. "What do the women customers do? Just watch? Or do they get up and dance, too?"

Sara laughs. "No, they don't get up and dance. But they will pay for lap dances sometimes, when their boyfriends want them to."

"What do the dancers wear?"

Sara shrugs. "Just whatever. Mostly dresses. The stretchy kind, so they can take them off easy."

"What do they wear underneath, though?"

"Underwear," says Sara, matter-of-factly. I see that she's teasing Haley more, enjoying withholding the information. She's like a teenager torturing her younger sister. After a moment she relents and expounds, "They have to wear G-strings. Sometimes they'll have on a colored bra, and sometimes no bra."

"I can't even imagine," Haley breathes.

"Sure you can," says Sara. "Just think of a bunch of skanky hos wiggling like worms so they can get a few dollars for drugs. Then imagine a bunch of dumb-asses watching them and touching themselves under the table." As if to punctuate Sara's words, one of the boys on the basketball court yells "Whoo!"

Haley grimaces. "Really? They touch themselves while they watch?"

Sara laughs. "No, not really. They probably want to, but they just sit there, mostly. Most of them just sit and watch. Some walk up to the stage and tip dollars to the girls. Then there'll be a few paying for lap dances. They stay pretty quiet, unless there's a bachelor party. Or unless they're drunken idiots."

"Are there a lot of drunks?" Haley asks.

"Not a lot," says Sara. "There's a two-drink minimum, and the cheap-asses just drink the minimum, as slow as they can. Some try to show off by buying a bunch of drinks and tipping big. Usually those types can hold their liquor. But once in a while we will get a drunk. Like, there's this one guy who comes in after work, sits down, and gets totally trashed on the cheapest beer. Once he's drunk, he starts with the lap dances. He'll pick out a girl and, while she's grinding on him, tell her she reminds him of his ex-wife, except that she seems nice and his ex-wife is a bitch."

My nose wrinkles in disgust. "I wonder what his ex-wife would say if she could see that."

"Here's the funny thing, though: He picks a different dancer every time. Blond, brunette, short, tall, big boobs, little boobs. He's bought lap dances from every chick there.

One of the girls, Lisa, told me he took a dancer home one night. You know, one of the dancers who turns tricks on the side. A hooker." Haley gasps at this, but Sara keeps going. "The hooker chick told Lisa that this guy paid her up front, but then, once they got in bed together, he started talking about his ex-wife again. And then he started crying. So she had to get up and leave him there. And we didn't see him at the club anymore after that."

"Did she keep the money?" Haley asks.

"Of course. She was a total skank," says Sara. She smirks at the memory, then adds, "But Lisa, the one who told me the story, wasn't a hooker or a drug addict. She was actually cool. A mom, like me."

I hear Lucia tell Jared, "Go to sleep. Have sweet dreams." Jared and Baby Junior are lying in the pebbles, mothered by Lucia and Monique. Monique says, "Hurry up and go to sleep. Mama's tired."

That seems like a pretty clear cue for us to gather our kids and go home. Well, except for Sara, who has to go to work now.

"Tell Geronima I said hi," I say to her as we stand at the crosswalk waiting for the light to change.

"All right," she says. She's not smiling anymore. Now that Haley's back is turned, Sara's lost the mischievous twinkle, the above-it-all swagger, and looks tired. Resigned.

She was putting on an act, for Haley's entertainment. Or for herself. Acting like her job is amusing, something she does for kicks, and not an unpleasant obligation for which she has to leave her kids at night.

I don't know if I could do what Sara does. Thank God I don't have to find out.

Alex

YESTERDAY WAS RAINING, but today it's not, and Mom says we can go to the park again. I already finished my homework. I asked her if Angelica and them are going, and she said yes. I'm putting my comics in my backpack to take with me. I'm taking my Venoms and some of the X-Mens, too. She might like those better, because they have more girls. Girls don't like it when movies and TV shows only have boys in them. That's why Mom and Dad used to fight when we went to the movies. That, and Dad didn't want Mom to put butter on her popcorn.

If I get married when I grow up, I won't care if my wife puts butter on her popcorn. It tastes better like that. But I'll probably get candy instead. Also, I probably won't get married. Mom said it's not easy to stay married, and that's why people get divorced sometimes. I just want to be by myself so I can do what I want and not have to argue about it with my wife.

I hope Angelica likes the Venoms, even though they don't have a lot of girls.

MOM SAYS IT'S good for me and Lucia to get exercise, but we only go to the park if the other moms say they can go, too. They like to sit on the benches and talk a lot. That's what they're doing right now.

Lucia and them are playing a stupid game. They're pretending the jungle gym is a house and they're grown-ups and Baby Junior's their baby. Lucia said Jared was the daddy, so she's the mommy and they're married. Then Monique said Jared would be her boyfriend. They don't know anything. They're pretending they're cooking dinner. Jared's only allowed to eat the fruit his mom brought. But I see him eating Lucia's goldfish crackers, too.

Me and Angelica are sitting on the swings, and she's reading the comics I brought. When she reads, she sticks a piece of her hair in her mouth and chews on the end. When she finishes the Amazing Spider-Man, I say, "Do you like it?"

She says, "It's okay."

We swing on the swings for a little while. Then she says, "Give me another one." I give her my oldest X-Man. She puts a piece of hair in her mouth and starts reading.

NOW WE'RE BEING spies. We went behind the swings, to the trees. Then we went around on the other side of the bushes. Now we're behind the benches, where our moms can't see us.

My mom is talking about my dad. She says, "So we went for about three months before Mike gave it up. But by that time, I was over it, too. All we ever did was repeat the same things over and over, in different ways. I'd say, 'Mike never helps me around the house.' And then she'd tell me, 'Can you look at Mike and tell him how you feel using "I" language?' And then I'd say, 'Mike, I feel tired and pissed off when I have to clean the house all by my damned self.'"

The other ladies laugh. Angelica's mom says, "That sounds stupid as hell."

My mom says, "It was. We never solved anything. After a while I felt like we were just there to give her the hundred dollars per hour."

I don't know who she's talking about. Maybe a lawyer or a judge. I know lawyers charge a lot of money.

Jared's mom says, "Well, there are good ones. I love mine."

"How often do you go?" my mom says.

"Every week, for the last three years, up until recently. Now I only call him when I need something."

Angelica's mom says, "Girl, what in the world are you talking about every week?"

Jared's mom says, "I don't know. Lots of things. My fears. Issues with my parents. Things that happened with my friends."

"And after three years he still couldn't fix you?" Angelica's mom says.

They all laugh. Jared's mom says, "That's not very nice, Sara." Then she says, "He usually just prescribes the drugs now. Maybe he did give up on fixing me."

Angelica's mom says, "Well, if y'all wanna give me a hundred bucks an hour, I'll listen to your problems all day long."

"Let's go back," I whisper to Angelica. I'm scared my mom might say more stuff about my dad and Angelica will hear it.

"WHAT HAPPENED TO your dad?" I ask her when she's finished with the third X-Man. We're back on the swings.

"I don't know," she says.

"Did your mom divorce him?"

She shakes her head. "They weren't married. I never saw him."

I say, "Not even when you were little?"

She shrugs her shoulders. "Maybe one time. I think he had black hair and green eyes. And he was tall."

I say, "Did he have dark brown skin? You're darker than me." I hold my arm next to hers. But she just looks at the dirt and kicks it with her foot. She's sad, I think.

I wish I hadn't asked her. Yesterday, at school, Ms. Hubacek asked if our dads could volunteer to make the haunted house for the Harvest Festival. Some of the kids raised their hands, but me and Devonique didn't. I told her, "How come you don't raise your hand, Big Mouth?" I said that because she called me "Kinderbaby" at lunch, and I know she hates it when I call her "Big Mouth." She didn't say anything. I was thinking her parents were divorced, like mine, but maybe her dad never married her mom either.

If I had a kid like Devonique, I probably wouldn't want to be her dad.

But if I had a kid like Angelica, I don't think I'd leave. I would try to see her on the first and third weekend of every month, like my dad does with me.

"Maybe he didn't want to leave, but he had to," I tell Angelica.

She looks up at me. "You mean because he fought with my mom too much?"

I say, "No, maybe he had to leave to do something important. Like for his job."

She thinks about my idea. Then she says, "Maybe he had to do a mission."

"Yeah. I bet that's why," I say.

After a while I'm tired of just sitting down, so I say, "You want to see how high I can push you?"

She says, "Yeah. Then I'll try to push you higher."

Maybe someday Angelica's dad will finish his mission and come back to see her. That'd be good. I'd be proud if my dad was doing something like that.

But I'm glad he's not. I'd be really sad if we didn't see him every first and third weekend.

Natasha

I WAS SUPPOSED to have another early dinner with Kate tonight, at Chick-n-Bix again. But I think I'm going to call and cancel on her, right after I finish this brief. That'll give her plenty of time to rearrange her plans.

It's not that I don't like her anymore, or that she's boring...No, that's it. She's boring lately. All our conversations are nothing but gossip about the women in my old neighborhood. And the longer I go without seeing those people, the less I care. Plus, I imagine her having dinner with the rest of them at the Chick-n-Bix up there and gossiping with them about me. What would she say? *That's right, Natasha's still divorced. Still a single mom. Poor thing.*

It's the fourth Friday of the month, so Haley and I have our kids. And Sara always has hers, of course. Maybe the three of us can get together in one of our apartments. Didn't Geronima say something about dinner? Or we could rent a movie. I'll call them after I call Kate.

All of a sudden, I'm looking forward to my weekend with the kids. It'll be fun. Yes, we'll do laundry and take the Blazer for an oil change. But I'm also going to make sure we do at least one fun thing each day, starting tonight.

❧

WHEN I TELL the kids we're going to Geronima's for dinner, Lucia says, "Yay!" and Alex asks, "Is Angelica going to be there?" He and Angelica have been getting close, I notice. But I don't think they like each other in a romantic way. They're still too young for that, thank gosh.

Angelica's a pretty girl. But I think Alex likes her because she's quiet, like him, and tomboyish enough to share some of his interests. Plus, they have things in common. I wonder if they've talked about their parents, about the fact that their dads don't live with them. No, I'm sure they only talk about school and Alex's comics. He's been trying to make her read his whole collection. Either she's being a good sport about it or she actually likes reading them. Good for her if she does. I can't get past the costumes and the cheesy dialogue.

Lucia wants ponytails with ribbons, like Tiffany always wears, so I'm trying to improvise something along those lines, when our doorbell rings.

I check the peephole and see a short, rotund woman in a khaki shirt and brown trousers. I open the door.

"Natasha Davila?" she says.

"Yes?"

"This is for you." She's smiling as she hands me an envelope. "Have a good night." And then she's gone.

I have a bad feeling about this. It's almost like . . .

"What is it, Mom?"

I close the door and open the envelope. Pull out a sheaf of paper, hoping it's not . . .

I see the double column of text at the top, with the family-court number stamped in the corner. Our case number handwritten on the line. Damn it. Goddamn it.

"Hold on, baby," I say to Alex. "I'll be right back. You guys keep getting ready."

The most private place in the apartment—my only sanctuary—is my bathroom. I go there now and close the door. Open the envelope, pull out the ticking time bomb inside, and skim its words.

> Service of Suit. November.
> Custody. Alexander Davila and Lucia Davila.

Alleges... Alleges what? *Neglect. Abuse.*

What the hell?

There's a whole section attached—not any type of court document I've seen before. It looks like something someone typed on a home computer. It's filled with sentences about... me.

> The Defendant, Natasha Davila, is neglectful toward her son Alex, not helping him achieve academic success. She fails to help Alex with his homework, despite his teacher's advice that he needs extra tutouring in spelling.

The word "tutoring" is spelled wrong in that particular way, and that tells me who wrote this: Mike.

> The Defendant has failed to adaquately prepare Alex for school. He had an accident (bathroom), and the defendant had not supplied the school with a spare outfit, as required in the Parent Handbook issued at the beginning of the year.

The Defendant does not provide Alex and Lucia with adaquate nutrition.

The Defendant verbally abuses Alex and Lucia, frequently yelling and using profanity in their presence.

Lucia needs new tennis shoes, but the Defendant refuses to purchase them.

For these reasons, the Plaintiff prays that the Court will turnover custody of Alex and Lucia to their father immediately, for the sake of their mental, financial, and academic well-being.

I can*not* believe this. He's got to be kidding me. Can he even do this—type a long, misspelled list of false accusations and append them to a court document? You'd think I would know, now that I work for lawyers. But they're not that kind of lawyers. Apparently Mike can do whatever he wants in the family-court system of Dallas. This proves it.

"Mom? When are we going to Miss Buena's?"

"Just one second, baby." I have to stay calm. Don't get upset. But it's too late for that. Then at least I shouldn't let the kids see how upset I am. Walk out of the bathroom, put the envelope on top of the dresser, and act like nothing's going on.

I can't believe he's doing this. He's out of control. Trying to get revenge. Pathologically lying. I can't believe he can make up lies like this and tell them to the court.

Could he literally be mentally ill? Maybe. That would explain so much...

Or maybe it's about child support. He wants to marry what's-her-name, so he's trying to get custody of the kids to keep from having to pay me. To make it so I have to pay him instead.

God. What am I going to do about this?

Call my lawyer, of course. Except...I still owe her twenty-five hundred dollars from the divorce. Joanne isn't going to take on a new development in our case unless I pay off that balance first. And she'll probably want another twenty-five-hundred-dollar retainer on top of that, like last time.

What am I going to do? I don't have enough money for that. I could put it on my credit card, but...No, I can't. I don't have enough there either. Not after the last round of repairs on the Blazer.

Why in the world is he doing this?

"Mom! Can you please hurry? Tiffany's gonna show me her new princess doll!"

"I'm coming, baby." God, I'm sweating through my shirt. I should change. No, I should cancel. I can't see anyone right now.

"Mom!"

I have to go out and act normal. "Hey. Here I am. Calm down, sweetie." Go to the dresser and lay the envelope face-down. Just like that. "Let me change my shirt real quick, and then we'll go."

"Hurry, Mom! I'm hungry!"

Keep moving. "I know you are, baby. Here we go. I'm ready now." Move forward.

"Alex, Mom's ready! We're going now!"

⌘

WE'RE SITTING IN Geronima's living room, eating dinner. The kids have already been fed and are playing in Tiffany's room. I've just spilled my guts to everyone. I didn't mean to—it just happened.

Geronima's horrified. "He did *what?*" she says. "He said you were neglecting them? To the judge?"

I say, "He sent someone—a process server, I think they're called—with a lawsuit. So he can try to get custody of the kids. The lawsuit has the list of allegations—of the things he says I'm doing to them."

"This happened today?" says Haley. Her brow is knotted in confusion.

"Just now. Right before we came upstairs," I say. I started it as a joke: "Sorry we got here so late, you guys, but I just found out my ex-husband is suing me." I didn't expect them to laugh. But I also didn't plan to ruin everyone's dinner, the way I'm doing right now.

Geronima walks over to me and bends down. She's . . . hugging me. With one arm, around my shoulders. I feel her cheek against the top of my head.

"M'ija. I'm so sorry," she says. She takes one of the tortillas from her plate and adds it to mine. As if to fortify me for the battle I'll have to fight. I'd laugh at her instinctive gesture, so characteristic, if I weren't struggling to keep tears from spilling down my face.

Sara says, "What the hell is wrong with him? What the fuck's his problem?" Then she catches herself, looks over at Oscar and says, "Sorry."

He shakes his head but doesn't say anything. Oscar's a

man of few words, but I take his expression to mean that Sara's cursing is warranted in this situation. He mumbles something I don't hear, then adds, "Not how a man should act."

"Where does he live?" says Sara. "We should go over there and kick his ass."

Haley shakes her head. "No, that won't do any good. Have you called your attorney?"

"Not yet."

Geronima's sitting now. "Eat, Natasha. You need to eat something."

We all take her cue. She's right. It helps to eat. I take a bite of the enchiladas with the good white Mexican cheese and chicken and tomatillo. Probably not the healthiest dinner, but it feels good to have something warm and delicious that I didn't have to cook myself. Now I'm glad we came here, and that I told them. It feels good to be listened to—to be nurtured like this.

After several bites, Geronima says, "I still don't understand. What did he say in the papers? How could he say that you're a bad mom?"

I try to explain. "He says I've been neglecting the kids. That Alex isn't learning enough in school and that I didn't do anything about his accident—you remember." They all nod, because I've already told them the story. "And he says...I don't know what. That I yell at them, or in front of them. That I say curse words. That Lucia's tennis shoes are getting too old and I haven't bought her new ones." I can't remember anything else from the list. It all sounds ridiculous now that I'm saying it out loud.

"That's so stupid," Sara says. "Is he for real? I know chicks who do way worse stuff than that. Shit, I do worse stuff than that."

Now I have to laugh a little. I can't help myself.

Haley says, "This isn't going to be a problem. Mike's just blowing off steam, obviously. Once you call your attorney, he'll get the charges dismissed."

And now I'm not laughing. "I can't call her. Not yet. I . . ." God, this is embarrassing to admit. "I owe her money, and she's going to want a retainer before she does any more work on my case. And I don't have enough to give her."

Geronima and Sara frown. Oscar shakes his head, like he's been doing throughout our discussion. But Haley's not buying my excuses. "She needs to take the case. You're her client. So you have to pay her a little later—that's fine. But you need to call her now so she can fix this."

I trade looks with Sara and Geronima. Eyebrows are raised. They know what it means not to have enough money. Haley can't understand.

I'll have to figure this out on my own, later. It's my problem, and I'll be the one to solve it, one way or another.

"You guys," I say, "let's talk about something else. I didn't mean to bring everyone down with my sob story."

"No." Geronima stands up and lunges toward me. Is she going to hug me again or spank me? No, she's leaning over to pick up Oscar's empty plate. "Natasha, don't be silly. You're not bringing us down. We're your friends." That said, she turns and carries her husband's plate to the kitchen.

"She's right," says Haley. "You don't have to feel bad about telling us. I mean, you've listened to plenty of my problems in the past couple of weeks."

"Yeah, seriously," says Sara. "I still think we should go out to your ex's house and beat the crap out of him, though."

"I wish it were that easy," I say.

A child emerges from the bedroom. It's Tiffany. "Grandma!" she bellows toward the kitchen. "Monique pushed Baby Junior, and Baby Junior's crying!"

"Aw, hell." Sara stands up. "I knew they were being too quiet over there." She takes her plate to the kitchen, then heads into Tiffany's room, saying, "Monique! Do I need to beat your little butt?"

Haley and I make comical grimaces at each other. By now we're used to Sara's gruffness with her kids. We know she won't actually hit them. At least not for an infraction this minor.

I need to check on Alex and Lucia. But first I should finish my food before it gets cold. Across the coffee table, Haley's watching me. I catch her eye, and she smiles. It makes me a little uncomfortable. I'm not used to whining to people and having them feel sorry for me. I have to change the subject. "Hey, where's Jared? I've been meaning to ask."

Now her smile disappears. "Oh, he's at Dave's. I dropped him off this morning."

"Really? So you guys aren't doing first and third weekends?" I say.

She sighs. "No. We're doing our own thing. Jared really misses Dave sometimes. And his bedroom, and all his toys. So I let him go visit more often..." She stops talking. Seems sad.

Great. Now I've taken the focus off my problems but made her feel crappy. I say, "Well, that's good, right? That you and Dave can make compromises like that, for Jared's sake." She nods, but doesn't look as if she agrees.

I'M ABOUT TO close the door when I hear her call my name. She's followed me back to our apartment. "Natasha, wait."

I have the impression that she's doing this specifically to catch me alone, so I tell Alex and Lucia to go on in, to give me a second to talk to Jared's mom. I close the door and stand outside it waiting for her.

"I wanted to tell you," she says, "but not in front of the others." And then she pauses. The chipped sconce on the wall lights the side of her face. She smiles, and it makes her look really young. She has a chameleon face, Haley. Usually I can tell that she's my age, but sometimes, in certain lights—or when she's laughing—she could pass for a teenage girl, with her pale hair and impossibly slim hips. How did she stay so thin after Jared? Some women just do, I guess.

"What is it?" I finally say. "Tell me." I hope it isn't something bad. Some sad secret. Not that I don't want to be supportive, but I have a lot on my plate at the moment.

"I wanted to tell you . . . I can give you the money. For your lawyer."

What? No. She isn't. Oh, my gosh. It's happening again—I'm going to cry.

"Natasha, are you okay?"

"I'm fine." I wipe my nose with the back of my hand, and it makes a noise, even though I'm trying to be ladylike. "Haley, you don't have to do that."

"I know I don't have to. But I want to. Please let me."

Are people always this nice to virtual strangers? Have I simply never noticed before? I say, "I can't let you. You barely know me."

"I do know you, though. You're my neighbor. Our kids play together. You're..." She takes a moment to think of the words. "You've been helping to keep me sane since I left Dave. It means a lot to me, to be able to have people like you and Sara to talk to. Maybe *you're* used to having tons of awesome, supportive friends just lying around since you left your husband..." We both have to laugh at that. "But whatever. The thing is, I have plenty of money, so it doesn't make a difference to me. Please take it. Consider it a loan, and if it makes you feel better about it, you can promise to pay me back someday."

I don't say anything. I can't.

She says, "I'm not going to leave until you tell me yes." She pulls her purse from her shoulder, mock threateningly.

I feel like I'm falling. The way they show people falling out of buildings, into trampolines being held by circles of firemen? That's me right now. Is this how it feels to rely on other people? I'm afraid yet exhilarated. Hopeful yet slightly panicked. And it's hard to say whether my feelings are normal, because I haven't been able to rely on anyone like this in a long, long time.

Natasha

HE SAID *WHAT*? That's ridiculous." That's Joanne, exactly the way I expected she'd react: as the calm voice of righteous indignation. I'm on the phone with her, in the hall outside the dentist's office while the kids are getting their teeth cleaned. Just hearing her use that word—"ridiculous"—makes me feel better about the whole thing. She's the lawyer here, isn't she? Therefore I have an official legal opinion stating that Mike's being an idiot.

"Okay. Here's what we're going to do. Fax me the whole thing, and I'll take a look. Don't worry about the hearing . . . You said November eighteenth, right? Great, right before Thanksgiving. But that's okay. I'll go to the hearing without you. I can tell you right now that the judge is going to order mediation, first thing."

"Really?" I say. I was picturing a big, dramatic court scene in which I have to take the stand and defend myself against Mike's allegations. I was already worried about what to wear.

Joanne says, "Yes. You know how this judge hates to sit there and listen to bickering. But we won't be able to schedule a mediator until after the holidays. You know what? I'm going to see if we can get Susan Graham. She wasn't available when you got divorced, but I think she's back in town now. She's the best, especially for cases like this. With any luck, whoever they assign will talk Mike into dropping the suit. This happens all the time. The men get upset over something petty and decide they want custody, but then they calm down and get over it. Let me guess—did you start dating again? Did he find out about it?"

"No, not really." I don't count the one incident with Hector as dating. And Mike doesn't know about that anyway. There's no use explaining to Joanne—reminding her—that Mike's already dating again himself. Like she said, he's probably upset about something petty. I'd guess it's because I embarrassed Missy at Alex's school, in front of the nurse and the secretary. And because I've been avoiding his phone calls since then. Too bad. Like Joanne says, he'll have to get over it.

The door to the dentist's office opens, and the hygienist emerges. She beckons me. Oh, no. Not a cavity, I hope. I hold up a finger to let her know I need a minute, and she disappears. I say to Joanne, "So is that all? Just wait for mediation?"

"Yes. Well, no. Natasha, before I continue with this case, there's the matter of my retainer."

"I know," I say.

"And I believe you still have a balance..."

"I know. I'm going to pay that. I can write you a check today." Now that Haley's check has cleared, I can.

"No, I know you're good for it," she says. "I'll send you a bill when we're done."

Good old Joanne. So trusting. And so successful and rich, presumably, that she can afford to bill me later. But I wouldn't have felt comfortable calling her when I didn't have the money to pay in full.

Time to talk to the dentist now, and see what else I'm going to end up paying for. But I feel a lot better than I have since receiving the summons. If Joanne says it's going to be fine, I believe her.

After we get out of here, I should call Haley and Sara. I want to get together with them tonight, so I can tell them the good news.

Sara

I BET YOU'RE wondering why I came here.

Yeah, you are. I could go talk to anybody. But you're the one who knows everything that happened with Natasha and her ex and their kids. So you already know that I'm a liar and a bad mom. But I came to see you on purpose. I want to tell you my side of the story.

First of all, whatever you think about me, I have to tell you that Haley's worse. I lied a little bit, after I first met her and Natasha. But she was lying to both of us the whole time. And I knew it, too. I could tell.

Wait. Hold up. I have to ask you one more time and make sure. You're not going to tell anybody what I'm telling you? Like the judge? Or Natasha's ex?

All right. I just wanted to make sure.

Yeah, I think so, too. It's going to make me feel better to tell *somebody* all this shit.

Alex

TODAY IS STUPID, because we have to review two-digit division and I've been knowing how to do that for a long time now, since Dad showed me. I already finished my worksheet, but Ms. Hubacek gets mad if I draw in her class. So I'll cover my paper with my book, and then she won't see me doing it. I'm going to draw Venom fighting Black Widow.

"Alex." Ms. Hubacek calls me. Maybe she's going to let me be her assistant, since I'm finished with my classwork. No, she only lets girls assist her. She's probably going to get mad at me for something. I leave my book on top of my picture and go to her desk.

She says I have to go in the hall and talk to some lady. She says the lady has permission from Principal Moyers to be there.

Out in the hall, there's someone waiting, but I don't know who she is. She's a black lady and kind of fat. She looks like one of the ladies at my dad's work, a little bit, but I don't think it's her, unless she got a different hairdo and put on red lipstick.

She says, "Hello, Alex. My name is Miss Gloria." She's definitely not the lady from my dad's work, because that one's name isn't Gloria. "Would you mind talking to me for a little while, Alex? I need to ask you some questions." She has a sticky name tag, like the one that all visitors have to wear, and she also has another name tag with her picture, on a string around her neck. It says GLORIA JOHNSON, CPS.

I say, "Are you a teacher?"

She says, "Not exactly. It's my job to help keep all the boys and girls in Dallas safe. I need to ask you a few questions to make sure you're safe, okay, sweetie?"

"Are you the police?"

She says, "No, sweetie. But I help the police sometimes. Why don't you come over here with me so we can talk real quick and then get you back to your teacher?"

She sits in one of the hall chairs that kids have to sit in when they make bad choices or when they need to take a test. I follow her and sit in the other chair. She takes a pen and a paper out of her little suitcase.

"Okay, sweetie. First question: Has anyone hit you recently? Has anyone been spanking you or hitting you anywhere on your body?"

I think about Angelica's mom hitting Monique on the butt, last time at the park. Is this lady going to talk to all the kids in school? I wonder what will happen if Angelica or Monique says that their mom spanks them sometimes. Will this lady call the police? I shake my head.

"Second question: Has anybody been yelling at you or calling you names? Any grown-up, I mean?"

Yes. I can think of two grown-ups who did that.

"Sweetie, you can tell Miss Gloria anything. Whatever you tell me stays right here." She does her hand on her mouth like it's a zipper. "I won't tell your mommy or your daddy what you say—it's just between us."

Who is she going to tell, then? The police? Principal Moyers? She's waiting for me to answer. I wonder what happens if I don't say anything. Will I get in trouble?

"Sweetie? Do you understand the question?"

I say, "Sometimes Ms. Hubacek yells at me. Me and the other kids. And sometimes my dad yells at me when I don't do good at football. But he doesn't call me names. He just says, 'Come on, Alex! Don't be such a wuss!'"

I want to tell her more about Ms. Hubacek being mean, but I'm afraid Ms. Hubacek will find out what I said and yell at me in class, in front of everyone. She's already more mean to me than before, since my mom talked to her about letting me go to the bathroom.

Maybe Mom sent Miss Gloria here to spy on Ms. Hubacek.

Miss Gloria says, "Okay, honey. I understand. What about your mommy? Does your mommy ever yell or call you names? Or hit you?"

Maybe she's testing me now, to see if I'm telling the truth. I say, "No. My mom yells a lot, but not at me."

Miss Gloria leans down and makes the little chair creak. She says, "What about your sister, Lucia? Does your mommy yell at her? Or hit her?"

"No. She never yells at Lucia. Lucia never even gets in trouble, and she does bad stuff all the time."

"But you do get in trouble?" Miss Gloria asks.

"Yeah. Kind of."

"For what? What happens, when you get in trouble?"

I think about the question. "Like, sometimes if I don't finish my homework or don't share with Lucia, my mom takes my video games away. Or she says I can't watch TV. One time she unplugged the TV and the video games and made me and Lucia clean our room. But that was Lucia's fault, because she put cereal on the floor for Mr. Beary." Miss Gloria just looks at me, so I say, "That's her teddy bear."

"Okay, sweetie." She writes on her paper a little bit, then puts it back in her purse. Then she stands up, so I do, too.

"Thank you, Alex. You did a great job," she tells me. I'm glad. Then she says, "Sweetie, do me a favor and let's keep this talk between you and me, okay?"

I think she means that it's supposed to be a secret. "You mean, don't tell the other kids?"

She says, "I mean, don't tell anyone."

I say, "You mean, don't even tell my mom and dad?"

She says, "Well, not unless they ask you. Your mom probably won't ask you." Then she leaves.

ANGELICA ALWAYS SITS next to Monique on the school bus. I'm supposed to sit with Lucia, but I never do. She likes to be up front with a bunch of kindergarten girls. Every time the bus goes over a bump, they jump up and scream. I like to sit with my friends in the back, where I can see everybody else. Like right now, I can see that Tiffany's started sitting next to Lucia. And I see Angelica looking out the window.

WE ALL GET off the bus at our apartment, with the other kids who live there. We say bye to Angelica and Monique. They knock on their door, and their mom opens it and waves to us.

My mom has to go to a class tonight, for her job. I remember that now, because Miss Buena is waiting by our apartment door. Tiffany and Lucia run over to her.

Miss Buena tells us, "Alex, Lucia, your mama's not going to be home until later. Y'all come on up with me."

I have the key to our apartment in my pocket, for emergencies. I could go inside if I wanted to. "Miss Buena, can we stay here? Or can Lucia go with you and I'll stay here?" If I stay here by myself, I can play video games for as long as I want without having to give Lucia her turn. I won't be scared, as long as Mom comes home before it gets too dark. "I'll keep the door locked until my mom gets home."

"No, m'ijo. You know I can't let you do that," Miss Buena says.

I don't even get to unlock our apartment and get my game. We have to go straight to Miss Buena's apartment, on the third floor. At least we get to ride the elevator.

IT'S BORING HERE when it's only us. Lucia's in Tiffany's room, playing with all her dolls. There's no video games and no computer, and there's only one TV. It's on some dumb show about fishing and we can't change the channel because Miss Buena said Mr. Oscar is watching it. But really he's just asleep on the couch. I can see his eyes behind his glasses. They're closed. So I'm sitting here reading the comics from the newspaper. They're boring, too. Miss Buena asked me if I had any studying to do, but I already finished all my homework in class today.

I wish I could've stayed in our apartment by myself. Mom told me this morning that I'd be too scared, but I know that I wouldn't be. I'm older now. I'm *eight*.

Maybe if I go in the kitchen, Miss Buena will give me another brownie.

The kitchen smells like a taco restaurant. Miss Buena's cooking something on the stove with both hands, and she's holding her phone between her ear and her shoulder, with no hands, so she can talk at the same time. It's rude to interrupt grown-ups when they're talking on the phone, so I wait for her to finish. Miss Buena's kitchen is full of chicken decorations. The calendar on the wall has a picture of a really big chicken wearing an apron. There are X's on the days that already passed. I can see that there's four more days until Halloween.

Miss Buena is saying, "No, that's what I said. She doesn't have to work because her husband pays for everything. . . . Right. Because he doesn't know. But she wants to work. . . . No, you know. So she can be on her own. You know how the girls are now."

She says some words in Spanish, just like my grandma does when she talks on the phone. Old people like to do that. Miss Buena says, "Girl, I know. That's what I'm saying. I'd live in a better place than this." She nods her head yes, then shakes it no. "No, her and the other one get along good. They've all been talking together when they go to the park with the little ones. . . . Right. The one who works at the club. . . . Yeah, that's what I said—that they'd all start getting along. . . . Mm-hmm. . . . What's that? . . . Which one, esta Natasha?"

She's talking about my mom now.

"Well, from what she's told me, her ex has been calling about the boy."

She means my dad. He's been calling Mom to talk about me.

"Hold on a second," she says. She turns around and sees me, then says, "Ruby, let me call you back, girl. I'm about to burn my chorizo over here." She hangs up the phone and puts it on the counter. "What's wrong, m'ijo?"

I want to ask her what she was going to say about my dad. What has he been telling Mom about me? What if it's something bad, like he's mad about the accidents at school? Or about me not sharing with Missy's baby?

No, I change my mind. I don't want to know. "Can I have another brownie, please?"

She smiles and touches my hair. "Of course you can, m'ijo." She turns off the stove and gets a paper towel from the roller that's shaped like a chicken. Then she goes to the butcher block and lifts the big pink upside-down bowl that's covering the brownies. "Do you want one with nuts or not a lot of nuts?"

"Not a lot," I say.

She puts a big brownie on the paper towel and tells me to go sit on the couch and be careful not to spill crumbs. Then she goes to the doorway and says, "Oscar," real loud.

Mr. Oscar comes in. He's yawning. Real fast, Miss Buena makes him a plate full of cut-up potatoes and eggs with orange stuff all over them. She opens her chicken-shaped basket and gets a tortilla and puts it on top of his plate. Then she opens a little chicken-shaped decoration that's full of hot sauce, and he puts it all over his food.

He looks at me and says, "You're not eating chorizo and eggs, boy?"

He sounds mean, but I can tell he's not. Old people like to pretend to talk mean sometimes. I say, "No, sir."

He says, "That brownie's going to rot your teeth."

When he talks, I can see that he has a gold tooth. Maybe from eating brownies. But he's also kind of skinny, and my mom says brownies and cupcakes make you fat. I don't say anything. We go to the living room and sit on the couch to eat. Mr. Oscar asks me, "How old are you, boy?"

"I just turned eight."

He says, "Just turned eight, huh? You must be the man of the house, then." I nod my head, even though I'm not a man. But I guess he knows that and he's just kidding. "You help your mama? Help take care of her and your sister?"

I nod my head again. But really, I don't know if I do take care of them. Maybe I don't.

He says, "You bring any toys up here with you? Books? Cards? There's nothing but girl toys in this house."

I shake my head. He said house, but I guess he meant apartment.

He says, "Why don't you watch TV, then? Put it on whatever you want." He gives me the controller, and I put it on cartoons.

Miss Buena's standing there watching us, and Mr. Oscar starts talking to her about doctors and medicine. When he's finished eating, he takes his plate to the kitchen, and she follows him.

I'm finished with my brownie. I pick up the crumbs that fell on the couch and take my paper towel to the kitchen to throw it away. When I get in there, I see Miss Buena standing at the sink looking down, like she was going to wash the dishes but she forgot.

Mr. Oscar goes, "Vieja? Gero, you listening to me?" She doesn't look at him, so he goes over next to her, where he can see her face, and says, "Gero, are you okay? When's the last time you took your medicine?"

She shakes her head and tells him, "I'm about to take it. I'm just thinking about Cristina."

Mr. Oscar says, "Ai, vieja." He goes back to the living room.

I have to hurry to the living room, too. I don't like to see

Miss Buena take her medicine. She has to give herself a shot in the arm, with a needle, like she's a doctor. I don't like to watch people get shots. And also, I want to get back on the couch before Mr. Oscar forgets what he said and changes the channel.

Sara

IT'S NOT LIKE I wanted to lie. At first I was telling the truth.

When I first saw Natasha, I remembered her, right off the bat. She went to high school with me. We had a couple of classes together, but we never hung out or anything. The reason I always remember her was this one time in gym class. There was this gang of girls who hated my guts, and our class had to play dodgeball against theirs.

None of my friends had shown up to school that day, so I was all by myself. And I was real skinny back then—even littler and skinnier than I am now. Don't get me wrong—I could take anybody in a fight. But we couldn't fight in gym, and these chicks were about to beat the crap out of me with a bunch of balls—those hard white ones that sting like hell.

So I was the last one standing on our side, and I was getting my ass beat by these ugly east side chicks, with everybody in the whole gym watching—boys' classes, too— when this chick Natasha stood up and walked back into the game. I remember she told me, "Don't just give up." And she started catching the balls and throwing them back at those ugly skanks. She was in sports or something, so she could throw harder than hell.

The coach came over and told her to sit down, and Natasha started talking back to her, saying it wasn't fair with twenty people against one. And she didn't even get in trouble for talking back. The coach just told us both to sit down. And I remember thinking, *That chick's not too bad, for a schoolgirl.* That was what we called them then, the chicks who never cut class or smoked or anything. The ones who followed the rules and did their homework.

So when I saw her at our apartments, in the laundry room, I remembered her. And I thought it was kind of weird that she lived there, and I figured she had just moved in.

Why? Because our apartments aren't the nicest place around, you know. I guess I figured someone like her would be living in town, in a house or something.

Someone like . . . you know. Someone who didn't grow up broke and messed up, like I did.

Yeah. I told her hi, remember me? All that stuff. I don't think she did remember me at first, but then she said "Sara," and I said right. She was looking at the sign Geronima had put on the wall for baby-sitting, and she asked if I knew anything about that. I'd been taking my kids to Gero's for a couple of weeks by then, so I offered to take Natasha up to meet the old lady. So we went up, and Gero invited us to dinner. And that was when we met Haley.

Yeah, that's right. I mean, I had seen Haley in the hall and the parking garage, but I never talked to her. And Gero had mentioned her a few times. She'd say, "My friend Haley just moved here. She's a real nice girl, with a little boy Monique's age. You should meet her."

And I thought that was weird, right off the bat. Why would an old woman have a friend like Haley—young and rich— and why would someone like Haley be living there in those apartments with her kid? Natasha told me Haley thought living there was an adventure or some shit. She said sometimes rich people think it's fun to pretend they're poor.

Haley told us later that her and Gero weren't really *friends*, but Gero used to take care of her and work for her mom. Basically, Gero was Haley's maid, back in the day. She told us that, and Natasha was like, okay, whatever. She's like that— she just listens to whatever people have to say and doesn't make comments or get all into their business about it.

But I thought it was weird, so I asked Gero about it later. She told me, "Haley's a good girl. She's going through some hard times right now and really needs some friends. I'm glad she's getting along so good with you and Natasha."

What did I think of that? I didn't know. To hear her tell it, Haley had everything with her husband. A nice house and plenty of money, and she didn't have to work. She didn't even have to mess with her kid if she didn't want to. She had her own maid and baby-sitter and all that. But she wasn't happy. She was on pills and who knows what all else, and she didn't want to be with that dude anymore.

Why do I say that? Well, she told us about the pills, right off the bat. Her doctor gave them to her for depression or anxiety or whatever. But I kind of suspected, when we first met her, that she was a pothead, too. You know how potheads act real flaky sometimes? Haley acted kind of flaky, when she wasn't freaking out about her kid. Then, later, when she had us over at her apartment, I knew it for sure. You know how potheads keep their places messy as hell and it has that smell? Well, she kept the living room and the kitchen pretty clean, but her bedroom was a total weed smoker's room. Clothes all over the floor, little boxes and trays laying around everywhere. Now that I think about it, she probably had a maid come over to clean the other rooms for her.

I was thinking that maybe she left her husband because she wanted to sleep around with other guys. Or maybe she'd already slept around and her husband had caught her. It sounded like he was a lot older than her. I thought, *Maybe the old guy can't get it up anymore.* You know? I mean, they have pills for that now. But maybe Haley didn't want to mess with him anymore. I didn't know. I just thought, *Well, whatever.* Because Natasha liked her, thought she was nice and funny and whatever, so I just went along with it.

Why? Because...because I liked hanging out with Natasha, and it was no big deal to hang out with Haley at the same time.

Why? Well, like I said, Natasha's pretty cool. She cracks me up. She knows a lot of stuff, and she's willing to help people, but she's not snotty about it. I never felt like she was looking down on me.

For instance, there were so many times that I thought, *Okay, this is it. Now Natasha's going to ditch me.* When I told them my kids had different dads and that neither of them paid child support, for instance.

Then I was ready for them to kick me to the curb when I told them I worked at a strip club. I didn't want to tell them, but I couldn't lie either. We were sitting there at the park, watching our kids play, and I thought, *Here it comes. I'm going to tell them and they're going to say, "Okay, we have to get out of here. Good luck with your life, you skanky ho."*

No, they wouldn't have said it like that. But you know what I mean. They would've been, like, disgusted.

No, they weren't. You're right.

I guess because they understood that I was doing it be-cause I had to. I was doing it for my kids.

No. Nobody could blame me for that. You're right. A good person wouldn't.

Well, anyway. I bet Natasha's sorry now that she was such a good person, huh? Because it totally came back to bite her in the ass.

Alex

WE DIDN'T GET real costumes this year. It's because my mom doesn't have enough money, since we don't live with our dad anymore. I'm wearing my Venom mask. Mom got my Venom pajamas and put some kind of glitter stuff on the web part, to make the lines show up. She said nobody will know they're pajamas, but I think they will. She made me put them on, with her black gloves. I don't want to go outside.

Lucia's a witch. She's wearing this shiny gray shirt that Mom wears to work sometimes, and it fits her long, like it's a dress. She has the witch hat we got for $2.99 at Walgreens, and she's super happy because Mom drew big eyelashes on her face with glitter makeup.

I wish we could go trick-or-treating with Dad, in the neighborhood where we used to live, where that one lady always gave us candied apples and we were allowed to eat them because we knew who she was.

Jared and his mom are waiting for us in front of Angelica's apartment. Jared's SpongeBob. His mom is dressed in regular black clothes, but she has cat ears.

Jared tells me, "I like your Spider-Man!"

Behind us the elevator buzzes and opens. Tiffany and Miss Buena come out, and Tiffany's dressed like a princess. She runs up to Lucia, and they start spinning around to make their dresses puff out.

Jared's mom knocks on Angelica's apartment door. Nothing happens. She knocks again. Then Angelica's mom comes out and says, "Hey. We're trying to hurry up and get ready in here."

Miss Buena says, "Well, can we come inside?"

Angelica's mom says, "Uh, yeah," and then we all go in.

Their apartment is kind of like ours, but with less stuff in it. Where we have our big beige couch, they have a little green one with flowers. Where we have our big bookshelf with the TV and all the DVDs and books and pictures, they just have a black table with a little TV on top. Angelica, Monique, and Baby Junior are sitting on the couch. They aren't wearing costumes.

Tiffany grabs Lucia's hand and tells her something in her ear, and they laugh.

Angelica's mom says, "Uh, I don't have their costumes yet. I was just getting ready to . . ."

Nobody says anything for a long time. Then my mom says, "Yeah, I had to make costumes for mine this year. We just threw this stuff together from my closet." I wish she hadn't told everybody that.

Angelica's mom goes, "Yeah, that's what I was going to do. Kind of throw something together." Then she looks around like she was getting ready to do something, but there's no clothes or glue guns or anything around her.

"Do you want us to help you?" Miss Buena says.

"Uh. Sure," says Angelica's mom. But I can tell she doesn't really want them to. But they're going to anyway. There's nothing else to do.

I hear my mom take a big breath next to me, like she does when she's getting ready to clean out the closets. She says, "What do you guys want to be? How about... Gypsy princesses?" She goes to Angelica and tells her, "You want to be a Gypsy princess, m'ija?" Angelica nods her head. Then Monique does, too.

My mom stands up straight and says, "Okay, we need scarves or tablecloths. Any kind of fabric. And maybe beads or necklaces. Do you have anything like that?"

Angelica's mom goes, "Uh. Maybe," and then walks into the other room.

My mom tells everybody else, "Let me run to our apartment real quick. I'll be right back."

Angelica's mom comes out of the other room with a scarf and a necklace. Then my mom comes back in the apartment with a whole bunch of scarves and necklaces, and a shirt, a belt, and some glitter paints and decorations from the box of stuff she always uses on our projects, plus the little zebra-stripe bag from her bathroom.

Then all the ladies get around Angelica and start putting stuff all over her like she's a Christmas tree. Except for Miss Buena, who sits on the couch and gives them ideas. Then Jared's mom says, "Oh, I just remembered. We have another costume upstairs. A pumpkin. Maybe it'll fit Baby Junior." She leaves.

Jared comes and stands by me in the corner. I make a pose like Venom. My mask is starting to itch my face, but I don't want to take it off yet. I like how I can see everybody through it but they can't see me.

When Jared's mom comes back, she's not wearing the cat ears anymore. She has a pumpkin costume, but my mom says it looks too big for Baby Junior. Monique jumps up and says she wants to wear it.

"Mommy," says Jared, "that's my costume."

"Yes, it is your costume, but it doesn't fit you anymore, remember?" his mom says.

He doesn't say anything else. I bet he'd start crying, though, if all these other kids weren't here.

Lucia and Tiffany and Angelica are all spinning around now. Angelica looks like a lady on TV, kind of. Jared's mom puts the pumpkin costume on Monique, and my mom puts makeup on Baby Junior's face so he looks like a clown. And then, finally, it's time for us to go. We all go out to the parking lot.

Tiffany and Miss Buena get in the car with Jared and his mom. We have the biggest car, so Angelica and them will ride with us. We have to wait for their mom to go get Baby Junior's car seat.

Mom says Angelica and I should sit all the way in the back, since we're the oldest. She means that we're the only ones who know how to behave.

MOM SAID WE could go to Walgreens and get me a flashlight. I remind her, and she has to call the other ladies to tell them to meet us there.

Walgreens has a lot of cool costumes, like Wolverine and Batman. And their Venom has plastic on the front so it looks like big muscles. Jared's mom sees me looking at it and tells me, "Aren't you lucky that your mom knows how to make better costumes than that?"

I say yes so she won't think that I didn't learn manners. I let go of the Venom costume and go stand at the front of the store with Mom and Lucia. Angelica and the others are there, too, waiting for my mom and Jared's mom to pay for the flashlights.

There's a big table full of teddy bears next to us, and Angelica picks one of them up. The sign says DOLLAR DAYS 2/$10.00, so she can get one if she has five dollars. Or if she has fifteen dollars, she can get three and share them with her sister and brother. I wouldn't—I'd keep them all for myself. But I don't like teddy bears. Only girls do. I have seven dollars and seventy-five cents in my pocket, left from the ten dollars my dad gave me. I'm saving it.

Angelica's mom comes up to her and grabs the teddy bear out of her hand. She says, "Put that shit down. I'm not buying that." I guess she's mad. When my mom's mad, she says "shoot" or "freaking." She only says "shit" or "goddamn it" when she's really, really mad. I think Angelica's mom is in a bad mood because she didn't want to go trick-or-treating with us. That's why they didn't have costumes, I guess.

I look at Angelica, but she doesn't say anything. She looks down so her hair covers her face, kind of like a mask. I could give her five of my dollars if she really wanted the bear. But I don't think she does anymore.

IT'S BETTER TO trick-or-treat when you're with a lot of kids, because sometimes the people get confused and give you two handfuls of candy by accident. It's good to have extra moms, too, because then they talk to each other instead of yelling at you to be careful and stay off people's grass.

There's a bunch of pumpkins and scary decorations in people's yards. The best was the Frankenstein sitting on the bench that made noise when you got close to it. Jared and

Lucia got real scared, but Monique ran up and kicked it until her mom made her stop.

I have to take off my gloves, because it's too hard to hold my bag with them. But everybody who gave us candy said my costume was cool and awesome. Especially the dads. We've only done eight blocks, but Baby Junior's tired and all the moms have to take turns carrying him. And Lucia and Jared are whining that their feet hurt, so we have to go back to the cars.

In our car I trade Angelica all my gummy snakes for her Sour Pops. Then she trades me her Powder Kegs for my candy corn.

Mom says, "Do you guys want to come over and hang out for a little while?"

Angelica's mom says, "Okay."

WE'RE PLAYING hide-and-seek with the little kids, but me and Angelica are playing spies, too. We're spying on the moms. It's easy. We take turns hiding in the hall and listening to them, and then we go back and make reports.

Angelica just finished her turn, so she comes back to the bunk beds and says, "General, I've returned." We salute to each other.

"Give me your report, Lieutenant."

"The enemy is talking about cat ears."

"Cat ears? Explain yourself, Lieutenant."

She says, "Your mom asked Jared's mom how come she took off her cat ears. Jared's mom said she didn't know. Your mom said it's not fair that only the kids get to have fun."

That's a boring report. Last time they were talking about the candies they used to have when they were little, and Miss

Buena said she's not supposed to eat candy, but sometimes she does anyway. That was boring, too. Now it's my turn again. Angelica salutes to me, and I crawl into the hall.

All the moms are sitting in the living room, just like before. They were eating the candies that none of us wanted, but now they're drinking wine and beer. I know Mom had a bottle of wine that one of her bosses gave her. But she doesn't drink beer, like Dad does. Someone else must have brought the beers from one of the other apartments. They're all laughing right now. Miss Buena tells my mom, "So what's going to happen next?"

Mom says, "We have to go to mediation. She said it won't be until after the holidays, probably. She's trying to get this woman to do it, Susan Graham. She's supposed to be the best mediator in the Dallas–Fort Worth area. That's what Joanne keeps saying anyway."

"Wait, I don't get it," Angelica's mom says. "What's she going to do? Listen to y'all and decide who's telling the truth?"

"Not exactly," my mom says. "She's supposed to help us reach an agreement on what to do. That's what we did before the divorce. A mediator helped us agree on how to split our property and decide on child support and all that."

Miss Buena says, "I don't understand. Why didn't he try to get custody back then?"

My mom says, "He didn't want to take care of them by himself. Now that he has Missy, he thinks he can get her to do all the hard parts for him."

She's talking about my dad and how he wants us to live with him. I guess Dad told her about that, and now they're going to talk to a mediator to help them decide if I'll be going over there or staying with Mom. But not until after the holidays, Mom said. I guess that means they'll decide after Christmas vacation.

"I found you, Alex!" Lucia says. She's behind me, coming out of Mom's bedroom, talking real loud. Monique and Tiffany are behind her. I crawl back to our bedroom before Mom and them see me and know I was listening to them talking.

We're all in my bedroom now. "You're it, Alex!" Lucia says. Then Tiffany tells Monique that her hair looks like scribbles, and Monique tries to hit her. Angelica has to grab them and make them stop fighting.

I cover my eyes and start counting so that Lucia and them will run away. Angelica stays next to me until they're gone, and then she says, "General, do you have anything to report?"

"No, not yet. Let me go back. Wait here."

We salute, and I crawl back to my listening spot. But Mom's not talking about us anymore. I wanted to hear what she was going to say—if she wanted us to live with Dad, too, or if she was going to keep us. Or what if she wants me to go with Dad and Lucia to stay with her?

Jared's mom is talking now. She says, "So are the dancers very pretty? I guess you'd have to have a really toned body, wouldn't you?"

Then Angelica's mom says, "Not as far as I can see. Neno's got girls in there that are fat. Girls with stretch marks on their guts, track marks on their arms, knife scars, mustaches, you name it. One time we had this girl with an extra finger on her right hand—like an extra pinkie, off to the side. She used that thing to hold her tips."

I hear my mom laughing. She says, "No she didn't. You're messing with us."

Angelica's mom says, "Nope. I swear to God, girl. I wouldn't lie about something like that."

They laugh again, but then Miss Buena says, "Sara, I wish you could find something better. I worry about you when you have the kids spending the night at my place. Aren't you scared, being there at night with those kinds of people? What if they're drug runners? What if they have one of those drive-by gang wars one night when you're working?"

Angelica's mom says, "Gero, you don't have anything to worry about. They aren't drug dealers, they're just normal guys. A lot of regular old boring guys just there to watch strippers."

I know what "strippers" means. It's ladies who take off their clothes, like in that song about the place in France where the naked ladies dance. I know because I heard my dad talk about it to his friend one time.

"Alex, come find us!" It's Tiffany. She's hiding right behind me, behind the bathroom door. I go in and tag her. Then I go into my mom's bedroom and tag Lucia and Monique. We all go back to my bedroom, and Angelica's waiting for me to tell her what I heard. But Monique and them want to play hide-and-seek again. So this time Angelica starts counting and makes them run away. Then she tells me, "What do you have to report?"

I say, "Your mom's talking about a stripper with two pinkie fingers."

She looks at me for a long time. Then she says, "You're lying."

I say, "Is your mom a stripper?"

She says, "No. She works at a club. She makes shots and cocktails."

I say, "What are those?"

She says, "Cocktails are fancy drinks for grown-ups. Like beer and wine with cherries and lemons on top. Shots are little drinks with no fruit on top." Then she moves her head forward so all the hair goes on her face.

I'm going to ask my dad if they have cocktails and shots where the strippers are.

No, I'd better not, because then he'll ask how I know about strippers, and I'll have to say it's from spying. He doesn't like it when I act like a spy.

Tiffany's yelling. We hear her say, "You're a cheater!" Then we hear Monique say, "No, you!" and Angelica has to go over there to make them stop.

EVERYBODY'S GONE NOW. It took them a long time to find Baby Junior, because he fell asleep in my mom's closet. Monique and Lucia fell asleep on the floor, so Monique's mom had to carry her back to the apartment and Angelica had to carry Baby Junior. Then Mom had to take Lucia's costume off and put her in bed. But I'm still awake.

"You want to watch TV with me, sweetie?" Mom says.

We watch the show about the detectives. At the end of it, I'm tired. Mom puts her hand on my shoulder and says, "Did you have fun, baby?"

I say, "Yeah." I didn't think I was going to, but I guess I did.

The show about doctors comes on. I almost never stay up late enough to see that one. I say, "Mom, do you want me to go live with Dad?"

She says, "Do you want to live with him?"

I say, "I want it to go back the way it was, when all of us lived together."

Mom doesn't say anything. I look at her to make sure she's not crying. She isn't, but she looks sad. "Baby, I wish we could go back to the way it was and everybody could be happy. But you remember we talked about this before. Your dad and I just can't get along anymore."

"I know," I say. "But I don't want to live somewhere else if you're not going to be there."

She leans over and hugs me, real tight and for a long time.

Sara

SO I WAS working at my cousin Neno's place. The strip club, out by the airport. Lucky's Cabaret, he calls it.

No, I wasn't dancing. I was only waiting tables. I wouldn't have danced at Neno's if you paid me a million dollars. Why? Well, first of all, every dancer there is either a crackhead or someone too old or messed-up-looking to get a job dancing somewhere else. Second, the tips suck, and they have to totally embarrass themselves to get them. Like, a guy holds up a dollar and the chick has to crawl all over the floor in front of him like she's a dog begging for a bone. I got more tip money from shooting the shit with the customers, making them laugh and stuff. I got free tequila shots, too.

How did I like it? I didn't. It sucked. But it was better money than I could get working at a cafeteria or cleaning bathrooms at the bus station. Better than minimum wage. But I hated that place. I hate my cousin Neno. He's a real bastard.

Like I said, though, working for him paid better than any other job I could get without my GED.

You sound just like Natasha. That's what she said, too: Why don't I just get my GED? I told her I didn't have time. When was I going to do that? When I was already working six nights a week at Neno's? Then I told her the truth: I never got it because I was too embarrassed. I said, "How's it going to look for some old chick like me to be getting her GED now, after all this time?"

We were sitting at the park by the apartments, watching the kids play on the jungle gym or whatever. I told her that I didn't want to get my GED when all the other people there would be younger than me and wondering what I was doing there.

You know what she said to me? She said, "I didn't think you were the type to care about what other people think."

Something like that. Like, she thought I wasn't afraid of anybody, so why would I be ashamed in front of a bunch of dumb-asses trying to get their GED, just like me?

No, she didn't say I was a dumb-ass. But you know what I mean. She was just like, "What are you afraid of?" And I thought about it later. And she was right. I'm not afraid of anybody—I'll fight anybody that wants to start something with me. But I'm afraid to go back to school.

After that? We quit talking about it, because that's when Haley showed up.

No, I didn't want to talk about it in front of Haley.

Right, because I was ashamed. That's funny.

No, not really...I just didn't want to give her the chance to say something annoying to me. You know? I mean, I didn't want her trying to give me advice. Haley could barely take care of herself, but she liked to give me advice or offer me money. If I'd told her, she would've said something like, "How about I drive you to the GED classroom and pay for your classes?"

No, she never *tried* to make me feel bad. But that's always how it came out. Like, she'd be telling me, "If you want, I can buy you a set of Baby Español DVDs, and then your kids can practice Spanish with Jared. If you don't have a DVD player, I can lend you Jared's and buy him a new one." And then, meanwhile, Jared—that's her kid—would be sitting under the swings eating dirt. Or he'd be getting ready to walk off into the street, and Natasha would have to jump up and chase him. And I'd be like, "Haley, you don't even know how to run your own life, so quit trying to run mine."

No, I never said that to her. But I wanted to.

I don't know. Natasha liked her, so I never said anything. I just let Haley run her mouth. You know?

Why? I don't know. Maybe because Haley was, like, better than me.

No, I don't think she was really better than me. That's not what I meant. I meant that she was...you know. Classier. Like, her and Natasha could talk about different things, like clothes from expensive stores or books or whatever.

Why did Haley like Natasha so much? Because Natasha listened to her whining and gave her advice. Like she was the mom and Haley was her kid. That's how Haley acted sometimes. Like a spoiled-ass teenager.

But now that all that stuff went down and Haley did what she did? I guess she's not a kid anymore.

I don't know if Natasha's been talking to her. Maybe. You think she'd talk to Haley but not to me?

Well, anyway. Here's the thing about the Cabaret: It sucked, but not because it had strippers. That part never bothered me. What made it bad was how Neno ran it. He treated all the girls like shit, and all the good dancers got out of there as soon as they could.

It was a little bit better if you were a waitress. None of the bouncers messed with me, since I was Neno's cousin. And I tried to keep them off the other girls—especially the ones I had trained. But Neno was an asshole, cousin or not. He'd give me the opposite hours from what I wanted, just to be a dick. But then he always had me covering everybody else's shift.

Why? I felt like I had to, back then. One, like I said, it was the only job I could get, without having my GED or anything. Two, he was paying me under the table so I could claim unemployment and do food stamps with my mom.

I know. That's ghetto as hell.

No, you didn't. But you were thinking it. You don't have to tell me.

Well, okay, you're right. I'm the one who feels like it was ghetto. But anyway, back then I felt like there was no way to get out of it. You know?

And then I met Natasha and Haley.

Yeah, they knew. I mean, they always knew about Neno's, that I was a waitress at the Cabaret. I told them that right up front.

No, that was the thing. It wasn't that they thought it was cool to work with a bunch of strippers—well, maybe Haley kind of thought it was cool, because she didn't know any better—but they didn't look down on me for it. It was like they thought I was there because I wanted to be, because of the money. And they totally believed that I could go get a different job whenever I wanted.

Yeah, exactly. After a while I started to believe that, too.

I would look at them and the way they did stuff and think, yeah, I could get a job with better hours, make a little more money, and then I could do more for my kids. Buy them better stuff. Get a better car so I could drive them around to places instead of just sitting around in the apartment all the time, watching TV and being pissed off at life.

Yeah, that's what I was thinking about back then. Making a better life for the kids and me. And then that's when Lisa came in and told me about the new place she'd started working at.

I was doing a day shift at Neno's for once. The girls were at school, and Junior was at Geronima's. The Cabaret was dead as hell for a Wednesday, so I was standing around watching whatever game was on the TV. Neno was out, and his sister was watching things in the office. This girl that used to dance there, Lisa, came in to get her last paycheck and some clothes she'd left behind. She'd had it out with Neno a week or two before and quit. I always liked Lisa. She didn't do drugs, and she didn't act stupid. She has a kid Angelica's age, and me and her used to talk sometimes, when she wasn't dancing.

So after Lisa was done talking to Neno's sister in the office, she came up to me at the bar and asked how it was going. We got to talking, and she said, "I started at a new place last week. Remember Caitlyn?"

Caitlyn was some chick who used to dance at Neno's a while back. Neno hated her. He always called her "that dyke bitch" and "that feminazi," so I definitely remembered Caitlyn. Lisa told me, "She's at this new place called the Dollhouse. Some lady from Houston came up and started it. It's not a club. It's private rooms only."

I said, "You mean it's a whorehouse?"

But she said, "No! It's like private dancing. Like VIP only."

I didn't know what she meant, but I knew that Lisa wouldn't turn tricks, so it must have been true. She told me she liked it a lot there, at the Dollhouse place, and that the pay was way better. Then she said, "You should come check it out. I mean, if you were ever thinking about dancing here."

See, I never told Lisa that I wouldn't be caught dead stripping, because she is a stripper, so that would've been rude. I always told her I was thinking about it but I wasn't ready yet or some shit like that. I kind of made it sound like Neno wouldn't let me, in a way. Because I didn't want to hurt her feelings. But now I was screwed, because she thought she was doing me a favor by offering me a hookup at this Dollhouse place. I couldn't just say no. So I said, "Oh, yeah, that'd be cool. Maybe when I get a few days off."

She went on and on about how nice it was—how much better it was than Neno's. She said one of her other friends had visited and was thinking about getting into it, if she could lose enough weight.

I figured she got some kind of bonus or something for recruiting new chicks into the club. Like a finder's fee or whatever. So I just told her sure, maybe, and then she left.

I DON'T KNOW what it was that finally made me go over there with Lisa. I was pissed off at Neno. I remember that. And I was . . . sad about Halloween. I felt bad, you know, about Natasha and Haley having to chip in to make my kids' costumes. Usually, you know, I'd just put some bandannas on the kids' heads, say they were hoboes, and hit up a few houses around the apartment buildings. But it's like if you want to hang out with people who have money, you have to spend money, too. Otherwise they're always trying to give you their stuff, and it starts to be a drag after a while. You know? I want to hang out with Natasha and Haley because they think I'm cool to hang with or their kids want to play with my kids or whatever. Not because they feel sorry for me and they're giving me stuff all the time.

I don't know. Maybe that's what I was thinking about, or maybe I was just bored. But I went with Lisa to her job, at the Dollhouse.

When was this? Good question. Um, maybe back at the beginning of November? Yeah, it was the first Monday, because the girls were back at school after Halloween.

It's over by Continental, the Dollhouse. You'd never know, because there's no sign or anything. It looks like a warehouse or something, with a big steel door. The only thing shady about it is that it's right behind this store called Erotix, where they sell lingerie and sex toys and stuff. Jackie owns that, too. The buildings are connected at the back. I didn't know that at first—Lisa and Caitlyn had to show it to me. There's security cameras all over both places, and you can get out of the Dollhouse and into the Erotix store through the back door, if you need to. If a customer gets out of control or if they get raided by the cops. But that never really happens, they said.

I don't know what I was thinking. That it would be like a normal strip club, like the Cabaret, I guess. Or maybe one of those fancy places, like the Treasure Chest down on 45. You know, a normal nightclub but with a few extra rooms where the girls could give private dances. But it wasn't anything like that. We went in the front door, into the waiting room, and it looked like a clinic, or the welfare office if they were closed down. Nothing but a counter and a couple of chairs. Nothing on the counter but a phone. Nothing on the walls except for the security camera up in the corner.

There was a guy there, waiting. He saw us come in and

jumped out of his chair and was all like, "Hello, ladies." Then he looked at me and said, "You're new."

Caitlyn told me not to talk to him. She pulled out a key and opened the big metal door behind the counter, and we went through with this guy watching us the whole time, like we were animals at the zoo. And Caitlyn was like, "We should've went through Erotix." And Lisa said she didn't want to give Jackie a reason to think she was late again.

They took me down the hall, past all these doors. Lisa told me, "This is our dressing room." And it was this big room with some couches and chairs in the middle and a bunch of lockers and mirrors on the side. Lockers like in gym class, I mean. And there was another chick sitting on one of the couches, just sitting there in her underwear, reading a book. Lisa and Caitlyn talked to her for a while, and then they introduced me to her, but I didn't say much, because I was weirded out by the whole situation.

It wasn't a club at all. I couldn't figure out what it was. I waited until the other girl took off and Caitlyn was messing around in one of the lockers, and I told Lisa, "This is a whorehouse, isn't it? Tell me for real."

And she laughed and said, "No. Well, not for me it isn't. All I do is dance here." And she said she'd show me the other rooms, where they do the dances.

And I was like, "Yeah, but where's your boss?" Because I expected that their boss, Jackie, would be there running everything and telling them what to do. But no, it was just a bunch of chicks hanging out, kicking back on the couches. Relaxing like they didn't have a care in the world.

When I first told Lisa I'd go there with her, back when I thought it was like a real club, I figured I'd sit at the bar for a while and maybe have a beer. Or maybe, who knows, I'd meet Jackie and talk to her for a while and see if she wanted to hire any new waitresses. It was funny—I even tried to dress kind of nice, just in case she'd want to hire me on the spot. I would've called Neno right then and been like, "Hey, fat-ass, guess who's not covering third shift tonight."

But it was so weird and different from what I expected that I didn't know what to do.

The phone rang, and Lisa said, "Caitlyn, it's for you." I saw she was looking up at something, and I turned around and saw all these monitors up on the wall behind me. One of them showed the front room, and I could see a guy in a suit standing at the counter holding the phone. The other screens showed other rooms, all of them with a little couch in the middle. Two of them had guys sitting on the couches, and I could see the top of somebody's head in the front of the picture, like right under where the camera must've been. And I figured out that those were the other girls who worked here, and they were dancing.

Is this boring as hell?

All right. Just making sure.

So the guy in the front was calling on the phone, and I guess he was Caitlyn's customer. And this whole time she was messing around at her locker, changing her clothes and doing stuff to her hair. When I looked at her again, she looked totally different, wearing nothing but a robe and a shitload of makeup. And the shoes—really tall heels, with platforms and everything.

She picked up the phone and said something I didn't hear, then waved bye to us and went out the door. Then Lisa went to one of the lockers and pulled out a flask of vodka. She asked if I wanted a sip, and I said okay, to be polite.

I saw Caitlyn on the cameras. First she went to pick up the guy from the front. Then, after a second, we could see them go into one of the rooms. The guy sat down on the chair. Then I saw Caitlyn's head moving around. Then I saw her reach out and throw something on him, on his lap. It was her robe. Then I stopped looking.

I told Lisa, "Hey, that other guy's still out front."

She rolled her eyes and told me, "Yeah, that's Marcus. The shoe guy."

I was like, "That's him?" Because Lisa had told me about him before, when she came to visit the Cabaret. This guy ran his own computer business. Made a lot of money. He came to the Dollhouse all the time and used to get dances from this chick Donetta. Donetta told the other girls all about him, how he was weird and creepy. He never wanted her to dance or even take off her clothes. All he wanted was stories.

Yeah, he wanted her to tell him stories, about the two of them. Lisa told me that most of the stories had to be about this guy Marcus being real little and Donetta, the chick, being real big. And she'd always tell him that if he couldn't behave, she'd stick him in her shoe and smash him.

Yeah. That's what I said. Real weird, right? Lisa said none of the other girls wanted to do that with him, 'cause they thought he was a creep. But he kept showing up anyway, just in case somebody changed her mind.

So that was the guy, standing out there in the front room. And Lisa had told me he was ugly, but now I saw what she was talking about. He was just weird, with googly-eyed glasses and an old-school Jheri curl and a big old butt like a woman's. And he was black, or maybe mixed. See, that was the thing I didn't know. He was black, and I'm thinking Donetta was black, too. And I'm thinking no one else would dance for him because of that. You know, because they were all white or Mexican or whatever, and they didn't like black guys. You know how people act.

Lisa started messing with me, going, "You could give him a dance if you wanted."

And I was like, "Why would I do that?"

And she said, "Remember when I was telling you about him, you said, 'Shit, I'll go tell some fool a story for a hundred dollars.'"

And I told her I was just kidding.

Then the phone rang again, and we looked up and Lisa said, "That's my client." It was a really old guy. He looked like somebody's grandpa or something. Lisa asked me if I wanted to go into the room with her and watch her dance.

I said no, that was okay. I was just gonna sit in the room and chill out. Then I looked around the room and didn't know what to do. I'd be there all by myself, and those other two chicks were going to finish dancing and come back, and I didn't want to sit there staring at them.

So I finally said okay, I'll go. By then we'd had a couple of sips each from Lisa's flask. She told me she always liked to get a little tipsy on the job—it made it easier. She picked up the phone and told the guy that she'd be out in a minute, that she needed to get ready for him. When she hung up, she told me they like it when they have to wait. We saw him sit down in one of the chairs, up on the monitor. I saw that Marcus, the shoe guy, was standing there all embarrassed. They wouldn't look at each other.

Lisa told me I had to get dressed. Well, to get undressed, really. And I was like, "What? Hell no." But she said it'd be okay, I could put a robe on and I wouldn't have to take it off. She said we had to act like I was a new girl getting trained, and it'd be weird if I went in there with my normal clothes on.

So I took off my jeans and my shirt real fast and let her put me in one of her slinky robes, from her locker. Then she whipped her clothes off real fast and threw on some lingerie thing and a robe on top of that. Then she said we needed makeup. I didn't want to, but I finally let her put some lipstick and extra eyeliner on me. Then she said we were ready, so we started walking out, but then she looked at my feet and was like, "Hold up. You can't go out there in those shoes." I was wearing these black flats. She said I had to wear high heels, like hers. I said too bad, because I didn't have any. She said I'd have to wear a pair of hers.

I really hate wearing other people's shoes. It grosses me out. Like, I'll get my jeans and stuff from the thrift store, but not my shoes. No matter how broke I am, I have to have my own shoes, even if they're just some clearance shit from Payless.

Why? I don't know. Maybe 'cause when I was little my mom always made me wear my brother's shoes after he grew out of them. And his were always nasty. I don't know.

Hmm? Oh, yeah. So she said I should wear her shoes. And I figured Lisa's a pretty clean-looking chick, so they can't be that bad. And she pulled out a red pair, to match the robe I had on, and I just closed my eyes and stuck my feet in them. And then we went.

I don't know. It was okay.

I mean, it wasn't fun or sexy or anything, but I sat there through the whole thing. I didn't get up and run anyway.

She just told him I was a new girl and I had to watch a few dances before I could start taking my own clients. And he was all like, "Oh, how nice. Maybe you'll dance for me someday." Like we were talking about a normal job and he was going to be my boss. I kind of wanted to laugh when he said that, but I just smiled and didn't say anything. I didn't want to piss him off and cost Lisa her tips.

He sat down on the little couch thing, and I was in a chair off to the side. Lisa put on her music—there was a little boom box in the corner and she'd brought a CD in with her. This slow song came on, and she took off her robe and started dancing around.

No, because I had seen her dance before, practically butt naked, at the Cabaret. And I'd seen plenty of customers sitting there getting off on it. But yeah, I guess it was kind of weird to be sitting next to them instead of serving drinks.

Really, though, it was mostly funny. He kept doing stupid shit, and I kept having to hold back from laughing at him.

Well, like, halfway through the first song, Lisa did this move where she turned around and bent backward, so her hair touched his lap. And when she did, he put his fingers in her hair, like it was rain or something, and he said, "Oh, *so* beautiful." Or something cheesy like that.

Oh, and then, at the end, when she was totally naked, she stopped and said she was thirsty, and that fool got up and poured her a glass of water from the table on the side. Then he told her he had a surprise for her. And she said okay, and she sat next to him on the couch. But he didn't touch her. He pulled a box out of his jacket and made her open it, and it was a freaking bracelet.

Yeah. A gold one. Like, the old serpentine chain that nobody wears anymore. But I guess it was real gold, because it was so thin and the box looked expensive, you know?

Yeah, she took it. She let him put it around her wrist, and it took him forever, probably because he had arthritis or some shit. Then, when he finally got it on her, she told him thanks and leaned forward and let him kiss her on the cheek. Like they were on some old-school date and she wasn't sitting there butt naked. Like she really liked him and wasn't only there because he was paying her.

Yeah, he paid her right there. Well, he left the money on the table. He had to put the whole fee—a hundred for Lisa and fifty for the door—on that little table as soon as he came in. That's the rule. But when he left, he put down some more money for a tip. After he was gone, Lisa showed me. She made two hundred dollars for twenty minutes of dancing.

Hell yeah, I was impressed. That's a lot of fucking money.

No, no one made that kind of money at Neno's. Are you kidding me? They would've been lucky to pull a twenty for a lap dance at that shit hole.

Sorry. I keep telling myself I'm not going to curse in here, in front of you. But I get all into it and forget.

Oh, man. I should've been out of here half an hour ago. Now I owe you extra. Shit.

Really? You sure?

All right. Thanks a lot. I'll see you next time, then.

Natasha

I SHOULD HAVE left Alex and Lucia at Geronima's a little longer so I could get some laundry done without having to drag them back and forth with me. The kids don't like staying in the apartment by themselves when it's dark out, but Alex *hates* doing laundry. He's dying of boredom and acts like he's undergoing torture just being here. What else is new, though? Lucia, on the other hand, is easier to please. She's examining the vending machines, completely fascinated by them, as if she never saw soda and detergent before. I guess they do look kind of exciting, lit up behind the glass like that.

Every ten minutes I glance around and make sure we're still alone—that Laundry Pervert hasn't suddenly appeared. If he does, however, I'll confront him directly, just like Sara did.

"Can we go to Goodburgers?" Alex asks. As if we didn't just eat chicken and mashed potatoes for dinner.

He misses the way we used to go there on weeknights sometimes, when we lived with Mike. He misses it the way I miss my washer and dryer. Feeling like a Scrooge, I say, "No, sweetie, we can't right now. Maybe this weekend." His scowl hurts a little, but I ignore it and hand him another pair of jeans to fold.

Do I wish I could afford to take the kids somewhere other than a fast-food drive-through? Yes. Do I wish we were someplace fun right now, instead of standing here folding our underwear while strangers parade through and stare? Of course. But wishes aren't horses, so dreamers can't ride, as my mom used to say, before I corrected her and she called me a smart-mouthed brat.

Thank God for Geronima at least. The woman's a freaking godsend. She actually enjoyed watching the kids. I can't believe she didn't even want me to pay her for it. I assume they're doing okay financially, probably living off Oscar's pension and the sale of the house they used to live in. But I'm glad Oscar took the money from me anyway.

I wish the kids had a grandmother like Geronima. As opposed to my mom, now that she's morphed into a bitter alcoholic. And Mike's prissy Baptist witch of a mother, who they never see anyway.

Everything's folded now, so I give Lucia my last few quarters, and she uses them to buy a miniature box of fabric softener, which transports her into paradise. Then I give Alex the lighter basket to carry, grab everything else, and tell Lucia to hold the door so we can head back to the apartment.

"This basket's hurting my hands," Alex says. Every step down the hall, he acts like he's going to drop it or keel over from exhaustion.

I imagine my mother standing here saying, "God gave you a whiny kid for all the times you were such a pain in the butt to me." I remember all the errands I ran with her as a child— me complaining and her telling me to shut up. Alex *is* a lot like I was as a child. And that's why I totally know where he's coming from.

I also know that the basket isn't too heavy for him to carry, though. It's only a third full—the rest of the clothes are on hangers, folded over my left arm, which is starting to go numb. Alex is upset because he's bored. We didn't go to the park today, and there's nothing on TV, and he's tired of all his video games and comics.

"It's a good thing we live on the first floor and not the third," I tell him. "You probably have just enough strength to make it." He scowls again. "Besides, I need you to carry the basket so I can keep one of my hands free."

"Why?" he says, dragging the word into two or three syllables.

"So I can be ready in case anything happens."

"Like what?" he says, skeptical yet interested.

I say, "Like monsters. Villains. Laundry assassins. I have to be ready to protect us." I indicate a skinny old lady coming down the hall in the opposite direction, carrying a scared-stiff little dog.

I see that Alex wants to laugh, or at least crack a smile. Instead he says, "What about Lucia? How come *she* doesn't have to carry anything?"

I look down at his sister, who is totally spaced out in a search for pennies on the hallway floor. I wonder if she even hears us. "Your sister's not like you and me, Alex. She hasn't yet learned our ninja ways."

He rolls his eyes at me, but I know he's masking a smile now. I swear, he's like a teenager already, the way he doesn't give me an inch. He's too smart for his own good, and for mine. I tell him, "We're almost there. You can make it. Hey, maybe we'll go to Goodburgers this weekend. If you behave and keep helping me out like a big boy."

"You mean like the man of the house," he says.

Now it's my turn to stifle a laugh. He must have heard someone say that on TV. "Right. Exactly."

IT'S NOT UNTIL the kids are passed out from an extra-long chapter of Harry Potter—and all the lights in the apartment are out, and I've showered and gotten into bed—that I can think about what *might* happen the next time I have a break. Not this weekend but the next, when the kids are gone again.

I probably *won't* call Hector. But what if I did?

Again, it's the shifting-sexiness thing. In theory he *isn't* sexy. Alone in the hotel room, magically, he is. It's just like how in the daytime I'm pretty sure that I'm not ready for any kind of relationship with a man, much less a sex-only thing with some sad divorced dad. But at night, here in the dark . . .

It's been more than three weeks since the last time, but I remember it like it's happening right now, right here under the covers. I reach down to help myself remember better. His weight on top of me, the strength of his arms. I can almost feel it right now, as if he's here with me. He's pushing, slamming inside of me. I do feel it. Oh, God, I feel it right now. Yes . . .

The phone rings. The freaking phone *would* ring right at this moment. God, and it's Mike. "Hello."

"Natasha. It's Mike."

I want to say, *I know it is, Sherlock.* Because of course it'd be him, calling when I'm trying to have a freaking orgasm. It fits right into his pattern of sucking all the pleasure out of my life.

"Natasha? You there?"

It's still strange to hear him say my name like this. Not that I want him to keep calling me Nat, or Natty, like he did when we were married. He used to say that the name Natasha didn't really fit me. That was something that he and my mother agreed on. She thought giving me such a glamorous name would ensure that I'd grow up thin and fabulous. She was wrong.

I don't know what he could call me now, to keep from sounding uncomfortable. Mrs. Davila? In the best-case scenario, actually, I'd never have to hear him speak at all. "Shouldn't you be preparing for your big lawsuit against me?" I say.

"That's what I'm calling about," he says. "I want to drop the suit."

"You do?"

"Yes. All you have to do is sign these papers I've drawn up, saying that Alex can live with me. Then I'll drop the suit and we won't have to pay the mediator's fees."

I sit up in bed. "Are you kidding me?" I say.

There's a quiet shushing noise in the background, and I wonder if his girlfriend's next to him, listening in.

He says, "Look, I'm not going to argue with you right now. I'm just letting you know. I'm checking into some stuff, and if you're not willing to consider handing him over to me, things are going to get a lot worse for you."

"What the hell are you talking about, Mike?" God, I hate to lose my temper, but it's too late. My heart starts racing like I'm in a physical fight. Who does he think he is, calling and talking to me like this?

He says, "See, you're already starting. I knew I shouldn't have tried to talk to you. I should have just went ahead with my plans." He uses his most irritating tone of voice, the one that's whiny and aggressive at the same time.

"You aren't trying to talk to me. You're threatening me," I say. "There's no reason for Alex to live with you. Why are you doing this now?"

"I'm not doing it *now*. I've been thinking about it since you left."

I have to work to keep my voice down, not to wake the kids. "That's a lie. You didn't even ask for custody during the divorce!"

He says, "Yeah, because I knew the judge would just give it to you, because you're the woman. But I should've done more research before letting them go. Now I'm thinking maybe the judge didn't make the right choice."

"*What* are you *talking* about?" I practically hiss. God, I wish I could reach through the phone and punch him. "You didn't even *want* custody! Don't pretend you're worried about the kids now!"

"I *am* worried about them! Living there in that rathole, with you and your bad temper. Who knows what's going on over there without me to watch?"

"Oh, my God." I feel the blood pounding in my head, just like it used to. We may as well be in bed together, screaming at each other in the middle of the night.

This is why I left him, the crap I refused to deal with any-more. And here I am being forced to deal with it. It's like there's no escaping him—or the misery he creates.

"Go to hell, Mike. You didn't care about the kids when we were living with you, so don't act like you suddenly started. Just because you never disciplined them and don't know how to do it now—"

He cuts me off, talking louder, exactly like he used to. "All right, shut up. I'm not listening to you. I didn't call to hear this shit. I just called to talk to you, in a reasonable way, but *you* don't know how to be reasonable. Listen to the way you're cursing at me now. That's one of the things I'm going to put on the list for the judge. You'll see what he thinks of that when he calls you in and takes the kids away from you."

"You . . . damned . . ."

And the phone is dead. That asshole hung up on me.

I call him back. It rings five times before he picks up. Then, before I can say anything, he hangs up on me again. My pulse is pounding in my neck, my hands, the tips of my freaking toes. I call back.

It rings three times and then goes to voice mail. I hang up and call back again. He's crazy if he thinks I'm going to sit here and let him say all those lies and not defend myself.

He picks up and hangs up again. It's okay. I can do this all night, you son of a bitch. I call him back again. Five rings and he picks up.

"Don't hang up, asshole."

"Natasha. It's Missy."

Oh, wow. That coward had his girlfriend answer the phone. "Let me talk to Mike," I say.

"I don't think that's a good idea right now," she says.

"I don't want to talk to you. I want to talk to Mike," I say.

"Natasha, I really don't think the two of you should talk anymore until you've calmed down some."

Who does this bitch think she is, sticking her nose in my business and telling me to calm down? "Missy, this doesn't concern you, so I don't care what you think. Hand the phone to Mike, please."

"I beg your pardon, but it does concern me, because it's taking place in my house."

What a freaking *bitch*. I hear Mike in the background. He says, "Let me talk to her."

But she doesn't give him the phone. She tells me, "I heard what Mike said to you, and I can see how it probably came out sounding different from what he intended—"

I say, "Missy, I don't want to talk to you. Either hand the phone to him or hang up."

"Well, I guess I'm going to hang up, then. It's getting late, and I don't want this to go on all night. We have work in the morning." She thinks she's some kind of mediator—some voice of reason. I don't need to be lectured by someone dumb enough to get involved with another woman's ex-husband, a man proven to be defective.

I tell her, "I have work in the morning, too. Your boyfriend's the one who started this. If you don't want any trouble, keep his ass from calling and threatening me."

She hangs up.

When I call back, Mike's phone doesn't ring. It goes directly to voice mail. I know better than to leave a message. I learned from our divorce that losing my temper on voice mail won't do me any favors. But I can't say *nothing*, so I say, "I just want you to know that you're going to be sorry you started this. The kids don't want to live with you." Then I push the hang-up button as hard as I can. But it doesn't take away any of the anger.

There's no *way* he's going to get custody. Like Joanne said, we'll go to mediation, he'll realize that his accusations make him look like a raving lunatic, and he'll drop the case. I know that. He's just trying to push my buttons, to torture me.

Knowing that he's wrong doesn't make me feel any calmer. And it certainly won't keep me from staying up and worrying until my alarm goes off six hours from now, at 5:30 A.M.

God, I hate him. I hate the way he makes me practically blind with rage, like a monster. Once again he's made me angry with myself, for not seeing what he was until it was too late.

Natasha

THE LAST TIME we went to Goodburgers...

The kids begged for strawberry milk shakes. I said no, then Mike said yes. "C'mon, Nat. We're trying to have fun here." Then he smiled, maybe winked at the sixteen-year-old girl taking our order. She gave him the same zombie expression that she'd give any other customer and handed him our buzzer.

The kids begged for quarters to ride the space shuttle in the game room. I only had two quarters, so Mike gave them a five-dollar bill for the change machine. Mr. Good Times to the rescue. Then it was him and me, alone at the table. So he took out his phone and began a long, in-depth conversation with it. Mike always had the most expensive phone with the newest technology—always the best avoidance device. I watched the interactions among the teenage staff. The boy refilling the ice in the soda fountains was obviously in love with the girl who took our order. The girl sweeping under the booths was obviously in love with that boy. I wondered how many of them would go to college and move on to better things.

I studied the pictures on the wall of our booth. John, Paul, and George looked the same as the last time I'd seen them there. Ringo was being overtaken, little by little, by the mold creeping up from the corner of his picture frame.

Our buzzer went off, and we went to pick up our burgers. I

led Alex and Lucia through the topping and condiment lines, helping them apply the perfect amounts of pickles, lettuce, ketchup, mayonnaise. Mike stood at the nacho cheese dispenser and leaned on the button until orange goo completely coated his fries.

Back at the table, I arranged the kids' plates, milk shakes, water glasses, and napkins around them before going to slap a little mustard on my turkey burger and fill my plastic glass with diet soda. "Hey, get me a cup of jalapeños, would you?" Mike called behind me.

Lucia didn't expect her milk shake to contain actual strawberries and spit a mouthful onto the table, thinking she'd sucked up a bug. That put Mike off his hot wings, so he took Alex to play the hoop-shoot game while I cleaned Lucia's mess. Mike and Alex came back disappointed in Alex's hoop-shooting prowess. Mike caught me reaching for one of Lucia's abandoned fries and said, "I thought you were on a diet."

The blond assistant manager made her rounds, stopping at every table to say the exact same thing, "How is everything? That's great. Let me know if I can get you anything."

When she got to our table, Mike smiled at her and made a cheesy joke. She laughed at his joke, probably in accordance with her Assistant Manager Training Manual, and wished him a good evening. When she walked away, Mike looked at me and said, "Wow. It's nice to be appreciated by *somebody*."

Because that's what he wanted, apparently—the same regard from me that a minimum-wage employee was forced to show him. That's what was missing from his life—me fawning on him because he'd deigned to have a burger with his family instead of staying late at work or locking himself in the garage for the evening.

THE CHEESEBURGERS AT McDonald's aren't as good as the ones at Goodburgers, but you can't beat the price of three Happy Meals. Sometimes we get the fruit on the side, and sometimes we break down and get the fries. Or we'll split an apple pie three ways. They taste really good, the fries and the pie that I eat without criticism.

Alex and Lucia usually ask for the boys' toy and I ask for the girls'. We put our favorites into the collection on the dashboard of the Blazer and toss the rejects into the Goodwill bag at home.

The kids tell me stories over their Happy Meals. Or sometimes they tell each other stories, using the toys to act out various scenarios, and I listen. In the playroom's playscape, Lucia hurtles herself fearlessly through space. Alex is more cautious, measuring twice and jumping once.

On the way home, we sing along to my Best of the '80s CDs, the ones I found after we moved to the apartment, that I hadn't heard since Mike declared his preference for country-western.

I DON'T LIKE being broke. I don't like having to work full-time or having to worry about the Blazer's maintenance in addition to everything else.

But I don't regret the decisions I've made. I have faith that in the future we'll look back on these McDonald's-and-two-bedroom-apartment days and say, "That wasn't so bad, was it?" Because it *isn't* so bad, everything considered.

Unless he takes the kids away from me. If that happens, none of this will matter, and I'll have nothing worth working for.

Sara

SO YOU KNOW what I'm going to tell you, right? After what I told you last week?

You don't? After all that about me going to see Lisa and Caitlyn at the Dollhouse, with that goofy guy Marcus sitting there in the front room waiting? And Lisa dancing for that crazy old man? No?

Well, that was when I did my first dance. That same day, right after I watched Lisa do hers.

No, with Marcus. I told Lisa I wanted to do it, and I took a few extra swigs of vodka so I wouldn't lose my nerve. She put some more makeup on me and sent me out in her robe and her red shoes.

Yeah, I still had my own underwear on underneath. But I didn't have to take the robe off, so it wasn't a big deal.

Right. All I had to do was stand in the room with him and talk.

Hmm? Oh, nothing. Just stupid stuff. I said what Lisa told me he liked—that I was big and he was little and that I was going to stomp on him if he didn't act right. I said some other stuff, too. I just kind of made it up as I went along, you know? I stood there talking smack to him for half an hour, and then I walked away with two hundred and fifty dollars.

Yep. Swear to God.

How did I feel? I don't know. It's hard to remember. Crazy. Kind of sick. But mostly like I got away with something—like I'd found twenty bucks on the street or stolen candy from a baby. You know? It was too easy. Too good to be true. I guess you could say I was in shock, kind of. Like when you hear some good news and you think, *No way this could be happening to me.*

No, I didn't stick around. I didn't want to leave Geronima watching Baby Junior for too long, and it was almost time for the girls to get home from school. But I did stop at the drugstore to get Geronima something—some little soaps and lotions in a basket, like a present for watching the kids all the time and not charging me an arm and a leg for it. And I got some little toys for the kids, too. Nothing too big, because I needed the money to last. But there were these little teddy bears that Angelica had liked the last time we were there, so I got three of them. Then I filled up the tank of the Impala for the first time in months—that thing had been running on quarters and fumes forever, and the fuel line was all full of sediment and shit. Then I went back to the apartments and picked up Baby Junior.

No, I didn't say anything to Geronima about the job. Not then. I just gave her the present—the soaps—and she was all happy. Then I took Junior back to our apartment and set up the teddy bears on the girls' bed, so they'd be surprised when they got home.

Yeah, they were. They liked them a lot. But I felt shitty, because Angelica was acting weird, like she knew I didn't have the money for toys and she had to pretend like she didn't really want hers. So I told her I got an extra-big tip at work that day and that I got her the teddy bear for being a good kid and helping me out with her brother and sister.

No, she still didn't act happy. She didn't smile or anything. She just said thanks.

It made me feel like shit. Like a bad mom. Because it's pretty messed up when you can't be nice to your kid without her wondering why. Poor Angelica was probably scared I was drunk or something.

But at the same time I thought to myself, *You know what? Everything's gonna change around here. I'm going to start making more money, and I'm going to buy my kids all the stuff they need, and I'm going to be home with them more, playing with them and listening to their stories.* You know? And it kind of sucked that I could only do all this stuff because I was working as a stripper. But at the same time, I didn't care. I felt like, it's time for us to have a better life, and I don't care how I have to do it.

Yeah. I'd made an appointment to see Marcus again in a few days, and I'd told Lisa that I'd meet with Jackie so she could set me up on the job full-time.

Yeah, I did.

How was it? Embarrassing. Like going to the clinic, when they make you take off your clothes and somebody you don't even know is staring at you and poking on you and telling you what to do. She told me I'd have to cover up my tattoo with makeup and redo my eyebrows and get myself waxed, and that I needed to go next door—to the lingerie boutique, Erotix—and get a bunch of nice outfits to wear on the job. But after we got out of her office, Lisa and Caitlyn told me not to worry, because they bought all their stuff at the Goodwill or from this real cheap costume store on the Internet, and no one cared. And they hooked me up with everything I needed for the first week or two, until I could make a little money and get my own stuff.

Yeah, I started doing it, just like that. I saw Marcus again, and Lisa sent her old man to me for one dance, and then some of the other regulars saw me there and started asking for me, and after a couple of weeks I had plenty of appointments.

Yeah, I did start having to take off my clothes. You're right.

I don't know. It's not really a big deal when you think about it. It's just a job, you know? It's not like I know these people in real life or care about what they think. If I start to get nervous, I just tell myself, "One more dance and you covered the electric bill. Two more dances and you made next month's rent. One more dance after that and you can get the girls a bunk bed." Stuff like that. Then, if I still feel nervous, I take a few shots of tequila. But I hardly ever have to do that anymore, now that I'm used to it. Most of my customers are pretty cool. They're not all freaks like Marcus. Most of them just want to chill out and shoot the shit with a naked chick for a while, like the guys at Neno's Cabaret did. Except these dudes make a lot more money, so they can watch girls dance in a private room instead of sitting in a filthy bar with a bunch of losers right next to them.

No, not really. I don't have to worry about it too much, because there's a lot of security. There's a metal detector on the front door. Then nobody gets through the door to our rooms unless one of the girls knows him or unless he comes with a regular and shows his license and all that. If a guy went into the room with one of us and then tried something weird, one of the other girls would see it on the monitor and call Jackie, or whoever was working at Erotix. That's usually Jackie's brother or one of her friends. Or if shit ever gets out of hand for real, there's a gun we can use. Not to shoot anybody, but to scare them away. Or we could just call the cops if we had to. But I'm not really worried about it. I've taken care of myself in way worse places, you know?

Yeah, we can call the cops. Jackie doesn't like to, but we can. What we're doing isn't illegal, as long as we're not having sex with the customers. And if Jackie finds out a girl's doing that, she kicks her out, fast. Same thing if they're doing drugs, or starting shit with the other girls, or trying to skim money off Jackie's cut. She's real strict about that stuff. She's not like Neno.

No, I still hadn't told Natasha and Haley. Or Geronima either. Well . . . I did tell them I'd changed jobs. They noticed I wasn't working night shifts anymore and that I was buying new stuff. Like, once I asked Natasha to take me to IKEA so I could get the kids a dresser, because it wouldn't fit in my car. And I asked them if they knew any dentists, so I could take the kids to get their teeth cleaned. So Haley finally asked me if I was getting a lot of tips lately, and I ended up telling them that I got a different job. I said I was working at Erotix and that the pay was way better there. I said they had to pay their cashiers real good salaries, because skeevy perverts went in there all the time and most people couldn't handle that. And that was why they didn't need me to have a diploma or anything either.

And they believed me. Haley asked if they could go visit me at work—she was crazy like that sometimes—but I said not until I was working there a little bit longer and the boss liked me better. That was all I could think of. I didn't want to lie even worse and pretend I worked somewhere better than that. But I didn't want to tell them I was dancing either.

Why? Come on. You know what people think about that stuff. Shit, the only reason I'm telling you about it now is because you're a stranger—and you get paid to listen to people's bullshit.

I don't know. Yeah, maybe, if I'd told them why and how much we needed the money. I guess they might have been okay with it. But I didn't want to find out. You know? It was like here I was, finally making enough money to hang out with them after work, to buy my kids some of the stuff that their kids had—to be kind of normal, like they were—but the only way I could do it was by stripping. I mean, if the whole idea was to be more like them so they'd want to hang out with me, how could I tell about the dancing? People like me can't have normal jobs that make decent money. We have to cheat. You know? Like, some guys deal drugs just so they can live in a house in the suburbs and send their kids to nice schools and give them piano lessons or whatever. Yeah, a lot of people deal drugs so they can buy a bunch of cars and gold teeth and shit. And some chicks strip so they can do drugs. But most of them just want to be normal, like everybody else. They just never learned how to do it the right way. You know?

I had this plan back then. I was thinking that I'd work for Jackie for a few months, save up some money, and take the classes to get my GED. Then, once I had that, I would get a regular job that I could tell Natasha and Haley about. Then I'd quit the stripping and forget it ever happened.

No, not anymore. Not after everything that's gone down. Why should I quit now? I'm making good money—better than I'd make working at some office. I'd be stupid to throw it away for nothing.

Well, I haven't really thought about it like that.

Right. No, I get what you're saying. Yeah.

Yeah, but if I did that, I wouldn't be able to afford to come here anymore. That'd be cutting into *your* money, right?

Oh, that's a good one. You're funny. You know, you're not so bad, now that I'm getting to know you better. You're pretty cool for a rich old white lady.

You're welcome.

Alex

I THOUGHT MOM was going to be mad that I forgot about my project until today, but she wasn't. She said she'd help me but that I had to do most of it by myself.

We turned off the TV and turned on Mom's CD player. We cleared off the table in the living room and laid out all the paints. Mom's on her computer in her bedroom looking for pictures of kingfishers and their habitats. I'm gluing my index cards to the poster board. Lucia's sitting next to me doing her workbook.

Mom calls me to her bedroom, and Lucia follows me over there. We go to Mom's little table in the corner, next to the ironing board, where she has her computer. It's showing all the pictures of kingfishers that she found. Mom says, "Well, the ringed kingfisher is this gray one with the rusty chest. All those super-colorful ones in your book actually live in Australia. But maybe we can show this guy catching a fish in his beak. That'd be good, right?"

I look at the pictures and find one where the kingfisher's standing on a stick in the water. "Yeah. I can draw him like that, but with a fish in his mouth. And maybe another kingfisher behind him, watching."

"That'd be awesome, baby," she says. "Do you want to sketch it out real quick here?"

I go get my poster board and my good drawing pencil. Lucia keeps following me, doing her gallop like she's a pony. Back in Mom's room, I look at her computer and copy the patterns on the kingfisher's head and chest. Then she finds out what kind of fish live in the Rio Grande so I can draw the right one in the kingfisher's beak.

Back in the living room, Mom helps me mix the colors on a paper plate, and I paint over my drawing in the middle of the poster board, between the index-card facts. It looks pretty good when I'm done.

"Alex, will you paint me a pony next?" Lucia says. "I want a blue one with orange spots."

"Maybe. Or I can just draw you one in your notebook and you can color it with markers," I say. Then I ask Mom, "What if Ms. Hubacek doesn't like my painting and says I should've printed out a picture instead?" Everybody else always prints pictures from the Internet for their projects. But our printer's out of toner, and we don't have time for Mom to print stuff at her job.

"Well," says Mom, "I don't see why she wouldn't like it. It looks really good, and everyone knows it's way more work to paint a picture than to print one. Plus, you can point out to her that you added a fish from the same habitat as the bird. You can tell her you deserve extra points for that."

I don't know if Ms. Hubacek will do that. But Mom's right about the picture coming out good. I like the way it looks. When I get my project back, I'm going to cut out the painting and put it in our room, next to my best drawing of Spider-Man fighting Green Goblin.

We clean up all the art supplies and put my poster board on the kitchen table so it'll dry. In the living room, the song on the CD ends and another one starts, the one about the guy who runs so far away. That's the song we always dance to. "Oh, yeah!" Mom says. "Watch out, y'all!" Lucia screams and runs into the living room. We follow her, and Mom turns up the CD player. Then we start to dance.

I like to do this dance Mom showed me called the Robot. It's funny. Me and Mom do that together for a little while, and then we do air guitar. Mom picks up Lucia and pretends they're dancing together like people do on the movies. Then she spins Lucia around, and they're laughing and screaming.

She can't pick me up anymore, since I'm big now. But she puts Lucia down and grabs my hands, and we spin around together like we're on a merry-go-round. We do it until I get dizzy, and then we crash into the couch, and then the song's over.

The next song is the one about the guy who lives in a big country. We sing the words with Mom, even though Lucia doesn't know them and says them all wrong. We're singing really loud, and then Mom says, "Hold on. Is that the phone?" She stops dancing and goes to her bedroom. When she comes back, she's talking on the phone, saying, "Yes. One moment, please." She tells me, "Alex, it's your dad," and hands me the phone. She turns down the CD player and says, "Why don't you take it in your room?" like she always says when Dad calls for us, so we can have privacy.

Lucia tries to follow me, but I tell her, "I'll come out when I'm done," and I close the door so she can't come in. She still doesn't understand what privacy means.

"Alex, how are you, buddy?" Dad says.

"Good," I tell him. "How are you?"

He says he's good. He asks me how school's been going, and I say okay. He asks how things are going at home, and I say good. He asks me where I am, and I say I'm in my room. Then he tells me, "Listen, buddy. You remember that conversation we had a while back? About how much I miss you and you maybe coming to live with me?"

I remember it.

"Well, I wanted to tell you that I'm thinking about getting you a computer. Your own computer, for your bedroom, so you can play games on it. And so you can do your homework, too, of course," he says.

I say, "Will it have a printer, with toner?"

He says, "Yeah. Of course. But, Alex, the thing is, I want to buy you the computer, but it costs a lot of money, and if you're not going to be here to use it . . . If you're only going to be using it twice a month, then it's kind of a waste of money. You see what I'm saying?"

"Yes." I do see what he's saying. I don't do my homework at Missy's house, so it'd be dumb to have a computer there.

Dad says, "Okay, good. Because I really want to buy it for you, but not if you're not going to use it."

I say, "What if you buy it and we put it in my room here? Then I could use it every day."

He laughs. "Well, yeah, I guess you could. But . . ." After a while he says, "The thing is, Alex, I really want you to think about what we were saying. About you coming to live with me. Have you thought about it at all?"

I did think about it a little bit, after he told me last time, but then I stopped. I know that even if I wanted to live with Dad at Missy's house, Mom would be mad if he told her that. Also, Dad never said if Lucia would come with me or not. I think Mom would get super mad if Lucia left her, too. Also, I don't know if I'd want to or not. Sometimes I think it'd be good, since Dad doesn't work as much anymore. He always says that living with Missy made him realize that family is the most important thing, and now he never works late anymore.

He's always taking Missy and Shepherd to the park and football games and stuff, and he's been saying that he's going to
take us all to Disney World this summer. So maybe if I lived
with him, he'd do all that stuff with me.

But then I think I'd be sad, because I'd miss Mom and Lucia, and I know Mom would miss me a lot. She'd probably
cry. I know she's sad when we go with Dad for the weekend
and she has to stay here by herself.

But that was before she started being friends with Jared's
mom and Angelica's mom and Miss Buena. Now she does
stuff with them when I'm gone, so maybe she wouldn't mind
if I left.

I don't want to ask her, though. And I know if Dad asks
her, they'll fight.

"Alex? What do you think, buddy?"

"I don't know," I say. I'm too scared to say anything else.

I hear him breathing in the phone, like he's tired or in a
hurry. "All right, buddy. It's okay. We can talk about it later,
all right?"

I say all right and ask him if he wants to talk to Lucia.
He says yes, so I go out to the living room and give her the
phone.

"My turn!" she yells, and then she runs to our room.

The music's real low now, and Mom's in the kitchen emp-
tying the dishwasher. She stands up and tells me, "I think
your painting's almost dry. Hey, baby, what's wrong? Are you
okay?"

I tell her that I'm fine. I ask her if I can watch TV now, and
she says yes.

Natasha

IT'S SATURDAY MORNING, and I have no plans. Unbelievable. I'm caught up on laundry and don't have any pressing errands to run. I could study my class notes from Wednesday's certification course, but I could also do that later. It's a beautiful clear day. I should go out and...

Call Hector?

No. Don't do that. Call Haley. I couldn't reach her last night and ended up talking to Geronima for an hour instead. But maybe Haley's free today and we can go walking at the mall. Burn some calories.

"Hello?" Her voice sounds scratchy, as if she's still asleep. It's already ten, but maybe she likes to sleep late when Jared's gone.

"Haley. Are you awake?"

"What? Yeah." She sounds bad. She must be coming down with something. "What time is it?"

"It's ten. Hey, I can call you back later if you're still asleep. I just wanted to see if you feel like hanging out. Go shopping or something."

She coughs. "I don't know. I'm pretty..." There's a long pause. She's sick, or she really is half asleep. "I'm kind of hungover, I think."

"Oh, really? Did you go out last night?" I'm a little surprised, even though I have no reason to be. She's an adult, isn't she?

She coughs again. "Yeah, I went to a party. A rockabilly party." I have no idea what that means. She says, "We partied... a lot. All night."

"Oh." I guess she wouldn't be in the mood for any mall walking, in that case. "All right. Well, are you going to be okay? Do you need me to bring you some coffee or aspirin or anything?"

"No, I'm good. I have green tea," she says.

We say good-bye and hang up. It's silly for me to be surprised. Haley's newly separated from her much-older husband. Of course she wants to do a little partying on her weekends off.

And it'd be really silly for me to wonder why she didn't invite *me* to the party. She probably wasn't at liberty to bring extra guests. Or—let's go ahead and be honest—she probably didn't think I was the rockabilly-party type. Not that Haley's that type either, actually. But maybe she's trying to change her image. Have some adventures, as she says.

I must look to her like an old, fat *mom*.

I'm being ridiculous, though. Because if she'd invited me, I probably would've said no. I *am* an old mom now, and I'm not even ashamed of it.

The phone rings. It's Sara, probably calling about Thanksgiving at Geronima's.

She says, "Hey, Natasha. How's it going? You busy?"

"No. What's up? Did Geronima tell you she wanted to get together for Thanksgiving?"

"Yeah, she did. But... um, I was calling to ask you..." She

sounds nervous. Why? She says, "You know that store called IKEA?" Not at all what I was expecting. I say yes, and she says, "Um, do you know where it is?"

I say, "Yes. It's out in Frisco." She's probably trying to apply for a job there. Poor thing.

"Frisco. How far away is that?"

"About an hour. Why?" The curiosity is getting to me now. I'm trying to imagine Sara in the yellow-and-blue uniform, lifting the big boxes of unassembled furniture and pronouncing all those Swedish words. I can't picture it at all.

"No reason," she says. "I was just thinking about going over there and checking it out. Seeing if they have a cheap dresser for the girls."

"You've never been?" I say. "They have all kinds of cheap dressers."

"Yeah. No," she says. "No, I've never been."

I say, "You want me to go with you? I need some stuff, too." It's true—I need something to make more storage room in our closets. One of those magical things that only IKEA sells.

"Nah," she says. "I wasn't trying to ... I don't want you to have to ..."

"No, let's go," I tell her. "We can take my Blazer. You're going to need a big vehicle to put your dresser in."

She relents, giving me something to do today.

"JESUS, THERE'S A LOT of shit here," Sara says as she rounds the corner from living rooms to offices, pushing her cart full of Baby Junior through the crowd. All around us people fawn over the desks in their rainbow shades of plywood. Monique's hanging on to the front of the cart like a stuntman in a car chase, and Angelica's walking next to me, proudly carrying my still-empty IKEA shopping bag. Traffic stops next to a curved desk topped by a cardboard computer.

"What does 'Galant' mean?" Angelica asks. Her voice is so quiet. I think it's the first time I've ever actually heard her speak.

Sara shrugs in total bewilderment, so I explain. "All the things for sale here have Swedish names, because this store was started in Sweden. 'Galant' probably just means desk."

She absorbs this information in silence, and I remember the first time I brought Alex and Lucia here. They asked the same kind of question, of course, but didn't stop there. Alex thought it was ridiculous that they didn't translate the names into English, and we ended up having a really long conversation about different cultures and marketing.

It's strange to be here with someone else's kids. But kind of nice, too. It gives me a chance to see how my kids measure up behavior-wise. And it gives me a chance to feel...appreciated. Angelica and Monique obviously enjoy any bit of attention I give them. And I enjoy being able to help Sara. She reminds me of my cousins, except she's more interesting. Funnier. Less ghetto, for want of a better expression, when you really get to know her. For instance, I can't imagine any of my cousins shopping at IKEA. They're strictly Walmart types. Not that there's anything wrong with that.

Yes there is. Walmart's disgusting. I'm proud of Sara for having better taste than that.

WE MUST HAVE burned at least three hundred calories walking through the IKEA maze and lugging Sara's dresser parts into the Blazer. So the gelato we're eating now? Practically doesn't exist.

"How'd you say you found this place again?" Sara asks me as she licks the dulce de leche off her tiny spoon.

"This is the neighborhood we lived in when I was married." And this makes two things that I miss about those days: the washing machine and this gelato place. I used to bring the kids here when Mike worked late, and back then it didn't seem like a big event. But now I realize that I used to take all that leisure time and extra money for granted.

Sara looks around the shopping center as if expecting to see my old house between the grocery store and the nail salon. "Nice."

Her kids decimated their sorbets a long time ago and are now hopping in and out of the drained fountain in the middle of the patio. I'm glad the sun's out, making it warm enough for us to sit here in our sweaters.

"I bet you're wondering how I have enough money to buy new furniture," Sara says out of nowhere.

I wasn't wondering, actually. But I smile politely, in case she feels like telling me.

"I got another job," she says.

"Oh, yeah? Congratulations. Doing what?"

She sits back in the iron chair and gazes across the lot at the cars passing down the boulevard. "It's kind of weird. I'm working at a lingerie place. You know, one of those places where they sell that kind of stuff. The sexy stuff."

"Oh, really?" I don't know what she expects me to say to that. But it seems like she's waiting for something. Approval? Understanding? "Does it pay better than your cousin's bar?"

"Oh, yeah," she says. "Way better."

"Well, there you go. Nothing weird about it, then," I say. "It's a job like any other, right?"

She gives a weak chuckle and nods. Doesn't say anything else.

I feel bad for Sara. It's obvious that she wants to make a better life for her children. But she has so much to struggle through. It's pretty clear that all she's ever known is poverty and family dysfunction. I can tell that it makes her self-conscious to be around people like Haley and even people like me, probably. But she wants to change. I saw her watching me at IKEA, mimicking everything I did, the way I examined the merchandise and spoke to the cashier. Then there was that tense moment when that woman gave Sara a "dirty look," and I could tell that Sara was holding back her impulse to curse the woman out. The way she'd curse out a pervert in the laundry room or anyone else she found threatening.

When that happened, she reminded me less of my cousins and more of . . . I don't know. Myself, maybe? Back when I was first dating Mike and was trying so hard to be the right kind of woman. The right kind of wife, eventually. I remember the first time Mike took me to a nice restaurant— a really nice restaurant, not the kind of chain place my parents would have considered nice. I remember sitting there sweating it out while the waiter dropped the napkin in my lap and asked if I liked the wine. Feeling unsure of myself in the same way that Sara must have felt his morning among all that Swedish gibberish. The fear of the unknown, battling with the desire to become someone *better*. I remember it well.

"I'm just glad to have a job," Sara says. "You know, life

was kind of sucking for me for a while there. I wasn't getting paid enough at my cousin's, and my freaking car was falling apart."

I don't want to be nosy, but then again yes I do. "So your ex still doesn't pay child support?"

"Who, Jorge?" she says. "He never had to pay until this past month, because the attorney general finally caught up to his ass. He's been all pissed off about that, and he wants me to bring him the child-support check and sign it over to him."

"What? Why would you do that?"

She shrugs. "It's his money."

"No," I say. "It's *your* money. He has to pay you. It's the law." I see Angelica glance up at us from the fountain, and I remind myself to keep my voice down.

Sara shakes her head. "I don't pay attention to that. When I decided to keep my babies, I told Jorge I didn't want anything from him. Because if it was up to him, I wouldn't have kept them. But he's been real good with them both, visiting them and helping out and all. Better than Angelica's sorry excuse for a father."

I've never heard a woman say anything like that before. "So you just...don't get child support at all?"

She shakes her head again. "I mean, he helps out, you know, when he can. He buys them stuff sometimes. But that's it. I never tried to take him to court, and I'm not down with the attorney general garnishing his wages on his new job. I never asked them to do that."

I think back to the conversation we had at the park, when Sara talked about raising her kids without their father's input. I say, "But those are his kids, too," even though I already have the feeling there's no use arguing with her.

"Yeah," she says. "But I didn't *have* to have them. I was the one who wanted to, not him."

I want to ask more: Did he ask her to have abortions and she refused? Why did she get pregnant the second and third time if she was already supporting Angelica on her own? She sounds so sure of herself that I'm dying to hear the logic behind the rest of it.

But then I look down at her children, playing quietly in the fountain, and I don't have the heart to ask. They're here already, so there's no use asking why. "You must think I'm crazy, then, getting into it with my ex-husband over the kids and the money," I finally say.

"No," she tells me. "That's different. You two were *married*, and he fucked that up. If I were you, I'd be taking him to court all day long."

It's funny the way she imagines me with more rights than she herself has, simply by virtue of a marriage certificate. Funny but sad.

"You know whose situation doesn't make sense to me, though?" she says. "Freaking Haley's. You know her husband has tons of money—you can tell. And he's letting her do this separation or whatever, where she gets to chill out as long as she wants while making up her mind about the divorce. And then he takes their kid whenever she needs him to. So what's the problem, right? Why even leave him? It's like he's giving her all this money, paying for her apartment and shit, and she doesn't even have to act like his wife. Must be nice."

I want to laugh at the way she's summed up Haley's choices, because sometimes I've wondered the same things myself. But instead I play devil's advocate and say, "Maybe they have problems Haley hasn't told us about."

"Like *what?*" Sara says.

"I don't know. Maybe the sex isn't good."

She scoffs. "Well, then she should make it better. *I* would."

I laugh, because I totally believe that Sara would. But for some reason I feel the need to defend Haley. Probably because I like her and want to believe she isn't just some flake. I say, "Maybe he hits her."

Sara jumps on that. "No, because why would she let her kid stay with him on weekends, then?"

"Well, maybe..." I don't know. Maybe she is a flake. Or a spoiled child, which is what I think Sara's trying to get at here. "She probably just doesn't want to live with the guy anymore. Does she *have* to stay with him if she doesn't want to, just because he has money?"

Sara sits there quietly for a little while, like she's seriously considering the question. "I guess not," she says finally. "But I sure as hell would."

I can't argue with her. Maybe, in her position, I'd feel the same way.

Baby Junior slips off the fountain's edge and falls into the shrubbery surrounding it. He cries out, and Sara and I jump from our seats, but he's not seriously hurt. Angelica hurries to help him up and brush the dirt from his hair.

Sara sighs. "We'd better take off, I guess. I have to do a bunch of laundry and stuff."

"All right."

As we load her kids back into my Blazer, it occurs to me that I haven't heard her yell at them once today. Sara buckles Baby Junior into the car seat. Monique is next to him, and her eyes are closing. Next to her, Angelica's bent over something in her lap. When I get into the driver's seat, I turn and see that she kept the inventory list full of Swedish words and is using a tiny IKEA pencil to make checkmarks on it.

I wonder if she's idly doodling or pretend-shopping for her future apartment. She looks up and catches me watching her in the rearview mirror. I meet her eyes and smile.

Sara

So THIS WHOLE time Haley was bugging me. She'd call me up on a Thursday night and ask if I wanted to go out. And I'd say, "You mean to the park, with the kids?" and she'd say, "Well, I was thinking you could leave the kids with Geronima and we could go to a club." Or she'd tell me about some show she heard about from the people working at the grocery store. Some weird punk-rock band or whatever. She'd say Jared was at his dad's and she wanted to have some fun. And I was thinking, *He sure does go to his dad's a lot.*

She came over one night before Thanksgiving. I'd been working at the Dollhouse for a couple of weeks already. She showed up at my place wearing jeans and a T-shirt, looking like a kid, and she told me she needed a big favor. I was like, sure, what is it? She said she was trying to get a job as a checker over at Earth Foods, but she needed references. And job experience. So she asked me if I'd cover for her and say that she used to work at the Cabaret, as a waitress.

I said I guess, but it would be kind of hard, since I didn't work there anymore. If they called the club, whoever answered wouldn't know any Haley Harrison. So she asked if I could call my cousin Neno and ask him to cover for her.

I said sure, I guess. I didn't want to, but it seemed like the least I could do. I mean, what else could I do for somebody like her? I wanted to be a good friend, you know?

Then she asked me if I thought she could say that she'd worked with Natasha, too.

I said, "I don't know. You know how Natasha is. She likes to play by the rules. Have you asked her yet?"

And Haley said that she hadn't asked her, but she wanted to see if I thought she could just put Natasha's name and phone number down and say she'd been Haley's manager at some job. She said, "If they called her and asked, she'd probably go along with it, don't you think?"

And I was like, "I don't know, Haley. I don't think that's a good idea." And then I looked at her close up, and I saw that she was stoned. Not a lot, but definitely buzzing. I remember thinking, *Is it just weed, or is she on something else?* Because she was kind of excited. Talking fast and stuff. And I was wondering how she was going to pass the drug test if they did want to hire her at Earth Foods.

Then she started asking if I could maybe get her a job at my place. And I didn't want to talk about that, so I told her we weren't hiring but I'd call my cousin and get her the hookup at the Cabaret.

I was hoping she'd take off then, so I could call him without her being there. But she wouldn't leave. She got all excited and started telling me how much she wanted to work at Earth Foods because she liked that they were all organic and shit. And how everyone who worked there was really nice, especially this one guy named J.D. And I was thinking, *Oh, so that's it. She wants to get it on with this J.D. guy.*

So I took the phone into my bedroom, and she followed me, practically peeing her pants, she was so excited. I was hoping Neno's sister would answer the phone and I could tell her real fast and get it over with. But of course Neno had to be the one to answer it. As soon as he heard my voice, he was like, "Where the hell have you been?"

And I was like, "I told you, I got another job."

And he was like, "That's some bullshit, Sara. Your mom's been asking me about you, wanting to know how come you haven't gone by and given her the unemployment checks and the WIC. She's pissed."

And I was like, "Well, she needs to call me if she has a problem."

And he said, "She's been calling you. She said you don't answer." Then he was like, "Look, Sara, I need you back here."

And I told him I wasn't coming back. So he started arguing with me, telling me this sob story about how one of his other waitresses quit on him. Then he said I should hurry up and go back to the Cabaret before I messed up on the new job and got fired. And I didn't want to hear that shit, so then he changed his attitude and started telling me that the customers missed me, that they were asking where I'd gone.

I said, "Who's asking where I went?"

And he told me the one guy came by and asked for me, that he knew my whole name and he wanted to know where I was working now.

And I was like, "You're full of shit, Neno." Because I never told the customers my name.

I finally hung up on him, then turned around and saw Haley staring at me like a kid who just missed out on Christmas. I told her, "Don't worry about that. My cousin's an asshole. But I'll call again later and talk to the others. I'll tell them to put in a good word for you."

She was all sad then, so I wanted to talk about something else. I said, "So where's Jared? With his dad again?"

She said yeah, and I said, "Well, that's good, that his dad's been spending so much time with him, right?"

She didn't say anything. For a long time, she didn't say anything at all. She was just sitting there on my bed, looking sad as hell. I told her, "What's going on, Haley?"

And she started crying. She said, "You can't tell anyone, okay?"

I said okay, and then she told me all this stuff. That Dave and her weren't separated at all. That he thought she was staying in a house with Geronima, because Geronima was her old nanny and was sick with some disease and that Haley wanted to spend time with her before she died. And that she brought Jared along so he could learn about his heritage or some shit like that. Because Haley's mom is half Mexican or something, and Haley told her husband she felt out of touch with that part of her culture and didn't want Jared to be out of touch with it, too. Or something. I didn't know what the hell she was talking about.

I said, "So let me get this straight—your husband thinks you're just chilling in some old lady's house, taking a little vacation?"

She couldn't say anything. She just nodded her head, and snot was already running out of her nose, she was crying so much. I got up and got her a roll of toilet paper from the bathroom, and I made sure the kids were still sitting in the living room watching cartoons. Then I came back and told her, "So your husband thinks you're coming back any day now?"

She said yeah. Then she started crying harder and said that she didn't want to go back, but she didn't know how to tell him. She thought if she got a job, she could just leave him cold turkey and tell him she was taking care of herself from now on. But she couldn't even get a job on her own, and every time she saw Dave, she was too scared to tell him what was up.

"Is that why you keep taking Jared over there? So you can tell him?" I said.

She said no, that Jared kept going over there because Dave wanted him to. And he kept asking her when she was going to come home, and she was running out of time.

I couldn't even understand half of what she was saying. She told me this was just like some other time, when she took Jared to some class in Portland for people who didn't want to eat flour or something. And another time when she told Dave they were going to Austin to learn Spanish for two months. She said she chickened out those times, too, and this was her best chance, because she had Geronima to help with Jared, but she was too scared to take it.

I tried to calm her down, telling her it was going to be okay and shit like that. I was wishing Natasha was there, because she would've known how to deal with this better than me. I got her to stop crying at least. I told her I'd help her get the job at Earth Foods but that she needed to lay off the weed for a while. She went, "I'm not smoking right now. I'm only taking pills." So I told her to lay off those, too, if she could. That I'd help her with the job thing but that she needed to get a grip and tell her husband what was up.

That made her start crying some more. She kept saying, "I can't. I'm not strong like you, Sara." She was freaking me out.

I told the kids I'd be right back, and then I hauled Haley's ass out of my apartment and upstairs to hers. I made her get in bed, got her some water, the whole nine yards. I saw the pills in her room, right there on her nightstand next to a dirty wineglass. They looked like some kind of painkillers, and they said somebody else's name. John somebody. I told her, "Whose are these?"

She said, "My friend J.D.'s. I told him I've been under a lot of stress, and he had those left over from his last dentist appointment."

I stayed there until she quit crying again. She was talking a bunch of weird shit. She asked if I thought a guy her age would want to live with her, even though she has Jared.

I said, "What do you mean? How old is this guy?"

She said, "Twenty-five." And I tripped out, because that whole time I'd thought she was in her thirties, like me and Natasha. I don't know why, now that I look back on it. I guess because she was always dressed up all the time, and she had her hair cut like an old lady's.

I told her I didn't know, that maybe she should think about living by herself for a while and not worry about any dudes until she got her shit straight with her husband. She didn't say anything to that.

I was thinking, *First thing I'm gonna do when I get out of here is call Natasha.*

I got up to leave, and she stopped me. She said, "Sara, please don't tell Natasha any of this, okay? I would die if she found out."

I said okay, I wouldn't tell her. I promised. What else was I supposed to do?

Alex

WE'RE AT MISS BUENA'S today, and Angelica's here, too. I told her we should play Spider-Man and she could be Mary Jane. But she wanted to be Jean Gray, so we're making up a new story.

Everybody gets in their places, and I tell Angelica, "Okay, use your powers on the monster."

She puts her hand on her head and does the telekinesis.

"You have to say words, though," I tell her.

"Like what?" she says.

"Something good, like 'I am fire! Take that, foul beast!' Or you can say something funny, like 'Try that on for size!'"

We make Baby Junior act like the monster again. Angelica puts her hand on her head and says, "I am fire! You will die, monster! Die!" She does her eyes like she's using her powers on Baby Junior. I lift him up like she's blowing him up with her mind. Then I throw him on the bed, like she dropped him and he died. It comes out really good, except when Baby Junior laughs.

"You're supposed to be dead now," I tell him.

Tiffany stands up so she's not in her cage anymore. "This is stupid. When do I get to kill somebody?"

"Mary Jane doesn't kill people," I tell her. "You have to wait in the cage until I come save you and Lucia."

"I don't want to play this game," she says. She kicks over the side of the cage that's made of books.

Then Lucia gets up and kicks the side made of pillows and says, "Me neither!" She always copies what Tiffany does.

I guess the game's over, then. Angelica says, "Monique, come out." Monique sticks her arms out from under the bed and screams, "Rawr!"

"No, dumb-ass," Angelica tells her. "Come out. We're not playing anymore." I can't believe she said a bad word to her sister. Monique rolls out where we can see her and says, "*You* dumb-ass!"

Tiffany and Lucia just look at Angelica and Monique with their mouths open. Then Tiffany looks at Lucia and says, "You're a dumb-ass." Then Lucia starts to cry. Then Baby Junior starts to cry. Then it smells like poop.

"Ew!" Monique screams. "Junior's Pamper!"

Angelica makes a noise with her mouth and says, "Hold on. I'll be right back." She goes out the door. Baby Junior crawls off the bed and starts pulling at his shorts. I think he's trying to take them off. Monique jumps up and slaps his hand. "No! Bad boy!" she yells. He screams and tries to bite her, but she holds his arm so he can't.

Angelica comes back in the room and tells me, "Do you know where Miss Buena is?"

I follow her into the living room, then into the kitchen. The pitcher's on the table with the sugar and a pack of mix, like she was getting ready to make us something to drink. But Miss Buena's not there. I know Mr. Oscar's gone, because he told me he had to go get his oil changed. Did he take Miss Buena with him when we weren't looking?

No, she's probably in the bathroom. Or in the other bedroom. We go over there, to the other bedroom. The door's open, but the light's off. We take a step inside, and I see her. She's sitting on the bed, talking on the phone.

She always talks on the phone, but in the kitchen. Why is she talking in here now? I look at Angelica, and we stand close to the door so we can hear what she's saying.

"I understand that, Robbie. I just don't understand why she won't call me herself.... No, I know that. I remember. I just wish ..." She sounds sad. "I don't know. Cristina's father, he doesn't know about any of this. I don't know if he would understand.... Yeah, I know.... What's that?... Well, all right, then."

She hangs up. Then she turns around and sees me there. "Alex, what are you doing there? You scared me."

Angelica walks around in front of me and says, "Baby Junior needs his Pamper changed."

Miss Buena stands up and says, "Okay, okay. I'm coming." Then she says, "You kids can call me if you need something. You don't have to sneak around like that."

Natasha

LORD HELP ME, but I'm here with Hector again. Same hotel room. Same shirt he wore last time, too, I think.

This time it's awkward, because of the last time. This time I have to tell him immediately that I don't want this to become anything serious, or even a regular occurrence. It's strictly a one-off, for purposes of stress relief. I've always been the type to get tense before the holidays, even when I don't have a vindictive ex-husband suing me for custody. Who can blame me for seeking a temporary escape?

Hector says he isn't looking for a serious relationship either. Of course not. He wants what I want.

That's really all there is to say. We're standing next to the bed, and now I really do wish it weren't daytime. The sun is blazing through the cheap curtains and right onto our bodies in a less-than-flattering way. I have two hours until the kids come back. That should make me feel nervous or guilty. But instead I'm thinking, *Hurry! Hurry!*

So I hurry and strip, and Hector does, too. This time I get on top. I push him back, onto the bed, and climb up like a cowgirl into the saddle. It's good that he's already hard. Sometimes when we used to try to do this position, Mike couldn't stay—

Don't think about that. Stop thinking about anything. Especially not Mike or the kids.

Think about the condom. He's handing it to me now. Oh, God. Did we use one the first time? Why don't I remember? I should think about the condom automatically, like they tell you on TV. It's the very first rule of safe sex. Why didn't I think about that?

Because I've been married too long. Because I have an IUD and I never think about anything except whether it's been five years since they put that in. Why do I still have my IUD if I'm not married anymore? Because I'm too busy to make the appointment to have it removed, and because it still has a year to go, and I feel like I should keep it the full five years and get my money's worth.

I'm fumbling with the stupid condom, and Hector takes it from my hand. He whips it out of its package and pulls it on real fast, like he's slipping into a pair of sweatpants. It looks like pantyhose in this light, like his penis has a stocking over its face and is about to rob a bank. It is. The First National Bank of Me.

Jesus. What am I thinking?

I haul my thigh over his torso. Is it wrong that I'm already super wet? Should I be ashamed? No, I should be ashamed if that's *not* the case, right? If we needed lube or something.

I look down at Hector, and he's so excited. He has this expression on his face like it's Christmas already and he's so anxious to open the present that his eyes are almost crossed. I want to laugh, but I don't. Mike always hated it when I giggled during sex. It was a "boner killer," he always said.

Stop thinking about Mike.

I like Hector because he just doesn't care. He's grabbing the fat on the sides of my butt and using it to push me up and pull me back down. He's trying to anyway.

I grab his hands with my hands, hold them still, there on my fat, and move myself up and down, the right way.

"Ohhhhhh," he says, like it's a slow-motion movie scene and somebody shot him. I laugh. I can't help it. I laugh, yet his boner remains.

AFTERWARD WE LIE there in a state of shock, like a pair of fish who just jumped out of an aquarium.

I can't help but ask, "Did we use a condom last time?" Now that the fun part's over, it's on my mind, bugging me.

"Yes, we did. Don't you remember?" he says.

I don't say anything. I don't want him to think I'm a slutty divorced mom who has sex without condoms. Never mind that he's apparently a slutty divorced dad who always has them on hand when he has sex with near strangers, here at his favorite motel.

"I have to leave soon," he says. "My kids are coming back at six."

"Mine, too," I say. "Wait—why are your kids gone? Do you have second and fourth weekends instead of first and third?"

"Yes," he says. "because I have custody of my kids. This is my ex-wife's weekend."

"Oh."

That's as personal as either of us wants to get, apparently, because we don't say anything else until after we're dressed and standing outside the motel room. And then we only say good-bye.

I'm crossing the parking lot to my Blazer. There's a man

sitting in a two-door economy car, watching me. He smirks at me as I pass.

Pervert. They're everywhere. This one sits in the parking lot and watches people leaving hotel rooms.

If I meet up with Hector again—I'm not going to, of course, but if I ever do—I'm going to tell him we need to find a nicer hotel.

I MAKE IT BACK to the apartment at five-thirty. Just enough time to shower and put on a mom-like outfit. Not that the outfit I wore to meet Hector was trashy or some special date outfit or anything like that. It was just a dress, like something I'd wear to work. Why would I put on something special to meet this guy when he's already seen me completely naked? It wouldn't make sense to try to look different all of a sudden. Which is why I didn't shave either. I only took the scissors and trimmed a little, and I felt stupid enough doing that.

Jesus. This is why I'm not ready to start dating yet. It's too much. Too many mistakes to make and petty details to worry about.

For instance, why am I even thinking about this now, going through this checklist of dating behavior to see if that's what I'm doing with Hector? I already told him this wouldn't be anything serious, precisely because I didn't want to obsess about it like I'm doing right now. Stop thinking about it. Move forward.

I'm standing in front of the apartments, in the cold, and Mike's supposed to be here with the kids, and of course he's late. Mike always loved to leave me hanging, waiting like a servant or like a dog tied to a park bench.

My phone rings. It's Geronima. "Natasha," she says in her

somewhat raspy voice, "what time are you guys coming over for Thanksgiving?"

I can't believe Thanksgiving's already here. It's this Thursday. "I don't know," I say. "What time is good for you?"

She talks to me about the time, the menu, and the characters on her favorite reality show. An old Tahoe pulls into the parking lot, and after a few moments I realize that Mike's driving it and Missy's in the passenger seat. It must be her car.

In my ear Geronima says, "I'll see you Thursday, then."

I hang up and prepare myself for battle. I hope Mike *won't* start anything with me, but if he does, I'm ready for him. And his little girlfriend, too.

I can see Alex and Lucia in the backseat now, sharing it with Missy's toddler son. They look tired. Maybe a bit anxious, anticipating the inevitable tension between their dad and me. Mike parks directly in front of me but doesn't make eye contact. I see Missy put her hand on his, on the steering wheel. To comfort him? Bolster his confidence? The kids clamber out of the back doors and join me on the sidewalk. And then Mike pulls away, without a glance in my direction.

Surprising. He must have talked to his lawyer, or to someone who advised him that threatening me wasn't the way to go. I wish again that I'd recorded that phone conversation. I should buy a tape recorder and start recording them all from now on, just in case. I'm going to ask Joanne what she thinks about that. Maybe if I catch Mike acting like a jerk on tape, it'll give me the ammunition I need to make him back off.

Sara

HEY. HOW'S IT going?

I'm okay. Kind of tired. They had some show at the school last night. Monique's class did a dance, and Angelica sang a song and played these little bells. It was cute as hell. But the whole thing took forever. We didn't get out of the school until nine o'clock. Baby Junior was acting like a brat at the end, and I kept having to grab him and put him back in his chair. But I took a bunch of pictures of the girls in the show.

Right, for black history. How'd you know?

Yeah, I'll show them to you.

Thanks. Yeah, you're right. She does look like me, kind of. Monique looks more like her dad.

Yeah, Natasha's kids still go to that school. I think she was there. I don't know. I didn't look around too much, you know? Her daughter was in the dance with Monique, though, so Natasha was probably there to see that. See, she's this one right here, in the purple shirt.

I don't know. Yeah, maybe. I didn't want to find out, though. That would've been embarrassing, if I'd walked up to her and she didn't want to talk to me.

Last time? Yeah, I remember. I was telling you that I called Neno, and he said my mom had been trying to get hold of me. She was mad because I'd quit working for him.

It's kind of a long story. There was a lot going on with that, you know? I used to do a bunch of messed-up stuff with them. Like, I'd work for Neno, but he'd pay me under the table, and he'd do something on his taxes to get an extra break. Then I'd file for unemployment and share the money with my mom. I'd get WIC for her, too. You know, the free food they give you if you're poor and have kids? I'd give my mom all the cereal and cheese and stuff, and that's what she and my brother would eat all day. Then, on top of that, she'd claim that me and the kids lived with her, and she'd get welfare for being the head of household for all those people.

No, hell no. Not anymore. I quit doing all that, and that was why she got mad.

I don't know. I told her I was doing my own taxes this year—Jackie hooked me up with this accountant guy who's helping me do it—and I told her I was using my real address, at the apartments. If she tries to claim me and they send somebody to her house, they're going to see she's lying. And if anyone asks me, I'm going to say I don't talk to her anymore. It's not even a lie.

What do you mean? I feel fine.

Oh, you mean because I don't talk to my mom anymore? I don't care about that. She never had anything good to say to me anyway.

I just mean, you know, she was always bitching at me about something. Complaining that I wasn't bringing her enough money or that I wasn't helping her do whatever stupid scam she was trying to pull. Back when she used to baby-sit the kids, she'd complain that they were brats and they never behaved. She'd say, "That Angelica's a little smart-mouthed bitch, just like you used to be." Which is a total lie—Angelica's nothing like I used to be. I was a brat. She's a good kid.

That's why I quit taking them over there. That, and I met Gero when she was first looking to do baby-sitting at our apartments. I was happy as hell about that—gave me an excuse to quit going to my mom's and listening to her bullshit.

You know what's funny? The whole time I was living with her, when I was growing up, she'd treat me bad. She'd slap me around and say it was because I was a brat. Then, when I got older, she started calling me a little whore. That's why I dropped out of school and took off with Angelica's dad. My mom thought it was because I got pregnant, but that didn't happen until later. I just had to get the hell away from her, you know?

So after all this time, she ends up being right. Her daughter's a whore now.

No, I'm just kidding. I'm just saying that's what she'd call me if she knew.

You're right. That's a good point. She was calling me names either way. You know what? Let's not talk about her anymore. What's that thing they say? Let's leave the past alone.

I don't know. You mean, do I feel bad when I'm doing it or do I feel ashamed of myself in general? When I'm there, it's no big deal. Taking my clothes off for those dudes is nothing. It's kind of funny, when I think about it. Sometimes I feel like I'm ripping them off, you know? They're paying me a lot of money just to see me naked and maybe for me to pretend that I care about them for half an hour. Meanwhile I'm dancing around thinking about stuff me and the other girls were talking about in the dressing room or what I'm going to get the kids for dinner. Like, the other day I had my Japanese client come in. He's this guy who likes to come in and look at my feet. He has one of those fetishes, you know, and my feet are the smallest out of all the girls'. So he came in, and I had just been looking at the videos on Caitlyn's laptop. I like to check out this site that has all these funny videos of cats, you know? Have you seen that one?

All right, so they have this one of a mother cat with all her kittens, and she's trying to walk around, but the kittens are trying to drink milk. So she gets up and takes off, and two of the kittens are hanging on to her with their mouths and they won't let go. So she's just dragging them around, and they're steadily sucking on her. I guess you have to see it for yourself. It has this funny music that goes along with it. So anyway, I kept thinking of those cats while I was dancing for my Japanese guy. And then I was thinking about getting a laptop for our apartment, so I can show the cat videos to the kids. Caitlyn said she'd help me hook up the wireless or whatever it's called. And then, next thing I knew, the half hour was up and I had two hundred extra bucks.

But I get what you're saying. You're asking if I feel bad about being a stripper. And I don't know. I guess it looks that way, since I don't tell people about it. But it's nobody's business anyway, right? I mean, there's a lot of people who don't talk about what they do for a living.

Sometimes I think, why should I be ashamed? Look how I grew up—all ghetto and shit, with no dad and a crackhead brother. Then I dropped out of school and had a bunch of kids with no dads. What else was I gonna be?

But at least I'm stripping in a good place, and I'm making more money than those skanks down at Neno's. Right?

No, I do remember what I said. I said I wanted to be a better mom, like Haley and Natasha. Well, like Natasha anyway. But it's different for them. They have it easier, because they didn't grow up like me.

Yeah, I still do. Didn't I tell you? I started my GED classes last week. But I need to make more money before I can quit the Dollhouse. I can't go back to how it was before, when we needed to pull scams with my mom in order to have enough groceries.

I guess you could say I'm ashamed, because I don't want people to know what I'm doing. But if they did find out, and if they knew why, I wouldn't feel bad about it. There's no shame in doing the best you can to take care of your kids, and right now this is the best I can do for mine.

I just wish I'd told Natasha everything, right off the bat. It probably wouldn't have changed anything, but at least I wouldn't feel like a damned liar and a sorry excuse for a friend.

Natasha

I'M GOING TO die and go to hell. That's what happens when you lie to your family on the holidays, right? I told my mother the kids were with Mike for Thanksgiving, which is true. Then, just now, I told her I couldn't make it to her house after all, because I was spending the day with some friends who didn't have families of their own. Which wasn't *exactly* a lie. I *am* going to Geronima's, but not until later.

Too bad. Who cares? I can't go to Mom's. I just don't want to hear her voice, especially not after she's filled up with Seagram's and Diet Sprite. She has my brother and his wife to eat with. That's plenty. I've already called my dad and wished him a happy Thanksgiving on his voice mail. That's plenty, too. He's doing fine by himself up there in Asheville.

The kids have been gone since yesterday. There's nothing to feel guilty about. So why do I feel guilty?

I don't. Not anymore.

"What are you thinking about?" Hector reaches over and brushes my hair back, so he can see my face.

"Nothing," I say. I scoot closer to him on the bed, turn onto my side so that my face is against his shoulder, as if he's taller than me. I pull the blanket over my legs. It's cold in here now, but his body's still hot.

"Is your mother okay with you not going over there for Thanksgiving?" he says.

"She's fine," I tell him. If he can ask that, I can ask a personal question of my own. "Are you okay not being with your kids?"

"Yeah, I'm fine. They'll have more fun with my ex," he says. "More cousins to run around with."

That's mature of him, to admit that.

The sun is starting to peek between the drapes. Hector turns toward me and wraps his arm around the small of my back. The medium of my back, more like. He buries his face in my hair, the way he likes to do, and says, "I'm glad you stayed the night."

I say, "I'm glad you found a nicer hotel."

He dips his head and takes my ear in his teeth, pretends he's about to bite. Moves his hand from my back to between my legs. Twirls his fingers and gently tugs. "I'm glad you don't shave."

I bite him back, on the neck, hard enough to make him groan, because I know he likes it. "What is this, your Thanksgiving list? All the things you're grateful for?"

He chuckles. "It's a good list, isn't it? I have a lot to give thanks for right now."

Me, too—for the moment at least. Hector moves down below the blankets, kissing as he goes, and I feel thankful indeed.

MAYBE I'M JUST being paranoid, but I could swear there's someone watching me as I say good-bye to Hector and get into my car. I feel someone staring, out of the corner of my eye. I turn and look across the street, and there's a flicker of movement in the windshield of a small silver car. No, that car's empty. It must have been the reflection of that tree's branches, moving in the wind.

Is that the same car from the other hotel? The one with the pervert who smiled at me? Or was that car more of a taupe?

I really am being paranoid now. I need to go to therapy or something. Why do I feel so guilty about this, when Mike's been sleeping with someone for months now?

Safe in the Blazer, I check my phone. There's a message from Joanne. She says that yes, I could record my phone conversations with Mike, but they wouldn't be admissible if we actually ended up in court, and that it's not worth doing if I'm saying anything inflammatory in our conversations myself.

Well, maybe I shouldn't bother with it, then. It's not like I really need tapes of our conversations anyway. I have to keep reminding myself: I'm not doing anything wrong. There's no reason any court would take my kids away from me.

Alex

I'M THANKFUL FOR: Mom and Dad, and Lucia, too, I guess. Our whole family and all my friends. All my toys and our video games and my comics. All my shows on TV. Recess and the days we get taco rolls for lunch in the cafeteria.

I'm *not* thankful for: The brussels sprouts, the green beans, and the freaky-looking yellow stuff on my plate right now. Cooked tomatoes. Social studies and Ms. Hubacek. Mean dogs and sleeping without a night-light. All the times that Mom and Dad fight.

Oh, wait. I'm also thankful for: The pies Missy made, that I can eat if I take one bite of this yellow stuff. The new football that Dad got me, that hurts my hands less. The dressing Mom always makes on Thanksgiving. I hope she made some today and is saving it for when we get home on Sunday.

Natasha

THE OTHERS ARE already here at Geronima's. Haley, Sara and her kids, Geronima, Oscar, and Tiffany. I walk in and smell delicious aromas that don't necessarily smell like turkey and all the trimmings. I see that Geronima still has all her pumpkin decorations out, the same ones she had for Halloween. But she's taken down the ghosts and more obvious jack-o'-lanterns. Oscar's on the couch, watching the parade on TV. Tiffany and Sara's kids chase each other in a quick circle around him. He says, "Hey, you kids," and they stream into Tiffany's bedroom and slam the door behind them. He waves me into the kitchen, where I find Haley doing a cooking presentation for Geronima and Sara.

"Don't you remember?" Haley's saying. "You'd say, 'Let's have party food tonight.' And you'd make those tiny cocktail sausages wrapped in batter."

"Pigs in blankets," Geronima says.

"Right. And you'd cut cheese into cubes and let me eat them with toothpicks. And then, when Mother got home, you'd tell her we had chicken and rice." I'm guessing she's talking about her childhood, back when Geronima was her nanny.

Sara's standing against the wall, out of the way, drinking one of Gero's Bud Lights. I say hi to everyone and set my casserole full of dressing on the counter. I see that Haley's already halfway into a bottle of sparkling white wine. That's probably what's brought on the wave of nostalgia. Meanwhile she's commandeered Geronima's microwave and half the butcher block with an assortment of bags, boxes, and bottles. We watch her pull a wheel of Brie from the microwave and decorate it with amaretto jam and pecan halves. Then she takes a tiny spreader and a box of expensive-looking crackers from her Earth Foods bag and uses them to complete the tableau she's created on the butcher block. "Here," she says, offering the spreader to Sara. "Try it."

"No thanks," says Sara immediately. "What is that, cream cheese?"

I accept a cracker topped with Brie and jam, and it tastes heavenly. "Good. This is really good, Haley." She beams at me like a child. "What are you drinking? Prosecco?" I say.

She says, "No, it's a cava. Try it." And she turns to the cabinet to get me a wineglass.

Geronima peers into the oven and says, "The brisket's almost ready."

"We're not having turkey?" I say.

Sara catches my eye, smiles, and shakes her head.

"I have turkey if you want it," says Geronima. "They had turkey breasts for a dollar ninety-nine a pound, so I got two. They're in the refrigerator. I can heat one up if you want."

I say, "No, brisket's fine. It smells great." Why not? If I can have Thanksgiving without my kids, without my mother . . . why not have it without turkey, too?

Haley hands me the glass of wine. She, Sara, and I clink glasses. "In thanks for this bounty," Haley says.

"To Turkey Day with brisket," Sara says.

"To eating and drinking," I say. "With friends."

Geronima clears the ever-present pots full of food from her stove, moving them to rooster-shaped trivets on the counter. Then she doubles up on pot holders—two in each hand—and opens the oven door all the way.

"Gero, let me do that," Sara says. She sets down her beer and takes the pot holders, bends down, and hauls up a giant roasting pan that must contain ten pounds of brisket and five pounds of golden, greasy brisket juice.

"Thank you, m'ija. Just leave it on the stove for a while, to rest." Geronima's perspiring, as if from Sara's effort. She's the one who needs to rest. I wonder how long she's been working in this kitchen, preparing for our visit, without a break.

"Let's go sit down for a little while," I say. "I'm tired from . . . driving over here." If I don't make an excuse to sit, Geronima won't.

We single-file it to the living room and arrange ourselves around Oscar and the TV. He gives us all affable glances but doesn't say anything. Oscar's a man long used to the company of women. He sits through our chatter, silent as a ninja but somehow never in the way. Is that why he and Geronima have stayed married for so long? Probably.

"So it's a long drive to your mama's house from here?" Geronima says to me as she blots her forehead with the skirt of her apron.

"What's that?"

"You said you were tired from driving. Your mother must live far away."

Oh, damn. This is why I should never lie. I'm not good at it. "I . . . um, I didn't go to my mother's."

"You didn't? Where were you, then?" Geronima's question

is completely innocent. How can she know that the answer isn't something I'm ready to make public?

"I had to go get something. To finish the dressing," I say. "The grocery stores around here weren't open, so I had to drive far away."

Geronima looks perturbed. "So you're not going to see your mama for Thanksgiving? Isn't she going to miss you?"

I don't know what to say to that. Will she miss me? I don't know. The only thing I'm certain about is that I don't miss her. So far this is turning out to be the best Thanksgiving I've had in a while.

Sara's raising an eyebrow at me. I know she isn't visiting her mother for Thanksgiving either, and I wonder if she's already explained herself to Geronima on that point. Haley, meanwhile, looks lost in her own world. She's staring at the TV but not registering the Snoopy-shaped float.

Oscar chooses that moment to join the conversation. "Gero, isn't it time for you to take your medicine, vieja?" I can't tell if he's trying to change the subject or if he really did feel the need to remind her. Either way, it makes her pop up and hurry to the bathroom. Baby Junior runs out of Tiffany's bedroom and nearly collides with Geronima's legs, causing Sara to call out, "Angelica, come get your brother!"

Once Geronima's behind the closed door, Oscar turns to me and says, "Never mind her. She's been sad that Tiffany's mama hasn't called her for the holidays."

That catches Haley's attention. She, Sara, and I exchange looks. We know that Geronima's only daughter, Cristina, lives elsewhere. It's been clear that they aren't close, but I wouldn't have guessed there was any strife between them. I venture a question, since Oscar's in the mood to talk. "Did Cristina spend Thanksgiving here last year?"

Oscar shakes his head. "She never does. Christmas either. We haven't seen her in five years, since Tiffany was born. But Gero's always hoping she'll change her mind and come back."

Geronima emerges from the bathroom at that moment, holding a bandage to her arm and keeping me from asking Oscar any more questions. It occurs to me for the first time that Geronima's diabetes must be pretty serious. She's talked about taking insulin before, but I always assumed she meant pills. Now I see the way she's holding her arm, and it reminds me of my father's mother and all the times I watched her, as a child, giving herself injections—before she died.

"Do you feel okay?" I ask. Now I feel guilty for coming over here, for practically forcing Geronima to cook us an elaborate dinner.

"I'm fine, m'ija. Good as new." She smiles at all of us and, magically, looks like her regular, energetic self again. "What are we doing sitting here talking? Let's eat!"

THE PARADE'S LONG over, the brisket's two-thirds demolished, and Oscar's gone to his bedroom for a late nap or a very early bedtime. Likewise Baby Junior's crashed out on Tiffany's bed, and the girls are sitting on the floor around him, playing with dolls in a food-induced zombie state. The rest of us are sitting in the living room picking at desserts and finishing the wine. Geronima's the only one still moving around the apartment. Every few minutes she pops up for one reason or other. Right now she's in the kitchen putting pots and pans full of soapy water on the stove, to soak away

the now-hardened rice, dressing, sweet potatoes, and pie.
She refuses to let us help her, and we're too drowsy to argue
much.

It's strange to be sitting here drinking at what feels like
a family party but without my kids. Bittersweet. Apparently
Haley feels the same way, because she's getting pretty emotional, now that we've made it through two or three bottles.
She keeps looking down at her plate of Brie and tearing up.

"Are you thinking about the parties you used to have with
Geronima?" I say.

She shakes her head. "No. I'm just..." And then a tear
breaks free and rolls down her face.

I see Sara giving her a cynical look. "Girl, please don't tell
me you're crying over a man." A man? Is Sara joking? Or does
she know something that I don't?

Haley sniffs and wipes away the tear. "It's not about him."

"Him who?" I say. There's something Sara knows that I
don't, and I'm annoyed. Or slightly hurt—both emotions feel
the same.

Haley won't say anything, so Sara explains. "She's into
some guy who works at Earth Foods. His name's J.D." Then
she asks Haley, "What happened? Is he being a dick to you?"

Haley sniffles again. "No. It's not about him."

I think back to the morning Haley was hungover and told
me she'd gone to a rockabilly party the night before. She
must have gone with this J.D. person. I can't believe she's
been dating and didn't tell us. Didn't tell me.

She says, "Nothing's happening between us. We're just
friends. I'm just...I miss Jared."

Now I feel guilty for being suspicious or jealous or whatever it was, and I reach over the corner of the coffee table

and put my hand on her arm. Of course she misses Jared. This is her first Thanksgiving without him, and he's her only child.

She's actually crying now. She says, "And Dave wants me to come back home."

"What's going on?" Geronima's back from the kitchen. "Haley, what's wrong?" She rushes over and sits next to Haley, to comfort her, probably the same way she did years ago.

Sara gives Geronima a quick recap. "Haley's ex wants her to go back home."

Geronima sighs. "Well, that's good. Isn't it?" She peers at Haley, who doesn't seem to agree. "Don't you want to go back? To work things out?" Haley can't answer. She's completely distraught.

Sara pipes up again. "She never told him she wanted a divorce."

"What?" Everyone looks at me. "I thought you were legally separated."

Haley coughs and sputters. "I'm sorry, Natasha. I wanted to tell you, but..." And she dissolves into tears again.

Sara leans over and explains it to me. "He thinks she's just visiting Geronima for a while. She doesn't have the guts to tell him she wants to leave."

I think back to everything Haley's ever said to me about her divorce, or her separation. And realize that she never said anything about either. She simply let me believe that Dave was her ex. A lie by omission.

And now I feel like an idiot.

Geronima's trying to give advice. "Why don't you just go back, m'ija? Tell him how you're feeling. He'd do anything for you. You know that."

"I know," sobs Haley. "But I don't want to him to do any-thing for me. I just want it to be over."

Sara visibly loses patience with her then. "You can't just wait for something to go away, Haley. You need to man up and tell him right now."

That's exactly what I'd say to her, albeit less harshly. But how is it that Sara knows all this—all Haley's backstory—and I don't? I didn't even think they liked each other that much.

The paranoia's coming back. This just feels too strange. What else is going on that I don't know about?

I stand, feeling a little wobbly. "I need to take off now. I have to . . . call my mother." It's the first thing that comes to mind. Hell, maybe I will call her.

"Natasha." Haley breaks away from Geronima and stands, too. "I'm sorry. I know what you're thinking—that I lied to you. But I didn't mean to. I just didn't want you to think . . . Well, I wanted you to think I was someone like you. You know . . . someone moving on with her life."

"It's okay," I say. Is it? I don't know, but she looks so miserable. And she's saying she lied in order to—what? Impress me? What can I say to that? "It's all right. Don't worry about me. Just worry about your situation. Get it taken care of. I hope it works out."

"I will," she says. "I'm going to call him tonight and explain everything."

I have to get out of here, right now. I don't feel so well all of a sudden. But I don't want to leave it with any of them thinking I'm upset. So I reach out and hug Haley. "Good luck, okay? Call me later and let me know how it goes." Then I hug Geronima and Sara good-bye. And then I hightail it out of there, so I can be by myself in my apartment for a little while.

Alex

AFTER THE TURKEY dinner and the football game, Dad says it's time to see the surprise he made for us. He goes to the bedroom where me and Lucia sleep when we spend the night at Missy's. I follow him to see what's there, and everything in the room is different.

"What happened to Lucia's bed?"

"Don't worry about your sister. She'll be fine in Shepherd's room."

Dad took the bunk beds out of our room and put in a new thing that's like a bunk bed except it has a desk on the bottom. It looks kind of cool, but I'm scared the bed will fall on top of the desk if I'm sitting there.

"This is where your computer will go," Dad says. He's standing under the bed. He has to bend down so his head won't hit it.

"I thought the computer was going to be at your apartment," I say.

Dad says, "No, that wouldn't make any sense. There's more room here, at Missy's house."

There's a new poster on the wall, of the Dallas Cowboys. I guess they took away Lucia's poster of that stupid pony show. Also, there's new curtains. They're blue with footballs and soccer balls all over.

Lucia comes in and sees how everything's different. Her

mouth opens up, and she makes the face she always makes before she starts crying.

"Hi, baby," Dad says.

Missy comes in behind her, carrying Shepherd. "Lucy, honey, come with me. I'm trying to show you something in Shepherd's room."

They go out, and I follow them. "Hey, buddy," Dad says behind me. But I want to go see what they got for Lucia.

It's nothing. Missy goes across the hall to Shepherd's room, and we see that there's a new bed in there. I guess it's for Lucia. It's white, with flowered blankets and pillows all over it. They had to push Shepherd's dresser into the corner to make the new bed fit.

"This is where you're going to sleep now, honey," says Missy. "Do you like it? I picked out the comforter just for you."

Now Lucia does cry, real quiet. She's a crybaby.

"Oh, honey. What's wrong?" says Missy. "Mike!"

I guess Lucia's crying because she doesn't like the bed. She doesn't really like stuff that's pink. Mom always has to get her light green or red and black. Maybe she's also crying because she doesn't want to sleep with Missy's baby. He's kind of a brat, and he cries real loud sometimes at night.

At least she doesn't have to be by herself. Now I'm going to have to sleep all by myself in a room with no night-light. Dad doesn't let us use a night-light, because he says he can see it through the crack in Missy's bedroom door and it keeps him awake.

Dad comes in Shepherd's room with us and tells Lucia, "Aw, sweetheart. Come here. Why are you crying?" She lets him pick her up like a baby. She likes to act like a baby sometimes. Dad says, "We thought you'd like our surprise."

Shepherd starts to cry real loud then. I think he's mad that Dad's carrying Lucia, even though Missy's already carrying him. Now Missy looks a little bit mad, I guess because Shepherd's crying. Or maybe she's frustrated that Lucia didn't like the blanket she picked.

I say, "Dad, maybe you should move Lucia's bed back to my room. She's probably scared to sleep by herself."

He looks down at me like he's thinking about what I'm saying.

Missy says, "She's *not* going to be by herself. She'll be with Shepherd."

Lucia squirms out of my dad's hands and slides back to the floor. She wipes the boogers off her lip and says, "Yeah! Wanna go back with Alex!"

I hate when she talks like a baby. But Dad always does what she wants when she acts like that. Missy looks really mad now. Probably because she hates when Lucia acts like a baby, too.

"Well, I guess..." my dad says.

"Mike," Missy says.

"What?" my dad says.

"I thought you said..." She stops talking and gives him a look, kind of like the way Mom used to look at him, right before they'd argue.

"I know, but..." Dad turns to me. "Alex, why don't you take your sister outside and throw the football around a little." He has to talk loud, because Shepherd is screaming now.

"It's dark outside," I say.

He looks up at the ceiling, then down at me. "Then take her to the living room, please. Put on one of your DVDs."

We go out of Shepherd's room, down the hall with all the

pictures of Missy and Shepherd on the wall, and into the living room, to the big blue couch. Lucia runs and jumps on it. Behind us I hear Shepherd stop crying. Next thing I know, he's coming into the living room with us. He climbs on the couch next to Lucia, and she makes the fart noise at him with her mouth. He laughs. He has snot on his lip, too.

I take out the stack of DVDs that Missy and my dad bought for us. Every time we come here, the Sammy Samaritan ones are on top. I move those out of the way and get down to the bottom, to Venom.

"Put on *Little Mermaid*!" Lucia says.

"No," I say. I put in Venom and go sit on the couch, in the corner with the biggest pillow.

When the cartoon comes on, Lucia says, "You're Venom and I'm Carnage." I tell her to be quiet.

In the other room, Dad and Missy are talking louder. I hear Missy say, " . . . your idea in the first place."

My dad says, "Well, what do you want me to do about it?"

Missy says something I can't hear, then, "Do you even know for sure that they want to live with us?"

I can't hear any more after that.

NOW LUCIA'S BED is turned so her head's pointing at the corner, like mine, except her body's by the window. I know she doesn't like that. There's freaky noises here at night. Missy says they're only frogs, but we didn't have frogs at our old house, and we don't have them at our apartment either.

"Alex," Lucia says.

"If you be quiet, I'll tell you a story," I say.

I see her nod her head. "Tell the boy and the girl and the witch."

She means the one Mom made up. "No," I say. "I'm going to tell a new one. Listen. Once upon a time, I was Venom and you were Carnage. But instead of enemies, we found out we were brother and sister."

She pulls the flower blanket up to her face, like she's scared. But I know she likes the story already. I make up a bunch of stuff, but she falls asleep before I can finish. She always falls asleep real fast.

Now she's snoring, so I don't have to say any more. But it's a good story, so I'll tell the rest of it in my mind.

Once upon a time, Venom and Carnage were brother and sister. They flew to the moon to find the source of their power.

On the moon they found a black substance oozing out of a big silver meteor. Venom collected it in a bottle made of kryptonite, and then they flew back home.

They knew that whoever swallowed the black substance would turn stronger, like them. Carnage wanted to give it to all her friends, even the ones who weren't superheroes. But Venom said no. He told her, "We only have a little bit, so we should only give it to people who really need it, who we want to be strong."

The first person they gave it to was Black Widow. She was already strong, but the black substance made her even more powerful.

The second person they gave the black substance to was Iron Man. It made him super strong, too. But now Black Widow was changed, and she had the same powers as Iron Man. So they decided to beat each other up.

Iron Man and Black Widow flew to a big mountain

where no one would see them. They shot lasers at each other. They jumped high in the air and hit each other in the face.

Black Widow said, "You can't control me! I'm smarter than you, and now I'm going to make you pay!"

Iron Man said, "That's where you're wrong! Only one of us can win, and it's not going to be you!" His girlfriend was watching and crying.

Venom and Carnage flew to the mountain and saw what was happening, and Venom knew what he had to do. He took the rest of the black substance and poured it all over himself so that it went inside him and took over his body, making him stronger than ever before. He was stronger than Carnage now, and even stronger than Iron Man and Black Widow. He grew taller than the mountain. His eyes turned glowing red.

When Iron Man and Black Widow saw him, they got scared and stopped fighting. "Please don't kill us," they said. "Tell us what you want us to do."

Venom said, "I want you to stop fighting and become allies."

"But I don't like him," Black Widow said.

"Yeah, me neither," said Iron Man.

Venom said, "I don't care. You have to get along. I control you both now."

So they all stopped fighting and flew back home. And they lived happily ever after, except when they had to fight other people.

The end.

Natasha

I'M GOING TO stop in front of Missy's house and honk the horn, exactly like it says in the divorce orders. I won't even roll down the Blazer's window. And while the kids climb into the car, I'll be mature and won't look at the windows of the house to see if Mike's watching me.

He *is* watching me. I see him peeking through her ugly 1990s plaid curtains. And now he's coming outside, exactly like the divorce orders say he's not supposed to.

The kids are inside with me now, Alex in front and Lucia in back, completely silent. They sense the tension, the coming confrontation. Why does he do this?

He walks around to my side and waits until I roll down the window. I'd rather drive away, but I don't want to create additional drama in front of the kids either.

"I have to talk to you," he says.

"I don't have anything to say." *Asshole. Bastard.* I'm not going to say those words. The kids won't hear me say what I'm thinking.

"I'll call you later tonight," he says.

I roll up the window and drive away. I've said nothing, but the kids are frozen in their seats. Afraid. I hear it in their silence, smell the fear in the air between us. Why does he do this—make them afraid? Make us all afraid?

"How was your Thanksgiving, guys?" I say.

"Good," they both mumble.

"Who wants ice cream?" I say, my voice creaky and thin. Good parenting skills there, offering calories as comfort. Great job, piggy.

Stop. Stop. Don't let him get you to this point.

The kids mumble nothing words.

"Or how about frozen yogurt?" I say.

Jesus Christ. Listen to yourself.

I HATE LYING here in the dark waiting for him. This time I'm waiting for the phone call, but it feels just like when we were married and I'd wait for him to come to bed and continue whatever argument we'd started earlier in the evening. Or I'd lie in a pool of imaginary sweat, right next to him, and wait for him to say anything at all. Or I'd wait for him to come home after I'd put the kids to bed with a story: *Daddy's working late so he can make extra money to buy you nice things.*

It feels the same now as it did back then, this constant strife between us. When does it end? What do I have to do to end it?

This is why people kidnap their own children—pick them up and haul ass across the border. Faces on a milk carton. "Last seen with mother." It's to get away from this—the unending unhappiness created by a single mistake.

Getting married was the biggest mistake I ever made, and yet it created Alex and Lucia, the best part of my life.

HOW DOES THAT happen, over and over? Everyone loves their kids—every normal person does—but everyone gets divorced. I bet I'm not the only one who lies awake fantasizing about some way—time machine, turkey baster—to have my kids, but without having any history with the other half of their DNA. I think about elephants, the way the females live with the babies and only visit the male elephants to get more babies. One of the girls at work calls her ex "the sperm donor." I wish that's all Mike had been.

The phone rings at 10:47 P.M. I answer without saying anything.

"Natasha?"

Don't say my name, this way or the old way. Don't speak to me, enemy. Villain who stole my youth. The clock on my nightstand ticks. The tree outside my window makes a miniblind-slatted shadow on my wall.

"What do you want?" I say.

His voice is raspy. "Listen. You're not going to win this one. You may as well just meet me this week and sign the papers." So now it's that easy, in his mind. He's so certain of getting his way.

"That's not going to happen," I say.

"Natasha, you don't want me to take you to court over this."

"Go right ahead. You don't have a leg to stand on." He's getting whiny-pitched already, but I keep quiet and steady. I won't let him upset me.

"No, you're wrong," he says. "I have a list. There's your temper, there's Alex's accidents at school, his slow physical development—"

"That's bullshit, and you know it," I say.

"—and then there's the company you've been keeping," he says.

Suddenly it makes sense. The man in the silver economy

car, watching me as I left the hotel. Both hotels. It must have been one of Mike's friends. Or maybe a detective. Oh, God, that's it—he found out that I'm sleeping with someone else, and he's jealous, angry that I've moved on, even though he's already done the same thing. That's why he's putting me through this.

I laugh. I can't help it. "You try to bring that up, Mike. Tell them I'm dating someone while the kids aren't here, then tell them how you're practically living with a woman out of wedlock and forcing the kids to live with her, too." It's ridiculous. Listen to how it sounds out loud. Why am I worried about this?

He says, "I'm not talking about that."

"Oh, you're not?" I'm sitting up now. I feel it happening— the tone of my voice, my lip curling into a sneer. I should hang up on him before I lose my temper, not waste any more of my night engaging in this. Where's his girlfriend? Shouldn't they be in bed together now? Is she lying there next to him, waiting for him to finish with me? Maybe that's what it takes for him to get aroused now—an argument with his ex.

I'm done with this loser. I'm hanging up.

He says, "I'm talking about your friends—those women you let baby-sit my children. The prostitute, the drug addict, and the old lady they hang out with."

"What?"

"Are you so desperate to keep the kids away from me, that you'd rather have them with people like them?" he says.

"What the hell are you talking about?" I'm sitting bolt upright now. What is he talking about?

If he's hired a detective, then he probably found out that Sara waits tables at a strip club, and he's exaggerating that into something worse. He's willing to lie about it to the judge. "She isn't a prostitute or a drug addict."

"Are you serious?" He laughs a fake laugh. "You don't even know who you've got watching our kids?"

I should hang up now.

"That friend of yours—the little dark one? She's a hooker. She works at a place called the Dollhouse up by Continental. You can see her half naked online and everything."

He's lying.

"And then your rich white friend? She buys pot every week from a thug who delivers to that rathole you live in. And last weekend she was partying at the house of a known Ecstasy dealer."

Oh, God. I feel sick. "You're lying."

"I'm not lying," he says. "Did you know or didn't you? God, Natasha—I can't decide which is worse. What's *wrong* with you? Don't you even *care*?"

I can't speak. I can't even breathe.

He presses on, pressing on me to get his way. "You can meet me tomorrow and sign the papers my attorney's drawn up. You can avoid going to court altogether."

Sara told us she was a waitress at her cousin's strip club. By the *airport*. Did she lie? Why would she lie?

Or maybe the question should be, why was I so quick to believe her?

And Haley . . . Haley hangs out with drug dealers? When? How?

I've already caught her lying to me once, though. What's wrong with me? How can I have fallen for this? Jesus. Are Haley and Sara scamming me in some way? How stupid am I? What kind of mother—

"Natasha? Are you still there?"

I make a noise. I can't help it.

"So are you coming to meet me or not? Will you sign the papers? I need to know right now."

There's nothing to say. There's no defense. I can't even explain it to myself.

I remember Sara telling us about the strip club like it was a joke. And Haley so quick to take interest in it. Then Haley's story about her ex...the way she made me think they were separated when they weren't. And Haley's been so freaked out lately—maybe she is a drug addict. How would I even know if she was? I don't know anyone who does drugs.

What was I thinking? I wanted to believe that I could trust these people, and I was stupidly, horribly wrong. Maybe I *don't* deserve to have custody of the kids. I can't even keep them safe.

"Natasha?"

Yes, I probably will have to meet him to sign the papers. I don't want this to go to court, do I? This is it. This is the end. He's going to take the kids away from me.

No. It doesn't make sense.

I hang up. I turn off the phone. I lie down again. But I already know that I won't fall asleep.

THIS TIME THEY deliver the subpoena to me at work. I accept it as graciously as possible, hoping the other girls will think it's a run-of-the-mill couriered letter and not a service of suit.

As soon as I can, I sneak the papers to the ladies' room, lock myself into a stall, and read.

In addition to the items listed before, the Defendant regularly exposes the children to the company of a prostitute, Sara Cardenas, employed by the brothel known as the Dollhouse.

The Defendant exposes the children to the company of a drug addict, Haley Harrison, who purchases illegally obtained prescription pills from former convict John "J.D." Chase.

The Defendant regularly neglects her duties as a parent in order to have a sexual affair with a man she has only recently met.

The Plaintiff prays that the Court will turn over custody of Alex and Lucia to their father immediately, for the sake of their health and safety.

Sara

I'M NEVER GONNA forget that phone call, because it made me feel so bad.

I was at the apartment, getting ready to drop Junior at Geronima's so I could go to work. It was right after Thanksgiving, so the girls were back at school.

I saw that Natasha was calling me, and I figured it was something important, so I quit messing with my makeup and picked up the phone.

The first thing she said, before I could even say hello, was, "Sara, where do you work?"

I was like, "What?"

And she goes, "Tell me where you work. Tell me the truth, right now."

And I knew then that someone had told her. I didn't know who—it couldn't have been Haley or Geronima, because they didn't know. They thought I was working at the lingerie store, just like Natasha did. So I was freaking out about that, wondering who the hell it was. But I had to say something, so I said, "I work at a place called the Dollhouse."

She made this noise into the phone, kind of like she was crying and kind of like she was going to throw up. She told me, "You lied."

I said, "I know. I'm sorry. But I had to."

She was so upset. I could hear it in her voice, but I didn't know why yet. She was like, "Why did you lie to me? You told me you were a waitress, and I didn't care about that, where you were working." And then she said, "But you're a prostitute. And you're a liar."

Yeah. That's what she said. A prostitute and a liar.

What'd I say? What could I say? I told her, "I'm not a prostitute. I'm only a dancer." But I felt like I was lying when I said it. You know? I mean, it was bad enough that she thought I was still a waitress. If I told her, "I got promoted to stripper," she'd be thinking I was dancing onstage in my cousin's club. But if she knew what I was doing for real, she'd probably call that being a whore. Right? Someone like her—that's how she'd see it.

She told me . . .

Fuck. This sucks. I don't want to talk about this right now.

Okay. Thank you. Yeah, just for a second.

Where are they, in the bathroom? Oh, I see the box over there. Okay. Give me a second.

I know. I'm not embarrassed because I'm crying. I'm embarrassed because it's such a shitty thing, the way it happened. You know? I'd give anything if I could go back and make it turn out different.

So yeah. She told me I was a prostitute and a liar, and I said no, I was only a dancer. And then she said, "I'm sitting here looking at the website, Sara. I'm looking at you naked online. What kind of dancer does that?"

Yeah, the website. I didn't tell you that part, did I? That was something Jackie made everybody do. We had our pictures on this website, so customers could see what we looked like before they came in. I didn't want to do it, but they made us.

And I thought it wouldn't be so bad, because it didn't have my real name, you know? How was anybody going to know to look for me on a stripper website with the name Raquel?

She found it, though, and she said she was looking right at it. So I started trying to explain everything to her. But she wasn't listening. She was so pissed off, you know? I don't think she could even hear me talking at that point.

She said... This is the part I remember the worst. The most. She said, "I wish I'd never met you. You've ruined my life."

And then she hung up on me.

IT WASN'T UNTIL later, when I heard from Geronima, that I figured out everything that was going on. Natasha had just gotten the extra papers from her asshole husband, telling her that she was a bad mother because she let her kids hang around with a prostitute and that he was going to take them away from her so they could be safe.

When I heard all that, I couldn't even blame her for being mad at me. She was right—I'd ruined her life. I'd fucked everything up.

I mean, yeah, her ex-husband had it wrong. I guess the detective he hired didn't do the full job, or else he told the truth about me and then Mike decided to make it sound worse than it really was. But it didn't even matter. He had dirt on Natasha, because of me. And because of that dumb-dumb Haley, too. It turned out that idiot she was trying to hook up with—J.D.—he had some minor record for selling X or whatever. And he was selling Haley weed, too. I don't even think she was smoking it—she was just buying a little bit every week so she'd have an excuse to see him. He only took her out one time, to some stupid party, and of course it turned out that the dudes running the party were real drug dealers, so Mike and his detective had a field day with that. It didn't even matter if it was true, what they were saying about Haley and me. They had enough to make Natasha look bad.

And so she had to quit talking to us, totally. She already looked bad enough just knowing us. But her lawyer said she had to do damage control and act like she wasn't our friend anymore.

Well, I guess she really wasn't, after that.

Yeah, you're right. It was hard. It sucked. I felt like shit about the whole thing, for a long time. I still do.

Geronima tried to talk to Natasha. She told her all about what I was doing at the Dollhouse and why. And later she told me that she thought Natasha understood and wasn't really mad at me anymore. But she still wouldn't talk to me. Of course she couldn't. And I didn't even blame her for that. She had to do what was right for her kids.

Haley? Oh, she never even talked to Natasha about it. She totally bailed as soon as she found out. Geronima said Natasha called and left Haley a pissed-off voice mail, the same day she called me. Haley heard that shit and couldn't deal with it. She packed up her stuff, packed up Jared, and took off.

Back to her husband's house, yeah. Of course. Where else was she gonna go? She called me a couple of times after she left, but it was either real late at night or when I was busy at work. Then, when I'd try to call her back, she wouldn't answer. But Geronima told me she'd gone to her husband to try to work things out with him. And I was just like, whatever. I mean, I felt bad for her. But I felt way worse for myself.

Yeah, my kids were still going to Geronima's, and she was still watching Natasha's kids, too. But not as much. I noticed that Natasha stopped taking her kids over there as much as she used to. And she quit taking them out to the park. And I felt bad about that, so I stopped taking mine to the park, too. You know? I didn't want her to feel like she had to stay locked up inside all the time, to keep away from me.

Yeah. It totally sucked.

Because I'd spent all this time feeling happy that she and Haley were around—that I finally had friends who weren't total losers, you know? For a while it was starting to look like things were changing for me, like my life was getting better. But of course I found a way to mess it all up. Just like always.

Natasha

LOOKING AT THE subpoena makes my stomach hurt. Literally. I want to throw it out the window, into these bushes behind the office parking lot, and drive away. Drive back home and act like I never saw it.

I don't even have to reread the words. Anytime I see a court paper with our family-court number typed on top—our court-case number, which I know by heart by now—I get actual cramps in my stomach. It's posttraumatic stress disorder, just like they say happens to the soldiers when they go to Middle Eastern restaurants. Seeing this paper makes me think of sitting in the hallway of the family-court building downtown. I can smell it—the paint, the piney wooden benches that remind me of school or church, all the people around us. Some were dressed up, like me. Trying to look like responsible parents and sweating through their polyester dresses and suits. Some weren't dressed up at all. Teenagers with tattoos and bandannas on their heads, wearing untied tennis shoes and constantly chewing gum into their phones. They were there for the same reason as me: We all had to spill our guts to the judge and hope he'd see our side of it. I was there to listen to him make decisions about my family that I was used to making myself.

I hated that judge, and I'm pretty sure he hated me. He never gave me more than a second glance. I wasn't allowed to say more than "Yes, Your Honor" or "No, Your Honor" when standing in front of him.

Mike, on the other hand, got to say whatever he wanted. He could go on and on with his explanations, and he could interrupt me or my lawyer whenever he wanted. The judge loved Mike. They kind of looked alike, the judge just a little bit older and fatter. And white, of course. All of the judges were old white men.

I still wonder if I made a mistake, picking a female lawyer instead of a man, like Mike picked. At least Joanne was straight with me. She warned me that the judge wouldn't like it if I looked too smart or too confident. "Cocky" was the word she actually used. I remember her saying, "Sound too cocky and the judge won't like you—he'll think you're an uppity feminazi who'll be mean to your kids. Sound too pathetic and he won't like you—he'll think you're a whiner who can't take care of kids properly." Meanwhile all Mike had to do was wear a shirt with buttons and speak with the same Texas accent as the judge, and he was golden. Freaking men. It makes me sick the way they stick up for each other, even when they're strangers.

But then again, it was the same with the women, too—our first mediator, the clerks, the woman who stood in for the judge, that one time—I had to be super careful about everything I said and did in front of them as well. I worried about my clothes and my makeup like I was wearing a costume in a play. I couldn't look too sloppy, too slutty, too successful, too feminine, too severe, too young, too old, too anything. While Mike could walk in wearing a trash bag and it wouldn't matter. He'd flirt with the women in the court. He'd *cry* in front of them, and they'd eat it up. Oh, look—a dad who cares about his children! How sweet!

I couldn't cry, though. Joanne said they wouldn't like that.

"You know how women are," she said. "They judge each other more harshly than they do men." Freaking women. It makes me sick, the way they do that.

MAYBE I SHOULD hire a detective, like Mike did. Would that help? Would my detective be able to dig up enough dirt on Mike to counteract all the dirt that Mike's dug up on me? Enough to make it worth taking out a loan for two or three thousand dollars to pay his fee?

Joanne said there's no use bringing up Mike's relationship with Missy unless I want to give him an opening to talk about my hotel visits with Hector. She said the best thing to do is lie low. Stop all contact with Hector, Sara, and Haley. Wait and let the mediator sort it all out.

But she didn't sound very confident. Sometimes I wish I could talk to her in person instead of over the phone. Does she look down at the phone in disgust, wondering what kind of mother she took on as a client? Wishing she'd billed me sooner, since I've already lost the case?

IF LOOKING AT the paper will make me sick, then rereading the words will kill me. But I don't have to reread them, because I know exactly what the words mean: I failed. I messed up. I picked the wrong women to befriend.

I picked the wrong apartment complex, probably. The wrong school. Wrong life.

It all makes sense when you consider that I picked the wrong man to marry, which is what brought me to this point to begin with.

What was the last thing I did right? If I had a time machine, how far back would I have to go to undo all the mistakes I've made?

This is stupid. Stop thinking this way. Why would I go back and undo anything? I wouldn't want to live my life again without having Alex and Lucia, would I? No. And there's no such thing as a time machine, so shut up. Get back to reality. Plan your next move.

The problem is, my next move will probably be planned by someone other than me. The judge. Mike. Joanne. The mediator. Someone I've never met. Any one of them could decide to take my kids away.

What if that someone is right? Maybe I've failed the kids one time too many and I'm not a good enough mother to keep them.

MAYBE I SHOULD just ask Alex point-blank if he wants to live with his dad. Save us all the drama.

No, don't do that. Don't put him in that position. Why, when there's no way he wants to live with Mike? Why would he want to, when he and Mike have practically no relationship at all?

Unless it's because Mike's trying to bribe him. I know Mike's trying; of course he is. And what if it's working? What if the mediator asks to speak to Alex and he tells her that he wants to leave me?

Oh, God. Okay, stop thinking about it now. There's nothing you can do about it right now. Just wait until you see the mediator, see how it goes.

God, help me get through this without going crazy. At least help me make it home through this damned traffic, and then through dinner without letting the kids see how stressed out I am, and then to bed, where I can finally cry alone.

Alex

Wish List

1. A better game system, if Mom can afford it
2. A new computer, but only if Dad will buy it without making me live at Missy's house
3. Comic books
4. New colored pencils
5. My own room, in a house where nobody's fighting

Natasha

THIS IS THE second time this horrible country version of "Jingle Bells" has come up on the CD player. I don't know why my mother insists on playing Christmas music when she only has the one CD. This time the annoying song is made more so by my mother's voice.

"What's wrong with you, crabby? Let me guess—I'm embarrassing you, right? You're embarrassed by your sad old mother?" She's saying this to me, practically whining it at me like a spoiled child begging for attention. I look up from the doll I'm trying to remove from its packaging, in order to gauge my mother's drunkenness. I thought we still had one or two cocktails to go before she became unbearable, but maybe I misjudged.

"Mommy, is Grandma being funny?" Lucia asks.

I say, "Yes. She's joking around." Alex looks up from his toy truck to see if *I'm* joking around, and I give him the cheeriest smile I can manage.

Mom's aged a decade in the past year. Or maybe it only seems that way because she stopped dying her roots.

No, she's definitely withered some, shrunk a few inches in her easy chair and in her perpetual purple robe with the quilted yoke and embroidered flowers. Next to her the giant fake Christmas tree doesn't have enough ornaments to cover the metal sticks holding up its branches. It looks like she gave up on it halfway through the job. When we were kids, Mom was a Christmas-tree Nazi. We weren't allowed to help her decorate it, because we couldn't do it right. No one could.

The room is gloomy and dim, because one of the bulbs in the ceiling fixture is burned out. Which is probably good, because it helps disguise the dust on everything, including the big brass lighting fixture itself. My brother, Daniel, and his wife are supposed to come over every other week to check on Mom, since they live way up here near her suburb. I can tell they haven't been doing it.

I can't blame them. Mom's always been rude to Tisha, and visiting her—listening to her complain and criticize everything—is sort of a downer. I'm getting situational depression just sitting here, as a matter of fact.

When was the last time we had a good Christmas in this house? Before Mom and Dad got divorced? Back when Daniel and I were kids, probably. Yes, it was the year I got my Barbie Dream House and my bike, back when I thought Mom and Dad's arguments were just jokes.

When was the last time I had a good Christmas at all, in this house or any other? When I actually felt everything they say you're supposed to—the love and the joy and the light—aside from the manufactured holiday cheer that I work so hard to create for the kids? Maybe way, way back when Mike and I were first dating, before I really knew him. Not the last few years with him, for sure. We'd fight on holidays more than the rest of the year, and always about the stupidest, pettiest things. Mike always complained about the plans I made, about everything I wanted to do, calling me "too much of a perfectionist" or a "spoilsport." If I wanted to wait until Christmas morning to open our gifts, he'd argue that we should open them Christmas Eve. If I wanted to make a special breakfast, he'd say he wanted to sit on the sofa in his boxer shorts and eat cereal instead. I wanted to take the kids somewhere—to see Santa or to a festival or a parade—and he wanted to stay home all day and watch sports on TV. It's true that I may have been a little OCD about Christmas sometimes, maybe even a little control-freakish. But at least I *cared*. At least I wasn't a selfish pig, like he was, as evidenced by the gifts he'd give us. Oh, Lord Jesus, the crappy gifts...

Mike gave two kinds of gifts: the selfish ones and the *hints*. He had the nerve to buy himself a TV surround-sound system and claim it was for me. He'd buy season tickets for the Cowboys every year, wrap them up, and write my name on them. Then, if I complained, he'd accuse me of being a hypocrite, saying, "You always want me to spend more time with you, so I'm trying to find something we can do together, and look how much you appreciate it!" Then there was the year that he gave me the StairMaster. And the year he gave me the gym membership. And the year he gave me a gift certificate for pole-dancing lessons.

He might as well just have wrapped pieces of paper that said "I don't care what you want" and "I wish I were married to someone else."

But I was used to Mike's assholery, after years of putting up with it, and I managed to find good things about Christmas, despite him. I always liked wrapping gifts for other people. I'd do the first batch with the kids, letting them decorate the packages for their grandparents and teachers and their dad, watching them giggle with glee over being entrusted with the secrets of who got what. And then there'd be the second batch of gifts, the gifts for Alex and Lucia that I'd wrap while they slept. And then, on Christmas Eve, I'd fill their stockings and sneak them into their rooms to find when they woke on Christmas morning. I didn't mind that Mike didn't help me, with the wrapping or with the shopping, because I enjoyed doing it so much.

And I liked the baking, back when we had that big kitchen. And I liked decorating the tree with the kids. And, of course, my favorite part of the whole year was always watching Alex and Lucia open their presents. Watching their faces. Their expressions in that moment were the payoff to my months of planning, searching, and shopping.

This Christmas is awful so far. I admit it: I've failed. I took a week off to spend it with the kids, and all we've done so far is laundry, errands, and watching TV. And then we came here to eat ham and dressing that smell as if Mom sneaked a cigarette while cooking. Daniel and Tisha have been bickering all evening. Mom pulled her yearly stunt of buying toys for Alex and nothing but clothing for Lucia. Good thing Tisha bought her the little dolls, or Lucia probably would've had a meltdown. And now we're sitting here watching Mom get drunk to *Miracle on 34th Street*.

Being a single mom sucks. I hate it.

No, *this* sucks. Being here, doing this. Why are we doing it? Why do we have to?

I stand. "All right, Mom. We're taking off." The kids follow my lead and start gathering their gifts. I can tell by Alex's face that he's relieved. I walk over to Mom's chair and bend down to give her an almost-hug on her shoulder. "Bye. Love you. Merry Christmas."

Instead of hugging me back, she glares up at me. "Let

me guess—it's something I said, right? It's always me, isn't it?" She's more petulant than angry. She'll probably pass out soon.

"Say good-bye to your grandma, kids."

They say it in unison. I pick up the sweater Mom gave me, which, like Lucia's, is a size too small, probably on purpose. I grab the pot holders and kitchen towels bestowed upon me by my brother or, more likely, his wife. We hit the door.

On the way to the Blazer, I see Daniel and Tisha standing in the front yard, in the dark, arguing. I wave good-bye to them, and then we're gone.

AS WE DRIVE home, Alex says, "What are we going to do *now?*"

I say, "Whatever we want. What do you guys want to do?"

That puzzles them for a second, but Lucia rallies quickly and says, "Go to sleep so we can wake up and open presents!"

Alex scoffs at her. "No. It's not bedtime yet." He looks at me in the rearview mirror and says, "Can we see a movie?"

"Sure. We'll have to rent one, though. I think the theaters are closed until tomorrow." There's a DVD vending machine at the McDonald's by our apartment. We'll stop there.

"Can we draw pictures?" Lucia says. "Can Alex draw me a pony? Can we read our book? Ooh! We can dance!" She's clapping her hands, popping up and down in her seat with excitement over the possibilities.

I say yes to all that, then, "Maybe, if you're good, Santa Claus will bring one of your gifts early and you can open it tonight."

Alex says, "You mean one of the presents you bought us?"

"Yes. Exactly." Hell, maybe I'll let them open all of them. There's no use waiting until morning, like we used to, if Mike's going to pick up the kids tomorrow at noon. We can open all our gifts now and stay up all night. I'll sleep tomorrow, when they're gone.

IN THE PARKING garage, I check for Sara's car. It isn't here.

I wonder if Sara and Geronima got together for Christmas Eve after all. I should have asked Geronima yesterday, when she called. But if I had, she would've tried to convince me to be friends with Sara again. I can hear her now: *Sara and Haley are good girls, Natasha. They're not like you, but they do the best they can.* And it's hard enough to deal with this situation without Geronima pulling at my heartstrings.

It must be awkward for her, with all our kids constantly together at her apartment and me not hanging out with the others anymore. I don't like putting her in the middle of my drama. I wish there were no drama at all.

Do I care if Sara's a stripper? Not really, now that I've gotten over the shock of it. What she does for money is her business. She's taking care of her kids, isn't she? It would bother me if she were a crack whore and the kids were starving or neglected in some way. But they obviously aren't. Shoot, considering the kind of mom Sara had, it's a wonder she's doing as well as she does. At least she was discreet about it—I never would've suspected if Mike hadn't told me.

As for Haley . . . I have to think that Mike was exaggerating or that the detective—if Mike really did hire one—got the story wrong somehow. I'll believe that she smokes pot. Big deal, a lot of people do. But partying with drug dealers? I can't imagine that. Not from her. Not that it matters anymore what I think. Geronima said she went back to her husband's house, so I no longer have to worry about avoiding her. I hope she's doing okay. I hope she's finding a way to be happy.

As we walk past Sara's door, Alex moves close to me and whispers, "Do you think they liked the gifts we got them?"

I say, "I hope so."

The bag isn't on her door anymore, so I'm assuming Sara found it. I hope she found it and took the gifts inside and opened them, and that they weren't stolen from their door. I used a plastic grocery bag so it'd look like something innocuous and so, as Alex noted, they'd be surprised.

Maybe I should've gone with the gift certificates in the mailboxes after all. That way I wouldn't have to worry about them getting stolen. But that would've been so impersonal.

Then again, maybe it should have been impersonal. I wanted to get them something, for the kids' sake, but I don't want there to be any obligation factor, for Sara to feel like she has to reciprocate in any way. And I don't want her to come over to the apartment to thank me.

No, I did the right thing. That's what you're supposed to do on Christmas, right? Give without expectations. I gave them gifts because I wanted to. That's the only thing that matters.

WHEN WE GET all the way down the hall to our own door, we see a bag hanging from the doorknob. A plastic grocery bag. Did Sara return our gifts? Were they insulted or offended? But there's also a thin box leaning against the door.

The kids are squirming with curiosity. I let Alex carry the packages into the apartment. Lucia says, "Open them! Open them!"

Alex opens the bag. "They're presents. For us!"

He's right. It's three gifts, wrapped and labeled with our names and signed with Sara's kids' names. There's also a sheet of paper. A note? "Let me see that, Alex."

He says, "It's for me." It's a drawing, seemingly of a superhero doing something dramatic. It has Alex's name on it, but this time in a child's writing. Angelica must have drawn it for him.

They beg to open their presents. I say yes, and they rip off the wrappings like madmen. Lucia gasps when she sees the tiny set of lip gloss and glitter nail polish. Alex's is an action figure, some kind of robot fighter. He studies it thoughtfully.

"Open yours, Mom!" Lucia commands.

Mine is a soft, irregular-shaped blob of red paper, practically shining with Scotch tape, the work of someone unaccustomed to wrapping gifts. It's also signed "Angelica, Monique, and Jorge Jr." in what must be Sara's blocky handwriting. I unwrap it. Inside is a folded square of silky fabric. Unfolded, it's a sheet of sheer blue, green, and gold. A scarf, like a Gypsy would wear. It's beautiful. Looking at it makes my eyes water.

My impatient daughter is ready to move on. "What's in the box, Mommy? Can we open that, too?"

Haley sent us books. Beautifully illustrated books for the children that look like they belong in royal nurseries somewhere—*The Little Mermaid* and *Robin Hood*. And beautiful, obviously very expensive stationery for me, engraved with my name. She must have been planning to do this for a while, then. And she must have paid a fortune to have the package delivered to us on Christmas Eve. Just as Sara and I did, she signed her gifts with Jared's name only. We all used our kids as fall guys, as if we needed excuses to be nice. To care.

"There's a letter, Mom," says Alex. He hands me an envelope that was left in the box. It says my name. I open it and read.

Natasha,

There's no way I can express how sorry I am for what's happened or for the effect my actions have had on you and your family. I can only hope that, in my absence, things will work out for you in the best possible way and that eventually you'll be able to forgive me. You were a good friend to me during a difficult time, and for that I will always wish you the best.

Haley

P.S. I know that you were planning to pay back the loan within the next six months. But please, please consider it an additional Christmas gift, and the least I can do for you under the circumstances.

Lucia runs into her room with her handful of treasures, and Alex follows her. I take the opportunity to hurry into the bathroom and use toilet paper to wipe my eyes and blow my nose.

I'm know I'm overreacting, here. I've been watching too many cheesy Christmas specials with the kids. But I can't help getting emotional. I hope that Sara and Haley liked the gifts I got them. And even though I can't talk to them anymore, I can still hope that they're having a good Christmas.

Sara

I FELT BAD about turning down Gero's offer to go to Mass, but I can't stand church. It's too damn boring. No offense.

But at least I went over there on Christmas Eve and gave them all presents. They acted like I gave them stuff they wanted, so that was good. Gero gave my kids little toys, and she got me a bottle of perfume.

Then they had to take off for Mass, and I didn't know what to do after that. I used to always go to my mom's, you know? But I couldn't do it this year. So I put the kids in the car and just drove around town. Angelica wanted to go to IKEA, and I had to tell her it was closed, like everything else. Then we saw that the movies were open, so we went and saw that one about the mouse that helps Santa Claus. Then, when that one was over, we snuck into *Speed Chase III*. After that we ended up going back to the apartment. Geronima had given us some tamales to microwave for dinner, and I cooked some rice and beans to have on the side.

Yeah, it was weird to hang out with the kids all day by myself. Weird but good, you know? Definitely better than being at my mom's.

Yeah, I felt a little bad about going off on her and not talking to her anymore. But then again, no I didn't. What was I going to do—drag my kids over to her house so we could watch my stupid brother get drunk with my cousins and their crackhead friends? Listen to my mom bitch about everything? Fuck that.

Sorry. I mean, forget that.

I thought about calling Jorge—Monique and Baby Junior's dad—but then I thought forget him, too. The last time we spent Christmas with him, we ended up sitting in his truck in the park at eleven at night, with Junior crying because his teeth hurt. I got Jorge a bottle of good cologne that year, and he didn't get us anything. He was too broke.

Really, I don't care about Christmas. I never did. People talk about how it's the most wonderful time of the year, when everybody's supposed to suddenly pretend like they give a shit about each other. But that's how it is for rich people, not how it goes in real life.

Speaking of rich people... Haley finally called me, a couple of nights before Christmas. She was trying to act like she was happy to be back with her husband, but I could tell she wasn't.

I kept thinking about her that night, on Christmas Eve, wondering what she was doing. Probably eating a big old turkey dinner with her family, next to one of those fancy real Christmas trees that cost more than all the normal ones. Not a shitty little fake tree from the thrift store, like ours. I wanted to go buy a better one from Target, but I waited too late. I just never felt like getting into the Christmas spirit, you know?

I wanted to be mad at Haley, thinking about her sitting there under her fancy tree. But then, instead, I thought about her old-ass husband putting his arms around her and kissing her all over, and I felt bad for her. Which was stupid, since she should've been happy to live in a nice house with a rich man who wanted to give her money. But now I can see how she didn't want to live like that, with some old dude touching her and telling her what to do all day. Honestly, I don't think I could either.

Oh, so I didn't tell you... When we got back to the apartment, we saw that Natasha had left us presents. They were in a bag, hanging from our doorknob. It was just a few little things, and the tags said they were from her kids and not her. But still, it was nice. The girls got a kick out of it. I wasn't expecting it, you know? Haley had given us presents before she took off, but I didn't think Natasha would do anything.

So I was really glad that I had gotten them presents, too, back when I went shopping for Gero and Oscar. Because I'd been feeling stupid about it, and I was planning to take them back to Ross Dress for Less and get my money back. But I never did, so we wrapped them up real fast and put them in the same plastic bag they'd used for us. Then I made Angelica run out and stick the bag on their doorknob. I already knew they weren't home, because I hadn't seen Natasha's Blazer in the parking garage. But I told Angelica to come back fast so nobody would see her. She got a kick out of that, I think. She likes doing sneaky stuff—pretending to be a spy or whatever.

The next day, on Christmas, I tried to call Geronima, but she never answered. Angelica told me she'd been feeling sad about the holidays, because she wanted to see her daughter but couldn't. Something like that. I didn't really pay attention when she first told me, but I wish now that I had.

We went back to the movies, and every time we'd go in or out of the parking garage, I'd check to see if Natasha's car was there, so we wouldn't run into her in the hall.

Why? Well, because. She'd said she didn't want to see me anymore, and I didn't want to see her either.

Yeah, I know. But I figured that was only because it was Christmas. You know how people get all mushy and emotional at Christmastime. I thought it was probably just her kids wanting to get gifts for my kids, you know? I didn't think she wanted to mess with me, so I left her alone.

Yeah, so Christmas ended up being pretty crappy for us this year. But in a way it was better than all the ones we've had before. I don't know what that says about us. Maybe you can tell me.

Alex

I DIDN'T WANT TO go to Missy's house today, because I was scared it'd be even more boring than Grandma's. But so far it's been pretty good. These waffles Missy made us are good, especially with the whipped cream and strawberries. Everything's decorated with those little funny nutcracker soldiers and fake berries. I told Lucia the berries were real, and she tried to eat one. That was funny, too.

I've had three waffles, and I don't think I can eat any more. Missy's picking up our plates and putting them in the sink. She's still wearing her apron with red Christmas flowers all over it, and she now has a gold bow in her hair. She looks nice.

"All right! Present time!" Dad says. He stands up, and Shepherd throws his plate down on his high chair and sticks his arms out, like Dad's going to carry him.

"Wait, wait," Missy says. She goes to the sink and comes back with a wet towel that has Santa Claus's face on it. She makes me and Lucia wipe our hands with it. "Okay. Ready!" Then she gets Shepherd out of his chair, and we all go to the living room, to the big tree with all the purple and gold ornaments, where all the presents are.

"Find the ones with your name on them!" Dad yells. "Find them and tear them open!"

Lucia screams and runs to the tree. Of course she trips and

lands on one of the presents. And of course it's one with my name on it. "Watch out, dummy!" I tell her.

"All right, calm down," Dad says. "Alex, why don't you help your sister find her gifts."

I go through every gift under the tree, checking the names. I make two piles of gifts next to the couch, one for Lucia and one for me. I tell her she has to wait for me to find all of them before we can open them.

My dad laughs. He says something to Missy, who's standing next to him, watching us. The only part I hear is, "just like his mother."

I tell Lucia, "Okay, let's just tear them open now."

Dad got me a Cowboys helmet, a Cowboys jersey, a bunch of new comic books, and an electronic dart game. He also got me a new video game, but it's the same one that Mom gave me last night. Should I tell him that? No, I'd better not. Missy gave me a remote-control truck, but she wrote that it was from Shepherd. Lucia got a bunch of girl stuff. Missy gave her a baby doll with yellow hair. It has a scary face.

I'm going to take my stuff to our bedroom. Maybe Dad will hang up the dartboard and show me how to play.

"Hold up, Alex, Lucy," Dad says. "One more thing. Missy, would you sit with me on the couch, please?"

We stop and look at him. Missy looks at him, too, like she doesn't know what he's talking about. I don't think she wants to sit on the couch either, because her apron has waffle dough smeared on it and she doesn't like when people get food on the furniture. But my dad's waiting, so she sits on the couch next to him and puts Shepherd on the floor. He starts crawling toward our stuff, but I push Lucia's baby doll in front of him, and that makes him stop.

Dad says, "Kids, I have a surprise for you, if Missy will go along with it." Then he sticks his hand in the pocket of his jeans and pulls out a little box. He holds it up so Missy can see it. I think I know what it is. "Missy, will you do me the honor of being my wife? And my kids' stepmother?" He opens the box. There's a diamond ring in it, just like I knew there'd be. Just like on TV. Now's the part where Missy says yes and hugs him, and he puts the ring on her finger. But she doesn't do that.

She looks at the ring for a long time. Then she says, "Oh, Mike." Then she starts to cry.

I guess it's because she's happy. Sometimes people do that on TV, too.

Natasha

THIS HAS TO be a bad omen for the New Year. I can't believe I'm almost late to the first freaking mediation meeting. Traffic sucking, my online map totally wrong, no parking...But here I am, damn it, two minutes before five-thirty. No strikes against me yet.

It looks like a building full of dentists' offices—silent hallways with beige carpet and rubber trees. Crooked letters on the directory say S. GRAHAM—SUITE 210. I can't find the stairs, so I take the elevator.

At the door that says 210, I push the buzzer, and after a few moments it opens and I see a woman standing there.

"I have an appointment with Susan Graham," I say.

"You must be Natasha. It's good to meet you," she says.

She's older than I expected, this mediator. She's wearing a Talbots sweater and flat sandals and looks like she might have been a hippie back in the day. She leads me through a short maze of rooms, all full of couches, tables, and tissue boxes. It's a little like the office where we had the pre-divorce mediation, but nicer. Warmer.

Ms. Graham offers pleasantries that I barely hear. I'm nervous. I'm not here because I want to be, I'm here because I have no choice.

At least Mike isn't here. That special torture doesn't take

place until our next appointment. So I get a chance to make a first impression that doesn't include me arguing with him.

Susan Graham and I sit at one of her tables, and she asks me to tell her about myself. I keep it brief: Born and raised here in Dallas, working at the law firm, raising my two kids. Divorced, obviously. Nervous laugh.

She tells me about herself, and it's a much longer story. I can't listen. I wish we could fast-forward to the real part of this interview. Let's get this show on the road. Quit wasting time with the small talk. She's saying, "...so once I earned those certifications, I became a counselor at my church. And I've been doing that for the last two years, in addition to running this business."

Wait. Stop. What? "You're a church counselor?"

She smiles a congenial-older-woman smile, her eyebrows lifting her fluffy goldish hair. "Technically, my title is outreach minister. I specialize in counseling couples and adults for Spring Lake Church."

Uh-oh. A Spring Laker. What does that mean? I don't even know. Maybe she's modern and open-minded and everything else they say on their billboards. Or maybe she smells the catechism classes on me and has already counted the first strike. But it's too late to worry about that now. It is, as they say, in God's hands now.

Once the formalities are finished, she opens the file on the table and pushes out a few papers. Among them I recognize the last e-mail Mike sent to me and to our two attorneys.

"This is quite a list your ex-husband has put together," she says with a twinkle in her eye, Santa Claus style. She's trying to be funny. Or trying to put me at ease before she swoops in for the kill, the way they do. She reads, "Prostitutes and drug addicts for baby-sitters. Illicit sexual relationship. Forcing Alex to participate in too many feminine activities. Neglecting Lucia."

I'm ready for this. "None of it's true. First of all, there's no prostitute or drug addict. He's talking about two women who live in my apartment complex, who've never even baby-sat for me. Second of all, Mike himself is living with a woman he's not married to. And—"

Before I can say more, she interrupts. "Natasha, don't worry. I've seen hundreds of lists like these. I'm sure you could make up your own list that sounds at least as bad."

Where is she headed with this? "I guess I could, if I wanted to be that way," I say.

"Obviously the children are well cared for. They're doing fine in school, and there are no third-party reports of abuse or neglect."

"Of course not," I say.

"So let's put this away for now," she says, literally pushing the file to one side. "What I want to know is, how would you say that you're doing?"

This is it. The big question. And I have to be really careful how I answer. I learned that during the divorce. Sound too confident and she won't like me—she'll think I'm an uppity career woman. Sound too pathetic and she won't like me—she'll think I'm a whiner who can't handle responsibility.

So what do I try right now? Because I'm not going to fall into the same traps this time, when it's more than just child support. I'm not going to lose my son based on some church lady's first impression. This is like a freaking job interview, where they ask you about your strengths and weaknesses. But way more stressful and way more crucial.

How about I try the truth? "I think I'm doing really well, considering the circumstances. Considering how little child support we get and the fact that this is the first real job I've had in a long time, I think I handle our finances pretty well and provide well for the kids. They aren't wearing designer jeans, but they have plenty of clean clothes to wear. I cook them healthy food. Lucia was getting chubby for a while, when we were still married, but that's under control now. The kids are doing well in school. I help them with their homework and projects. Alex is good at art and math, and I'm looking into a special program for him this summer, at an arts organization in our neighborhood. Lucia might be good at sports, like I used to be, so I want to put her in soccer. But nothing too competitive—just for fun and so she can meet more girls her age. Um . . ." What else can I say? "I monitor the kids' TV and video games and make sure they aren't watching anything inappropriate or spending too much time . . . I read to them. Not every night, not anymore, but . . ." *Okay, stop talking now. You're not helping yourself anymore here. You're starting to sound desperate.*

Susan Graham laughs. She's laughing at me. Oh, God. This is not good.

"No, no. I'm sorry," she says. "Natasha, I meant, how are you *doing*? You personally. It must be stressful, to go from being a homemaker to a single mother, working full-time. How are you handling the stress?"

"Oh. I thought you meant . . ." I laugh, too, to show her that I'm free and easy and likable and confident in my ability to be whatever she's expecting me to be. But I don't know how to answer her question. How am I *doing*? How do I handle the stress? I say, "I don't really handle the stress. I just do what needs to be done."

She makes a face at me. Partly a smile, partly the face you'd make if you were looking at a puppy who'd just fallen on its face. I gave the wrong answer, didn't I?

I'm starting to have a sickly feeling. It's circling my stomach, under the stupid button-down blouse I put on to impress this woman, that's now too tight in the waist and forces me to sit here holding my breath. It's the feeling that things are swirling out of reach, and I can't control what's going to happen. I want to vomit. I want to get up and leave the room, but I can't. I have to sit here and face this woman and do whatever I can to sway her to my point of view.

"Listen, Ms. Graham..."

"Please, call me Susan."

"Susan, fine. I just...I don't want to whine to you about my problems, okay? I really just want to find out what's going to happen with my children. I want them to stay with me. Can you tell me what you think your decision is going to be? Or tell me what I can do to keep my kids? That's all I care about. That's why I'm here."

She sits back and smiles that eerily serene smile at me, like a saint on a postcard. Why? Does she *want* me to have a panic attack here?

She says, "You know I'm not going to decide whether Alex and Lucia stay with you."

I sigh, because I do know that. *But what the hell do you want from me?* is the unspoken question between us. And furthermore, *Why am I* paying *to be here?*

She opens the file on the table in front of her, reads something inside, and says, "Your divorce was finalized more than a year ago, correct?" I nod. "And since then you and Mike have been in and out of court several times."

"Right. Mostly at his request, though, so he could lower his child support."

She says, "Right. But my point is these are issues between you and Mike. There's nothing serious going on with the kids that requires the judge's immediate intervention. Wouldn't you agree?"

"Yes. Of course." Yes! She sees it my way! I'll be out of here in no time, and Mike will be sorry he ever started this.

She leans forward again and puts her hand on the table, almost like she's reaching for mine. But I stay still, hands on my lap. She says, "My job here is to work with you and Mike to decide what's best for Alex and Lucia. To keep you from having to drag this into the courts."

"So . . . you're going to advise us on how to decide who Alex and Lucia should live with?" I must look stupid now, like I'm missing something. But I don't care. I need to know what's happening and where this woman stands.

She shakes her head. "No. I'm going to facilitate a discussion in which you and Mike decide what's best for *everyone*."

I don't have anything to say to that. Wait, yes I do. "That's not going to happen, Susan. You haven't met Mike yet, have you? He's totally unreasonable. He doesn't listen to anyone. It's his way or the highway, basically. That's part of why I left him."

She laughs at that. "Well, why don't you let me give it a shot anyway? It can't hurt, right?"

I shrug. "I guess not. Unless you end up with the same headache he gives me."

She laughs again. Then she looks at her watch. "Well, our time is just about up." She stands, so I do, too. "Natasha, before I see you again, I'd like you to think about stress and how you deal with it. I'd like you to come up with a list of ways that you take care of yourself emotionally, or ways that you think you might like to try. Can you do that for me?"

This is starting to sound like something from a cheesy movie or a self-help book. I can tell she really means it, though. She seems like a nice person in general, so I humor her. "Sure. Yes, I will."

"Thank you." She reaches out to hug me good-bye, which seems like an inappropriate thing to do. Maybe even borderline sexual harassment. But she's older, so she probably doesn't see it that way, and I go ahead and let her hug me a little.

She hugs me a lot. It feels awkward.

Then it feels okay all of a sudden. Warm. Nice. Safe, in a way.

This is totally corny, but it almost feels like . . . like she's a mom. An older mom who's more experienced than me, who knows what I'm going through and wants to help. Which, if I'm lucky, might actually be the case.

NOW THAT I'M in the Blazer, on the way home, I feel sorry for this Susan Graham. She really doesn't know what she's in for with Mike. Yes, she's definitely more on the ball than the previous mediator was, and she seems to believe that she can handle him. But that's what I thought, too, throughout our marriage. That I could handle Mike and his constant bitching, negativity, and neglect. And I couldn't. It escalated as the years went on. It wore me down, and I had to give up. And since the divorce it's gotten exponentially worse.

I can't believe she gave me *homework*. A list of ways I deal with stress, or would. Should. Could. Am I supposed to type it up and print it out for her? Create a slide presentation, maybe?

It's easier to find my way back home than it was to find

her office. Left, right, left, and I'm back on the freeway. It's a little chillier now that the sun's gone down. Time to turn on the heat, aim it at my extremities.

The fact that I can't think of anything to put on Susan's list—is that an issue? Should I be concerned?

When am I *not* stressed, first of all?

My stress isn't the kind that needs handling. It's the stress of everyday living. Do I wish I had a maid and a nanny so I could relax more? Sure. Is that going to happen anytime soon? No. So I take care of my business, without whining about it.

When was the last time I was *really* stressed? Easy: Mike pulling this lawsuit on me. Finding out that he's trying to take the kids away.

And how did I deal with it? Or how did I want to? I wanted to . . .

Black hair pale skin scratchy stubble hotel bedspread . . .

No, don't think about that now. Drive the car. Cut around this slowpoke and keep your focus on the road.

What did I actually *do*? I cleaned the kitchen floor. Yes, that's how I handle stress.

Be honest, Natasha. You yelled at the kids first, and then you cleaned the kitchen floor.

Be *honest*. First you yelled at the kids. Then you cleaned the kitchen. And then you ate, you piggy. You ate that big piece of cake you said was left over for the kids but that you kept hidden in the very back of the refrigerator.

I ate. Late at night, in my bed, tears and snot running down my face.

God. I'd better think of something else to put on the list before I see this woman again.

Alex

I'M GLAD ANGELICA'S here today, because the last two times we came to Ms. Buena's, she wasn't. And I can't see her at school, because second grade and third grade have recess at different times.

Mom said we're only staying here for a little while. So I tell Angelica we should play spies first, by ourselves, and then we can play X-Men until my mom comes to pick me up. She says okay.

We tell Lucia and Tiffany and them that we're going to make them a surprise in the other room and they have to play dolls until we come back. Baby Junior's too little to know that dolls are for girls only, so he likes to play with the big one that has a flowered dress. Tiffany takes all the dolls out of their boxes, and me and Angelica go to Miss Buena's room. Miss Buena's in the kitchen.

We sit down behind Miss Buena's bed to plan our mission. But first Angelica says, "Your mom is mad at my mom."

I say, "No she's not."

She says, "Yeah she is. That's why y'all never come over here when we're here anymore."

I'm thinking about that. I don't know if it's true.

Then she says, "That's why they never take us to the park anymore." She's right.

I say, "Why's my mom mad? What'd your mom do?"

Angelica doesn't like it when I say that. I can tell. She puts her hair in her mouth to chew on it, then spits it out. She's looking down, and I know she's a little bit mad. She says, "My mom didn't do anything. She said it's because of your dad. He doesn't want them to be friends anymore. I heard her tell somebody on the phone."

I don't know if she's playing a trick on me. I don't think my dad knows Angelica and them.

But maybe he does, and maybe he thinks they're trashy. He says that sometimes, if people have old, beat-up cars like Angelica's mom does. He says they're trashy and don't like to work hard enough to buy better cars.

I don't care what kind of car they have. I say, "Well, my dad never said I can't play spies with you."

She says, "What if he does say it?"

I say, "It won't matter, because spies are secret. So we'll keep being spies, and he won't know." She doesn't say anything. But I can tell she's not mad anymore. So I say, "Let's do our mission now, before it's too late."

Today's mission is to spy on Miss Buena before Mr. Oscar comes back from the drugstore. Every time Mr. Oscar leaves the apartment, Miss Buena calls somebody named Robbie on the phone and talks to him about Cristina. Cristina's pregnant, and she's almost ready to have her baby. Mr. Oscar doesn't know, because he got mad at Cristina a long time ago and never talks to her anymore. He thinks Miss Buena doesn't talk to her either. She doesn't, but she does talk to Robbie. Angelica was the one who found out that Cristina is Tiffany's mom. She got that information from spying on her mom. Angelica's a really good spy sometimes.

Miss Buena comes into her bedroom and says, "Alex. Angelica. What are y'all doing? Y'all aren't playing doctor, are y'all?"

I say, "No, we're playing X-Men."

She says, "Well, why don't y'all go play it in the living room. Or watch your cartoons. I have to do something in here. I'll be out in a little bit."

We say okay and go to the living room. Miss Buena closes the door almost all the way. That means she's going to get on the phone. I go turn on the TV so she'll think we're watching it. But instead we go sit in the hall by her door, to listen.

Something happened. Miss Buena is saying, "Oh, my God. I can't believe it. Oh, my God!"

"The baby died," Angelica whispers.

"How could it die?" I whisper back. "It's still inside her."

Miss Buena says, "Is he doing okay?" Then she says, "Six pounds. Oh, my gosh." Then she says, "Oh, thank God. I'm so glad, Robbie."

Angelica says, "The baby didn't die. She had it already."

Miss Buena says, "I want to. But do you think she wants me to?" Then she says, "I really do want to, Robbie. But...I don't know. I have to talk to Oscar first. I should tell him."

Then she listens for a long time. Then she says, "When?" Then she says, "That's too soon. You can't travel with the baby that soon." Then she says, "Oh, my gosh. I don't know. I don't know what to do."

Then the apartment door opens, and Mr. Oscar's back. He comes in and puts a bag on the table. Then he says, "What are y'all doing?" to me and Angelica. We stand up. I hear Miss Buena say, "I have to go. I'll call you back."

She comes out of the bedroom, and I say, "Miss Buena, we were going to ask you if you can make us quesadillas."

She puts her hand on my head and says, "Of course, m'ijo. Let me go heat up the sartén." She goes to the kitchen to heat up the black quesadilla pan. Mr. Oscar sits down and picks up the TV remote. Me and Angelica go back into Tiffany's room.

Junior's crying. Angelica tells Monique, "What did you do to him?"

Lucia says, "He's crying because Tiffany said his doll looked ugly."

It takes Angelica a long time to make Junior stop crying. Then Miss Buena comes in and says, "Alex, Lucia, your mama's here."

Mom doesn't come inside. She waits for us in the hall. We have to hurry up and grab our backpacks. I say, "Bye," but Angelica doesn't look at me.

In the hall I want to ask Mom if she's mad at Angelica's mom and if she's really not allowed to talk to her anymore. But Mom's walking too fast for me to say anything, and she doesn't look like she's in a good mood for questions.

Natasha

THIS IS A scene from a nightmare.

"No, *you* shut up. You let me talk now. Shut *up*."

This is like a joke, a bad cartoon. The cat and the mouse who hate each other but won't leave each other alone.

"You're always talking. You *never* listened. You think you're more important than me and everyone else."

What is Susan thinking as she watches this? I can't even look at her. I'm ashamed, but I can't stop.

"No, *you're* wrong. You're exaggerating. You're *lying*."

"This is why I left you. Who could live with someone like you?"

"What are you talking about? This is why *I* left *you*."

There's a click. It's Susan. She's set down her phone on the table. The phone has a timer, and it shows ten minutes. Her Christmas vest—black with red poinsettias—should keep me from taking her seriously. But the vest has some kind of teacherlike authority, apparently, because Mike and I stop yelling.

Susan says, "Well, we've spent one-fifth of our session on this so far. How do you feel? Better?"

We don't answer.

"Is it helping? If so, we can continue. Would you like some water, either of you? Your throats must be getting hoarse."

I take the opportunity to make my case. "No, it's not helping. He didn't come here to compromise. He came to make accusations and try to convince you that I'm some horrible mother who deserves to have her children taken away."

Susan looks in my direction and starts to speak. Mike, neck turning red and threatening to pop out of his shirt collar, says, "Tell her what *you* came to do. You want to sit there and act like Little Miss Perfect and like I'm too stupid to know how to take care of *my* kids."

Susan looks at him, then back at me. "Is that true, Natasha? Is Mike too stupid to take care of the kids?"

Yes, he is. But I say, "It's not that he's *stupid*. It's that he never cared about taking care of them until now, and now he's only pretending to care in order to punish me."

She turns to Mike. "Are you doing this to punish Natasha?"

"No." Yes, he is.

She asks him, "Is Natasha a horrible mother?"

He pauses like he has to consider the question. He says, "Not always." God, I hate him. Just roll over and drop dead, you hateful, smug bastard. "But she's selfish. She puts her own needs before theirs. And she has a bad temper, and she takes it out on the kids."

I open my mouth to contradict this bullshit, but Susan interrupts me. "Okay. So we have an overview of what you perceive as each other's parenting faults. What about your positive traits? Natasha, what does Mike do *right* as a parent?"

I feel myself giving her a look. This is some cheesy *Afterschool Special* crap. I don't see why I should give Mike any compliments at this point. "I don't know."

"Nothing?" she prompts. "Come on. Tell me one thing."

Only so I can't be blamed for not trying here, I say, "I guess he's good at playing with the kids. Taking them outside and riding bikes and stuff." Then I throw in, "Since he has time to do that and I don't."

Susan nods, then turns to Asshole. "Okay. And what do you say, Mike? What is one of Natasha's good parenting traits?"

"She doesn't have any," he says, fat chin sticking into the air, waiting for me to jump over the table and punch it.

"Oh, come on, now," Susan says. "She doesn't have *any*? You married a woman without one good parenting skill, got her pregnant twice, and let her stay home with your kids for eight years? If that's true, what does it say about you as a dad?"

Ouch. You go, Susan. I'm surprised she said that. Mike's surprised, too. His eyes go wide, and he says, "Well, she wasn't bad the *whole* time." He pretends to have to consider some more, then says, "I guess she's good at scheduling stuff. Making sure the kids get to school and all their appointments on time, I mean."

Susan nods. "So we can agree that each of you has good traits. Each of you has strengths that the other may not. Agreed?"

I don't want to nod, but I do. Mike barely tips his big head.

Susan flips a page on her clipboard and picks up her pencil. I take the opportunity to swallow hard a few times. My throat *is* getting hoarse, actually, and my lips are starting to chap from all the talking. Yelling. Susan clears her own throat and says, "Let's try a little exercise. I'm going to read a list of roles that parents are often called on to play. I want you think about each role and tell me which of you plays it most often. Ready?"

We nod.

"Disciplinarian."

"Me," I say. Obviously it's me. I'm the only one who cares about making the kids behave.

At the same time, Mike jerks his head in my direction and says, *"Her,"* as if being a disciplinarian is a bad thing and he's pinning the label on me before he can be accused of it himself.

"Okay," says Susan, making a mark on her clipboard. "Social planner."

"Me," I say again. No contest.

"Her," says Mike.

"Motivator."

I have to think about that one, but Mike chirps, "That's me," so I let him have it.

"Adventure seeker."

"Me again," Mike practically crows. I'll let him have that, too, since it isn't actually a parenting skill. I'm guessing whoever made this test had to throw in some fake ones so the bad parents could score at least a few points.

Susan nods, then says, "Nurturer."

That's me.

"Dreamer."

That one makes no sense, so it's Mike.

"Housekeeper."

Me. Who the hell else would it be?

"Repairperson."

Mike, I guess. But I've had to do more of it since he's been gone.

It goes on and on, and I get it now. We each have our roles. Neither one of us does everything. But... "I just have to point out," I say, "that Mike gets all the fun parts. And I'm guessing that his girlfriend takes on the hard parts for him, just like I used to."

"Right," he snaps. "Which is why the kids should live with me. Because with me they'd have a two-parent household."

Jesus Christ. What an asshole. I turn to go off on him.

Susan speaks before I can. "So, Mike, will you tell the kids that? Will you tell Alex and Lucia that your girlfriend can take their mother's place and they won't need Natasha anymore?"

That shuts him up for a second. Then he says, "Well, no. Not exactly like *that*."

"This is important," Susan says. "This is something I need each of you to keep in mind. When you're calling each other names, you're also calling Alex and Lucia's parents names. Do you know what I mean?" She turns to Mike. "Would you walk up to Alex and say, 'Yo' mama's so selfish, she doesn't care about you as much as she cares about herself'? Would you let anyone else talk to him like that?"

On the one hand, I want to laugh at Susan's attempt at ghettospeak. On the other hand, I'm angry because I know Mike has said things like that in front of the kids, and yet he's sitting here shaking his head like he's never bad-mouthed me in his life.

Maybe, though, it's because those words sound so harsh coming out of this stranger's mouth, and he doesn't want to believe that he'd talk to the kids like that. Maybe she's actually getting through to him.

"What about you, Natasha? How would you feel if someone walked up to Lucia and said, 'Your father doesn't care about you—he's only pretending to in order to get back at your mother'?"

Okay, this isn't fair. It's not the same in my case.

It stings. Yeah, it would hurt, and I'm a jerk when I act like that in front of the kids. I admit it.

"These aren't things we want our children to believe, are they?" she asks us. No, they aren't. She's like a kindergarten teacher, scolding. But she's right. "And these things aren't true, are they? Don't we know that?"

Yes, we do. I hate Mike's guts, but I do want to believe that he cares about the kids. I glance in his direction. He's glancing at me. Sheepish.

For a while after that, neither of us yells.

Alex

ANGELICA MUST'VE BEEN wrong, because we have to go to Miss Buena's all the time now. I asked Mom why, and she said because she has a lot of appointments after work and they're going to last until January's over. I said, "Doctors' appointments?" and she said, "No. It's grown-up stuff, baby. Boring stuff."

So we're back at Miss Buena's again today, but this time Angelica and them aren't here. It's only me, Lucia, and Tiffany. I hate when it's like this.

Miss Buena's on the phone again, but it's no fun spying on her by myself. Maybe she'll say something good, though, and I can tell Angelica next time she's here with me. So I go stand by the bedroom door to listen.

She's sad. Or mad. Or scared.

She says, "Robbie, no. Just wait." Then she says, "What if I come right now?" Then she says, "I'm coming right now. Please tell her. . . . I don't know. Please wait for me."

She comes out of the bedroom real fast and scares me. She says, "Alex. Oh, God. Alex and Lucia." She looks around the apartment like she's trying to remember something. Then she says, "I'm going to have to take y'all with me."

I say, "Are we going to see Robbie and Cristina?"

She looks down at me. "How did you . . . ?" Then she says,

"Yes, m'ijo. We're going to see them, real quick. Real fast. Go tell your sister and Tiffany, okay?" Then she goes to the kitchen.

I go in Tiffany's room and tell her and Lucia that we're leaving.

"Is Mom here?" Lucia says.

"No, dummy," I say. "We're going to visit Cristina and Robbie."

I know that Lucia doesn't know who they are, but I think Tiffany does. I guess Tiffany knows that's her mom, because she looks at me for a long time, with her mouth open.

Miss Buena comes in the room. She's not wearing her apron anymore, and she has on black tennis shoes instead of slippers. "Okay, kids. Come on. We're going to take a ride real quick. Tiffany, guess what? We're going to visit your mama."

She already has her purse and her keys. We follow her out of the apartment and down the hall to the elevator.

Natasha

THIS SUSAN GRAHAM is some kind of miracle worker. I've never seen Mike listen to anyone's opinions so respectfully, much less a woman's.

She's telling him, "I understand that, and I believe you when you say that you aren't doing this to hurt Natasha. But do you understand that because of the way you've chosen to do it, that's how it comes across?"

Mike nods.

Susan says, "I want you to look at Natasha and tell her, right now, why you're doing this."

I don't need Mike to look at me. I don't want him to. But I want to cooperate with Susan, so I compose myself and look him in the eye. I'm surprised to see that his eyes are glistening.

"Listen, Natasha. I'm not as good with words as you are, but I'm going to try. The reason I want the kids is . . . It's not because I think you're a bad mother. I just had to say that, because I knew you'd never agree to let me have them. But I want them to spend more time with me now, because I know I didn't spend enough time with them when we were married. I know that now, okay? I see the way Alex is . . . He's like a little carbon copy of you. Even to the point that he's scared of bugs. And I'm not saying there's anything wrong with him being like you. I'm just saying it's made me realize that he's never learned anything from me. I see the way he looks at me when I try to talk to him. It's like he doesn't even know who I am and he's just listening to be polite. And that's because I wasn't around enough."

"Well," I say, "that wasn't my fault."

Susan raises her hand. "Natasha, no one's saying it's your fault. Let Mike finish."

Mike gives her a quick smile—a nervous smile, not his usual smirk—and heaves a big sigh before continuing. "I know you think I only want to do this now because I'm with Missy, because I'm going to try to get her to take your place and act like the kids' mom. But that's not what's going on. If anything, Missy was the one who helped me see that it's not too late for me to have a better relationship with them. She doesn't agree with how I've been going about it. But . . . well, what else was I supposed to do? You weren't going to listen to me any other way."

I can't believe this. *Can* I believe this? Is he telling me the truth now, finally?

Susan puts her hand on Mike's. "Thank you for your honesty. I know those weren't easy words to say."

I guess he was telling the truth. Susan believes him, and she's too smart to be fooled by bullshit.

She extends her other hand, puts it on mine. "We're out of time. But I think we're in a very good place now, don't you? When we meet next week, I'd like you to try to think of ways that we can help repair Mike's relationship with Alex—with both kids—without hurting each other in the process. Can we do that?"

We both nod like children in a classroom.

By the time we leave the office, my eyes are wet and, I'd

almost swear, Mike's are, too. I walk out to my car slowly, feeling like I've spent the past hour and a half doing a year's worth of work.

As I climb into the Blazer, my phone rings. It's Geronima. She's probably wondering what's taking me so long. "Hello?"

"Hello, Natasha? This is Oscar."

"Oh, hi, Oscar." Why would he be calling? Hopefully not because anything's wrong. "What's . . . How are you?"

He says, "I was calling to ask if you'd heard from Gero."

"You mean since I called your apartment earlier? No. What's going on?"

"Oh, nothing." His voice is quiet, like he's turning away from the phone. "She must have taken them to the store or something."

It's seven-thirty now. No, almost eight. It was four when I called and talked to her last. "How long have they been gone?" I say. He doesn't respond. "Oscar?"

He sounds like he's coming up from underwater. I can barely hear him. "That's the thing. I wasn't here when they left. But it must have been a while."

Is he confused? Did he just wake up? I turn my phone's volume all the way up and ask him, "Did you call her?"

"No. I can't. Her cell phone isn't working, or it's off or something."

A sick feeling . . . "So Geronima is gone, with Alex and Lucia? Maybe she took them back to my apartment. Maybe Alex wanted to go play his video games."

"No," he says. "That was the first thing I thought of. I already went over there and knocked. I tried Sara's apartment, too, but they aren't there."

I'm starting to worry now. But it isn't time to give in to

panic. "Oscar, let me hang up. I'm going to call the phone in my apartment and make sure they aren't there. I'll call you right back."

He agrees, and I hang up on him to dial our number. Damned old people and their refusal to turn on their cell phones. I have a phone at the apartment just because it came free with the cable. Otherwise I'd *only* use my cell. I call and hear our phone ring. The answering machine picks up, and I hear my own voice, nasal and unwelcoming, stating that I've reached my own number. Where are they?

I call again. Still no answer.

They probably went to the store, like Oscar said. I'm sure there's nothing to worry about. I call Geronima's apartment again, and Oscar answers in one ring.

"They aren't at my place," I tell him. "They probably did go to the store. Maybe her cell needs to be charged."

"Maybe," he says. "But I always stay on her about that. She has a charger in the car, so I don't have to worry when she's out driving. I keep calling, but she must have it turned off." *He* sounds worried. That bothers me, even though logically there's nothing to worry about. The sick feeling returns. It's getting darker. Colder. The wind has picked up and is licking at my windows.

Oscar says something I can't hear. There's static on the line. I feel locked out, trapped where I can't see what's happening. I want to start driving, back to the apartments or to wherever the hell my kids are right now. It's making me angry that I don't know.

I hear him sigh. "She's been so upset lately. I thought it was because of Cristina, and Christmas, or maybe this thing with you and Sara and Haley. But..." He's waiting for me to say something. I don't know what. He says, "I'm sorry. I hate to call and worry you like this. But I'm worried myself. She left her insulin here, and it's almost time for her to take it."

The sick feeling melts away, and in its place there is steel. Like a steel rod in my body, holding me up. A metal calm. "I'm on my way. Wait for me there."

I start the engine. I make him promise to call me if they come back or if she calls. Now I need to hang up the phone and drive.

There's tapping at the window. It's Mike. I roll it down to see what he wants.

He's not teary-eyed anymore. He looks the same as always: like he's spoiling for a fight. "What are you doing, waiting for me to leave first? You think I'm going to go back in and talk to Susan behind your back?"

And I see now that he was planning to go back inside and talk to Susan behind my back.

He says, "No, you were probably planning to go back in yourself. Yeah, well, I'm not going to let you do that." There he goes, with his constant projections of guilt. But I don't have time for an argument with Mike right now.

I shouldn't tell him. I should just drive away. But no, I'm not the asshole here, so I say, "The kids are missing. Their baby-sitter—my neighbor, the old woman—took them to the store three hours ago, and her husband hasn't heard from her since."

"What?" He looks around like there might be someone lurking in the shrubs around the parking lot, springing to at-tack. "What did you...Why didn't you call her cell phone? What are you doing? God, Natasha, I knew you shouldn't have...See, that's why I...You should have—"

"Her cell phone is turned off," I say. "I'll find them. I'm going to the apartment now."

Leave him. Now drive.

Call Geronima's cell phone. No answer. Okay, then keep calling every few minutes.

Drive fast. Not *that* fast. Cut around this slow car, but be careful.

Think.

Men with guns, hijacking the car. Geronima on the side of the road, heart attack. Alex and Lucia and Tiffany still in the backseat, crying. Afraid.

Don't think about that. But go ahead and call the police. Watch out for that torn piece of tire in the road.

The woman says, "This is 911. What is your emergency?"

Tell her. Keep your voice clear.

"Ma'am, I can't help you with that. You're going to need to call the non-emergency line."

Memorize the number. Hang up. Dial it. Watch the road.

The man says, "Police."

Tell them. Keep your voice calm.

"Okay, what is your name, ma'am?"

Answer the questions clearly. Don't let them waste time by asking you to repeat.

"What about the license number on the vehicle, ma'am? Do you have that?"

Tell them you'll get it and call them back.

Someone holding a gun to Geronima's head. She's dead on the side of the road. Now the gun's at Alex's head, and Lucia's watching, and—

Stop that. *Focus.* Try her cell phone again. Drive the car.

Alex

CRISTINA AND ROBBIE must live far away, because we've been driving for a long time. I was playing my new Game Blaster that Dad got me for Christmas, but now my fingers are starting to hurt.

We're far away from our apartment and my mom's work. For a while we were next to the freeway, and Miss Buena stopped at a gas station so we could get out and go pee. But now I can't see the freeways or any of the big buildings anymore. We're just driving by a bunch of old houses and trees.

I turn around and I can see Lucia. She's still holding one of Tiffany's dolls, but she's not playing with it anymore. She's staring out the window. Tiffany's staring out the window, too, but she looks like she's falling asleep.

"Does my mom know where we're going?" I ask.

Miss Buena says, "We're just going real fast. We'll be back before your mom comes to pick you up."

"But what if she comes back early and doesn't know where we are?" I say.

"We're almost there," she tells me. "I'm just about to find it."

"Alex," Lucia says, "I left Mr. Beary in my backpack."

She's saying that because she's scared. She only remembers that bear when she's afraid of something. I don't want her to start crying like a little baby, so I turn around and tell her, "Don't be scared. We'll go back and get him in a little while."

I'm not scared. I'm only worried that if Mom comes back early from her appointment and we're not there, she's going to get mad. She's been mad a lot lately. I think the appointments are about my dad, because she's always mad and quiet like that when she sees him.

Maybe they're going to the courthouse, like they used to. Maybe they're going there to fight about me and Lucia and whose house we're going to live in. I hope that's not why, but I bet it is. That's what Mom was talking about, I bet, with the other ladies in the park. That's why she's been mad but pretending she's not. I wonder if she's at the courthouse with Dad right now. I wonder what they're saying.

I don't want to move to another new place, but I don't want to stop seeing Dad either. But I also don't want him to take me away from Mom and Lucia.

I should've told Dad that I didn't want a new room at Missy's house. Then he and Mom wouldn't have started fighting again.

It's too late to fix it. I should've told my dad that I wanted to keep seeing them both. Or I should've told Mom. Even if they would've gotten mad at me. But now it's too late.

Now we're driving where there's hardly any houses. It's just a lot of trees. It's getting darker, and some of the trees have scary shapes. There's a broken truck next to one of them. It doesn't have any wheels.

I wish we weren't going to visit Robbie and Cristina right now. It's taking too long. I want to go back home.

Miss Buena has the radio on. It was playing old songs when we started driving, but now the station's messing up, so she turns it off. She's driving real slow and leaning forward so she can see better. She says, "Where is it? Did we already pass it?"

I say, "Are we lost?"

She says, "No. I just can't find the street we're supposed to turn on."

I say, "Why don't you call Robbie?"

She says, "Good idea." She pulls over on the side of the road and stops. There's nothing around us now except tall trees. I think we probably passed the right street and went too far.

Sara

W<small>E WERE AT</small> a used-car lot when I got the call.

I'd saved up fifteen hundred dollars by then, and I was thinking about getting a newer car instead of wasting any more money on fixing the Impala. I was trying to decide between a crappy old Pontiac and a crappy old Chrysler, both of them with too many miles for the price. Monique and Junior were running around between the cars, with Monique yelling crazy stuff like, "I'm the professor! You're the wolf man!" Angelica was looking at the cars with me, and she said, "Mama, your phone's ringing."

She has way better ears than me. I looked at the phone, and it was Natasha. I thought, *What does she want?* I didn't know if something bad had happened, or if she just wanted to talk, or what.

She said, "Sara. Hey. Are you busy?" and I said, "Kind of, why?" And she said she was sorry to bother me, but Geronima took off with her kids and no one knew where they went. Because they'd been gone for a long time, and Geronima forgot to take her medicine. And she was just wondering if I'd heard from her.

And I was like, "Oh, shit." I hadn't talked to Gero since the day before.

And she said, "Okay, well, thanks," like she was going to

hang up. She sounded serious as hell, and I knew she must have been freaking out.

I said, "Did you call Oscar?" and she said he was the one who called her to tell her they were missing. I asked her if she was at the apartment, and she said she was on the way over there and she had to hang up.

I was scared then. I didn't know what to think. I told Angelica, "Get your brother and sister. We have to leave right now."

So she got them, and then we peeled out to the apartments.

Natasha

I UNDERSTAND THAT, but in this case I think it's completely warranted. It's three children with an old diabetic woman. I'm sure you see the severity of the situation. Yes, I'll wait. No, actually, let me speak to your supervisor myself. It'll save time."

Someone's following me from the parking garage. I hear the footsteps speeding up behind me.

"Yes, I've already spoken to the police. They're working with us. Should I have them call you? Yes, I understand that it takes time. That's why I'm calling you now, to get the process started."

It's only Mike. Keep going. Take the stairs, they're faster.

An officer's already here at Geronima's, standing outside her door. Good. Mike appears from the stairwell behind me, out of breath. "Natasha. Wait. What are you—"

I tell him, "Her cell-phone company is working to locate her phone signal, in case she turned it back on but is out of range or whatever. But it'll take a while." Mike sighs. Ignore him for right now. Talk to the policeman instead. "Officer . . ." Read his badge. "Officer Brown. I'm Natasha Davila. Thank you for coming out."

The apartment door opens, and Oscar lets us in. I introduce everyone, and Oscar reexplains the situation to Officer Brown. I let him, without interrupting.

Officer Brown has questions. I answer them clearly, without letting myself become upset. I need to stay calm so the
police can do their work as efficiently as possible.

Mike interrupts. Mike is upset. Now he's pacing and perspiring. He goes to the kitchen and makes a call. "No, not
yet," he says. "Damn it, I know. We're waiting to find out." I
ignore him.

I keep calling Geronima's number. There's no answer. I'll
keep trying.

There's a knock at the door. Oscar opens it. It's Sara with
her kids.

"Hey," she says. I let her hug me, quick. "What do you
need me to do?"

Good question. "Just . . . think. Think of where they could be."

Sara sends her kids to Tiffany's room. Good idea. Get them
out of the way. She goes to the kitchen. She'll see Mike there.
Will he say anything to her? Don't worry about that now.

Officer Brown says, "Well, Mr. Buenaventura, Ms. Davila,
that's all I can do right now, is file the report. We'll put
out the APB and get the alerts going on the highways, of
course."

That's all he can do. He's leaving now. Sara comes out of
the kitchen. "Have you eaten?" she says.

No. There's no time.

She hands me something, and I eat it. She hands me water,
and I drink. She does the same for Oscar—it's a cookie—and
he thanks her. Mike is hovering in the background.

"Okay, so tell me again what's the last thing that happened," Sara says.

Oscar tells her the same thing he already told me. Nothing
new, but maybe someone new hearing it will make a differ-

ence. Now Mike's eating a cookie and Angelica's hovering in the background, listening.

Oscar says, "I called the grocery store and had them page her, but they said she's not there. They're checking to see if anybody remembers seeing them." That's good. Oscar's smart.

I say, "What about restaurants? Maybe La Sultana?"

"Taqueria las Brisas," Sara offers.

I'm on the phone calling Information and getting the numbers. It doesn't take long to call each one and find out that they haven't been there. We need to get back into the cars and drive until we find them. Standing here isn't doing anything.

Angelica sidesteps slowly to her mother and whispers.

"What?" says Sara. "Angelica, let the grown-ups talk right now."

The girl speaks louder. "Maybe they went to see Cristina."

Oscar looks down at Angelica with a start. "Where did you hear that?"

Angelica clears her throat. She's nervous, not used to this kind of attention. I realize that I've never heard her speak more than one sentence before. She says, "Miss Buena's been talking to Robbie. He's Cristina's boyfriend. They had a baby."

"What?" says Oscar. He's surprised. This is news to him. He says, "She's still with that punk? They had a baby?"

Angelica nods. "I think so. We heard Miss Buena talking about it on the phone. She said the baby was six pounds. Robbie wanted her to come see the baby, but she said she had to tell you first."

Oscar stares at her. "He wanted her to go see the baby in Alabama?"

Angelica shakes her head. "They live here now. They came

back. That's why Robbie called Miss Buena, because they came back. Miss Buena only talks to him when you're not here."

Oscar is shocked. We all are. Sara says, "Girl, how in the hell do you know all that?"

Angelica looks down at the floor. "We were playing spies," she mumbles.

This is important. This is a good thing. I fall to my knees in front of her so that we're face-to-face. I put my hands on her arms and say, "Angelica, that's good. I'm glad you were playing spies. You can help us now."

She meets my eyes. She bites her lip, looking exactly like her mother for a split second. She's nervous, but I can see that she wants to help. And she's not stupid. Thank God Angelica's here and she's a smart little girl.

"Sweetie, can you tell us where Robbie and Cristina live? Did you ever hear Miss Buena talk about that?"

She thinks back, thinks hard. I imagine I can hear the thoughts flicking through her head, like a file of index cards. She says, "No-o-o . . . Well . . . one time she asked him, 'It's a trailer? You mean like a mobile home?' And then she said, 'Well, I guess mobile homes can be nice.' "

I stand. "A mobile home. That means it has to be outside the city limits." My mind flips through its own index cards now. Where do people live in mobile homes? "Angelica, did she ever say where they lived? What neighborhood? Was it in Dallas or another town?"

She's straining to remember, I can tell. "I don't know. Maybe?"

"Fort Worth? Did she ever say Fort Worth? Or Abilene? Denton? Scarborough?" Sara and Mike look at me like I've gone crazy. Why aren't they helping? Why aren't they thinking of towns with mobile homes?

Angelica shakes her head. "No."

Oscar says, "Red Oak. Did you ever hear her say Red Oak?"

Angelica turns to him. "I think . . . maybe. Yeah. She said, 'So y'all ended up back in Red Oak.' I remember now."

Red Oak. That isn't far from here, is it? A half hour, I think. I bend down and hug Angelica. I could cry from relief, from happiness that she's here right now and that she's a nosy little girl with such a good memory.

Oscar's telling us, "Cristina used to hang out with some hoodlum kids in Red Oak. If Robbie's the one I think he is, that's where she met him."

Everyone falls silent and absorbs this. Oscar's looking down at the floor. In concern? Shame? He says, "After Cristina had Tiffany, we said we'd take care of her so she could finish school and keep working. But instead Cristina started running around wild all the time. Drinking, drugs, all that. Then she went to live with this Robbie kid, and . . . I didn't like that. He was . . . he wasn't like us. I told her if she was going to live with him and end up pregnant again, I didn't want to see her anymore." He takes a deep breath. This is hard for him, telling us this truth. "She left us and left her own daughter. She moved away with this Robbie kid to Alabama. Since we sold the house and moved to this apartment, we've lost touch with her."

I see the surprise on Sara's face and the utter bewilderment on Mike's. Angelica's quietly listening—she shouldn't be in the room right now. She's already heard too much about our grown-up problems, obviously.

Oscar continues, "When Gero started baby-sitting for you and Haley, I thought it was good for her. It made her happy to have so many kids in the house and people to cook for. But then she started talking about Cristina again, after all these years, and saying she felt like we made a mistake. I should've known she was talking to them again. I should've paid more attention." He sighs. "I'm sorry, Natasha. To both of y'all," he adds, indicating Mike with a nod. "Sorry y'all got dragged into this mess."

"I'm going," I say. "I'm driving to Red Oak."

"Wait," says Sara. "You can't just run off without knowing where they're at."

"That's where they are," I say. "That's the only thing that makes sense. I'm going. Call me if you hear anything."

"Wait," they say. I can't hear them. I'm on my way.

GOD, PLEASE LET them be safe. I'll do anything. Please let Geronima be okay without her medicine and able to drive safely. Please let them be somewhere brightly lit, easy to find. Please watch over them and don't let them be hurt.

God, I know I haven't spoken to you in a long time, and I haven't been a very good person lately. I've been angry and judgmental, and I haven't taken time with the kids like I should. I'm sorry for that. And I'm sorry I never pray or give thanks. I am thankful for everything we have. But I need your help now, please.

I promise that once they're back, I'll be a better mother: Be more patient with them. Listen to them more. Get along better with their dad ...

God, I swear I'll do whatever it takes. Do you want me to stop fighting with Mike? I will.

Do you want me to accept Missy as their new stepmother? I will.

God, if you want me to let Alex live with Mike . . . If you want both of them to go . . . I feel like that'd kill me. I hope that's not what this is about. But if Alex wants to live with Mike and Lucia wants to go follow him, then I promise I'll let them and I won't complain. And I won't let them see that I'm unhappy, even if I can barely stand it. I promise. And I'll work with Mike to make everything good for the kids, to keep them happy. I swear, God.

Please just let me find them, and let them be safe.

Alex

MISS BUENA KEEPS trying to call Robbie, but her phone isn't working. "I think we're too far out," she says. "Alex, do me a favor, m'ijo. You hold the phone, and I'm going to drive. You tell me when the phone starts working again." She hands me her phone.

"What do you mean?" I say.

She takes it and points to the corner of the screen. "I forgot to turn on my phone earlier. But now it's on and I can't get a signal. See these little lines, how they're flat? When we get closer to the signal, the lines will get bigger. You see?"

I say yes, and she starts to drive. "Tell me when they get big."

We have to go for a long time, kind of.

Lucia says, "Alex, I'm scared."

"Don't be scared," I tell her. Then I look at the phone and I see that one of the lines got bigger, just like Miss Buena said. "There's a signal," I say. "There's a line."

"Okay, good. Let's call Robbie and get better directions." She pulls over again and takes the phone. But when she calls, no one answers. "Where are they? Why don't they pick up?" she says.

I don't know. "Maybe their phone doesn't have a signal now."

Miss Buena says, "Maybe." She starts to look worried. She's getting a little bit of sweat on her lip, like my dad does when he works in the garage. But it's cold outside, and it's starting to feel cold in the car, too. She says, "Alex, do me another favor. Look in the glove compartment and get me one of the peppermint candies that's in there."

I find one at the bottom of all the papers and give it to her. She opens it and says, "You can have one, too, if you want."

I say, "No, thank you. I don't like mints."

She says, "Well, see if the girls want one."

I turn around and see Lucia staring at me. I try to give her the candy, but she doesn't take it. Tiffany's asleep all the way now. Her face is pressed against the door.

"Well," says Miss Buena, "I guess we should keep looking."

She turns on the radio again, but it takes her a long time to find a station that works, and the one she finds doesn't have music, only news and people talking about stuff. The deejay's talking about the Dallas Cowboys. It's getting darker, but Miss Buena keeps driving.

I take out my Game Blaster and restart it, but this time on the easiest level. I turn around and give it to Lucia. If she thinks about the game instead of looking out the window, she won't be afraid. She takes it from me. I say, "You have to jump over the spikes. Don't fall in the water." She starts playing it. That's good.

Now we're out of the trees and back to the part where there's streetlights again. There's houses, too, but they're skinny ones with little steps instead of porches. Some of them have lights in the windows. One has men sitting in front of it. It looks like they're drinking sodas or beers.

"We need to pull over," says Miss Buena. "I need to figure out—" Then, she says, "Oh, no."

"What is it, Miss Buena?"

"We're about to run out of gas."

That means we need to go to a gas station. We passed one a little while ago. "Maybe we should turn around," I tell her.

She says okay and pulls over off the road a little bit. She checks to make sure no other cars are coming and then turns our car around and starts going back the way we came. It's really dark now, and we can barely see anything except the streetlights and sometimes lights from somebody's house far back in the trees.

"Oh, no!" Miss Buena says again, but this time louder.

"Looky!" Lucia says real loud.

There's a big animal in front of our car. A deer. It jumps real high. The lights from our car shine on its eyes and make them turn red.

Miss Buena slams on the brakes and turns the car real hard. We run over a bunch of bumps and then skid into the grass. I can feel it under the tires.

The deer's gone. Lucia starts to cry. Now Tiffany's awake, and she starts crying, too.

"I'm sorry, m'ijos. I'm sorry," Miss Buena says. Then she opens the door and gets out. I undo my seat belt and lean over to see. She fell on her knees in the grass next to the car. She's coughing and holding her stomach. I think she's going to throw up.

The radio turned off. The car's all lit up now, because the door's open, and it's making a beeping noise.

Lucia's crying even louder. "I want to go home!"

I call Miss Buena's name, but she doesn't answer. She has her head against the car door with her eyes closed. She's making little noises like a kitten. I don't think she can hear me.

I don't know what to do.

I wish I had my Venom mask. I feel like if I had it on right now, I'd know what to do next.

Natasha

THERE'S A GAS STATION ahead, and I need directions. I don't want to stop, but I have to. Maybe I shouldn't have driven out here like this. I'm in Red Oak but have no idea where to go. I should have looked up the various trailer parks in the area or . . . something.

But there's nothing happening at the apartment either. Every time I call, Oscar and Sara sound more and more hopeless. The police aren't doing anything. Nothing's happening. I have to find them myself, before it's too late. I can't stop thinking about . . . God, don't think about it. Just find them.

I'll stop really quick to ask the gas-station clerk where the trailer parks are. Maybe . . .

Mike. Mike's followed me here. That's his car pulling up beside me. Through the window he says, "Natasha, wait."

I don't want to wait. I don't want to talk to him. There's no time to waste. I just want to find out—

"What are you doing?" he asks.

"I'm going inside to find out where the nearest trailer park is."

I go inside and ask the woman behind the counter. She tells me about Sunnyside Park, on this road, and Rainbow Park a few miles away. But she says there are other trailers all over the town, not in parks but on their own land.

Fine. Sunnyside first, then the others. I'll drive to every trailer in Red Oak if I have to.

Mike stops me again when I come out. "Natasha, wait. Look. I have it." He holds up his phone, one of the expensive ones with the fancy screen. It's showing a map. "Sunnyside Trailer Park," he says.

He can help me. "Give me the phone," I say. "I'll take it with me."

"No, I'm coming with you." He points the remote at his car, locking it, and follows me to the Blazer. "They're my kids, too."

There's no time to argue. I need to keep moving. He gets into the passenger seat, and we drive.

Alex

LUCIA IS CRYING so much she's hiccupping. "Alex! I want to go home!" Tiffany's crying, too, and saying, "Grandma! Grandma!" I wish I knew how to drive, and how to drive us back home. Or if there wasn't enough gas, I'd...

We have to call Mom. I say, "Miss Buena, we need to call my mom." But her eyes are still closed. She's making noises like she's having a dream.

Her phone is in her purse. I open her purse and find it in one of the pockets. I open it, but the light doesn't come on. Maybe it's broken.

No, I think it's asleep, like my Game Blaster goes to sleep when I stop playing it. I push one of the buttons, and the light comes on.

I know Mom's phone number by heart. I dial it, but nothing happens.

A truck comes up the road. I see its lights. Can it see us? It's a stranger. Should I honk the horn or should I hide? The truck passes by.

"What happened?" says Miss Buena, real quiet.

I have to keep trying. I press the button with the picture of the green phone. Nothing happens. Then I see that the lines in the corner of the screen are flat again. There's no signal.

The last time we found the signal, we were farther that

way, by the gas station. But Miss Buena can't drive us there now. She's too sick.

What if I walk that way? If I walk just a little bit, can I find the signal and call my mom?

I open my door. Lucia screams, "Alex, no! Don't leave!"

I say, "I'm not going far. I have to find the signal again, so the phone will work and I can call Mom to come get us. Y'all stay here with Miss Buena."

Tiffany's crying so loud I can barely hear anything. Lucia says, "Don't leave us. I'm scared of the dark."

I say, "I'm going to leave the door open, so the light will stay on. Don't be scared. I'm coming right back. Look—take off your seat belts and scoot up. You can watch me out the window."

That makes them stop crying a little bit. Lucia takes off her seat belt and wipes her nose on her dress. Then Tiffany copies her. They scoot way up so they can see me get out of the car and walk in front of it. It's hard to walk here, because the grass is really tall. I can see the tracks where Miss Buena ran over it and flattened it out. It looks red from the car's lights in the back.

I walk around to Miss Buena's side and see her sitting in the grass next to the car. "Miss Buena? Are you awake?" She looks really tired, like she fell asleep right there. She kind of looks like Tiffany now, with her face pressed against the car and a little bit of slobber coming out of her mouth. "Miss Buena, I'm going to try to call my mom. I'll be right back."

Lucia and Tiffany are watching me. I wave to them, and they wave back. There's a lot of little bugs flying in the air between us. I guess they came up to see the headlights. Now

I have to start walking toward where the gas station was. I press a button on the phone so it'll light up again and I can see the signal.

Now that I'm getting far away from the car, everything is super dark. I shine the phone like a flashlight to see where I'm going. There's a white thing in front of me. What is it? It's just trash. I keep walking. I turn around and wave at Lucia, but I don't know if she can still see me. I can't really see her anymore.

I have to keep walking, even though it's dark. I don't want to, but I'm the only one who can do it.

I'm really far now. The car looks like a house, real far away.

The phone light blinks off, and everything turns black around me.

There's a noise behind me, in the trees. I want to go back now. I want to run.

I can't. I have to keep going. Lucia and them are waiting for me. If I don't call Mom, what's going to happen to us?

The phone lights up. It rings, real loud. It scares me, and I jump, like in a monster movie. I look at the screen. It says Robbie.

"Hello?"

"Who's this?" It's not a man's voice. It's a lady.

I say, "This is Alex. Who's this?"

She says, "This is Cristina. Are you with my mother?"

It's Cristina. Miss Buena's daughter. I say, "Miss Buena—your mother—drove us out here to visit you and your baby. But we got lost, and she's sick now. She can't drive the car anymore. I'm trying to call my mom to come get us."

She says, "What? Where are y'all?"

I say, "I don't know. We're out by some trees, where it's dark. I think we went too far past your street."

She says, "Where's my mother?"

I say, "She's sitting by the car. She can't talk. I had to walk far away from them, so the phone could get a signal and I can call my mom."

She says, "Shit. Damn it. Stay where you are . . . What's your name?"

I say, "I'm Alex. My sister is Lucia, and Tiffany's with us, too."

She says, "Tiffany? Shit. Stay where you are. Me and Robbie are coming to find you. No . . . Is my mom okay? Can you call 911? No, I'll call. Oh, but I don't know where you are. Can you call 911, so they can find you? And tell them to send an ambulance for my mother? I'll call them, too, but you have to call from where you are so they can find you. Please."

I say okay, and we hang up. I dial 9-1-1. There's another noise in the trees, but I'm going to ignore it. I can't get scared right now. Miss Buena needs me to call.

"This is 911. What is your emergency?" a lady says on the phone.

"Hi. We need help. We ran our car off the road, and now Miss Buena—my baby-sitter—is sick and needs an ambulance to come get her."

"Hold on. Who is this? How old are you, son?"

"This is Alex. I'm eight."

"Alex, can you tell me where you are, son?"

"No, we're lost."

"Stay on the line, please. Don't hang up." I don't. I hear the lady talking to someone else. Then she says, "Alex, are you in Red Oak?"

I say, "I don't know. Maybe." That sounds familiar. Maybe that's what Miss Buena said earlier.

The lady says, "Are you with Geronima Buenaventura? Is she your baby-sitter?"

I say, "Yes. That's Miss Buena's name. Do you know her? Do you know where we are?"

She says, "Her daughter just called. Stay on the line. Don't hang up. We're going to find you right now."

I say, "Okay." I hear other people talking in the room with her.

Then she says, "Okay, we have you now. We're coming to get you, Alex. Hold tight. You can stay on the phone with me until the ambulance gets there."

I say, "Thank you. But I have to call my mom now."

She says, "What? Okay. But stay where you are. Wait for the ambulance."

I say okay and hang up. Then, real fast, before the signal can go away, I call Mom.

I hear her voice. She says, "Geronima? Where are you?"

"Mom, it's me."

"Alex!" She sounds like she's crying. "Alex, where are you, baby?" I hear someone else with her. He says, "Where are they?" It's Dad, I think.

I say, "I'm in Red Oak with Miss Buena and Lucia and Tiffany. Are you coming to get us?"

She says, "I'm trying to, baby. Where are you? Where's Miss Buena?"

"We ran out of gas, and then a deer came and we went off the road. Miss Buena's sick. She's in the grass. I had to leave everybody in the car and walk far away so I could get a signal to call you."

"Oh, God," says Mom. "Alex, we're coming to find you. Your dad is here with me. But you have to help us. Do you know what street you're on?"

"No," I say. "I told you, we're lost." I feel like crying now. It's stupid, because now Mom and the ambulance are coming to get us. I don't have to cry anymore, but I still feel like I'm going to. I say, "I called 911. They said they know where we are and they're going to send an ambulance to get Miss Buena."

"That's good, Alex," Mom says. "You did a good job. Now tell me what you can see, baby."

I can't see anything. There's nothing here but me, the trees, and Miss Buena's car, far away. I look all around. "I see trees and the street. One of the trees doesn't have leaves. Wait—there's a sign next to it."

"That's good!" Mom says. "What does the sign say?"

"It says . . . 'No dumping. Sub . . . subject to five-hundred-dollar fine.'"

"Oh," Mom says. I guess she still can't figure out where we are. I hear Dad talking to her. He's saying, "Ask him what he can see around him."

I look around some more, in case there's anything else.

"There's another sign," I tell Mom. "But I can't see what it says. It's kind of far, and it's turned the wrong way." And it's dark. The sign's across the street.

"Baby, can you go look at it and tell me what it says?"

I don't want to. I'm afraid to move. But I want Mom to find us.

"Alex, are you still there?"

"I'm here. I'm going to look at the sign," I say. "Don't hang up, okay?"

She says, "I won't."

I look both ways, and then I run across the street. I get up to the sign. "It says 'FM two-three-seven-seven,'" I tell Mom.

"Farm to Market Road twenty-three seventy-seven," she says. I hear Dad say okay. Then he says, "We just crossed it. Go back." My mom says okay, and then she tells me, "That was good, baby. We're not far from you."

"Which direction on 2377?" my dad says.

"Alex, I need you to think hard now," my mom says. "I know there's nothing but trees where you are now, but can you remember anything you passed before you got there? A house, a store, another street sign?"

I think about it as I look both ways and run back across the street. "There was a gas station. We passed it a little while ago."

"Good!" says Mom. "Good job, Alex!" She tells my dad about the gas station, and he says, "I'm looking it up."

I hear my dad saying something to my mom. Then Mom tells me, "Alex, I need you to do one last thing. I need you to tell me what kind of gas station it was. Do you remember what the sign said? What it looked like? There are a lot of gas stations around here, and we need to find the right one."

I try to remember.

"What color was the sign? Was it called Red Oak Gas Station?" she says. "Did it say R-E-D O-A-K?"

"No," I tell her. "I can't remember what it said. I just remember it had a picture of man on it."

"What kind of man?" Mom says. "Like a man with blue overalls, like Mario?"

"No. It was one of those...the men that live under rainbows on the cartoons."

Mom says, "A leprechaun. Mike, it's an old Diamond Sham-rock!" I hear Dad say, "Got it. Ten miles," and then Mom says, "We're coming right now for y'all, baby."

"Okay." I don't want to hang up on her, but I have to go back to Lucia and them now, so they won't be scared. "Mom, I have to go back to the car with Lucia. But when I go, the phone's going to lose the signal and hang up on us."

She says, "Are you sure you don't want to stay on the phone, baby?"

I want to, but I can't. I say, "I have to go back. Lucia's scared." She says okay, and I say, "Hurry and find us. Hurry, okay?"

She says, "I am, baby. I'm coming to get y'all right now."

I start to run. If I run real fast, I won't have time to think about the noises in the trees or the things in the grass. I hear Mom saying, "I'm almost there. I'm almost there," over and over, until the phone loses signal again and I can't hear her anymore. I keep running, all the way to the car. Lucia and Tiffany are watching me through the window. Miss Buena's still sitting in the grass.

"They're on the way," I tell Miss Buena. Then I open Lucia's door and tell them, "They're coming to get us."

The ambulance is coming. I hear it, far away. And now I see its lights, red and blue, coming down the street.

Lucia starts to cry again.

I say, "What's wrong with you? They're coming to get us right now."

She says, "I was scared they were never coming!"

She's so dumb sometimes. I always knew that Mom would find us. Especially with my help.

Sara

SO EVERYBODY WAS back at Geronima's apartment again. Her daughter, Cristina, and Cristina's boyfriend, Robbie, were there, too, with their new baby. I figured out why Oscar was pissed about their daughter taking off with Robbie. It's because he was black. But I could tell that he felt stupid about that, after Robbie showed up and turned out to be a good guy. And the baby was cute as hell, too. Plus, Oscar was so glad that they found Gero and that she turned out okay, you know. All she needed was a shot or an IV or whatever, and she was totally back to normal by the time they got her home. So they were all in the living room, talking about everything that'd gone down and how Robbie was going to start a new job in Louisiana and all that. Geronima was happy because she got to see the baby before they left and because Cristina gave her their address in Louisiana and said they could bring Tiffany to visit. Natasha was happy because her kids were okay. The kids were happy to be hanging out together, and they were running all over the apartment.

So I went into the kitchen to get Geronima some more water, and there was Natasha's ex. He was walking back and forth, beating on the backs of Geronima's chairs like they were a drum set. I had already gotten a good, long look at him earlier, and I knew exactly who he was. And I thought,

*What's he doing hiding in here when everybody else is out
there talking to the old lady and the kids, making sure they're
okay?* I know he hates Natasha's guts because she dumped
him, but that's his kids' mom, you know? He should've been
out there with her, telling the kids everything's gonna be all
right. Something. What kind of man hides in the kitchen like
that?

It pissed me off, and I guess that's why I decided to do
what I did. But I didn't want to let him know that I was pissed
off. It was like Natasha says—getting loud and violent with
people doesn't do any good. They just call the cops on you.

So instead I walked up to him and said, "Hey, how's it
going?"

He stopped moving around and sort of smiled, nervous
like, and said, "Okay. It's okay, now that we've found them."
He looked at me some more, and then he noticed who I
was. I saw it on his face: Him thinking, *That's the stripper. The
prostitute. That chick I narked on so her own friends wouldn't
want to hang out with her anymore.*

But I just smiled at him, real cool, and then I went back to
the living room.

After a while Mike took off. He came out and told Natasha
he had to get back home and he'd call the kids the next day.
She said okay, and he left.

I waited a few minutes, and then I told Geronima I had to
run to my apartment to check on something and that I'd be
right back. But I didn't go to my apartment. I ran down all
the stairs to the first floor, and I got there right when Mike
was coming out of the elevator.

I said, "Hey, Mike." He turned around and saw me, but he
just nodded and started walking to the parking garage. So I

said, "Hey, wait up a second," and I followed him out. I was glad it worked out that way, with the two of us in the parking garage where it was kind of dark.

I said, real cool, "So I haven't seen you around lately."

He said, "What do you mean? You don't . . . Have we met before?"

I said, "No, we never met, but I've seen you where I used to work, at the Cabaret."

He looked around real fast then, like he was worried somebody would walk out and see us there together. He said, "I don't know what you're talking about."

I took a step closer to him, close enough to freak him out. But I stayed real sweet, kept smiling, and said, "Sure you do. You used to go to the Cabaret some nights after work. You'd have a few drinks and watch the girls dance. You took one of the dancers to your apartment one night. Remember?"

Yeah, that's what I'm telling you. As soon as I saw him that night, I knew who he was. He used to go to the Cabaret and get totally trashed after work, and one time he hired one of the girls for a night. But when he got her home, he was too drunk to get it up. And she came back and told everybody about it.

I'd never met Natasha's ex before that night. But as soon as I met him, I recognized him.

So I told him that, and he took a step back and hit the wall. He said, "All right, look. I don't know what you're trying to say, but—"

And I was like, "I'm not trying to say anything. I'm just wondering if Natasha knows that you like to hang out at strip clubs and pick up hookers. Because you seem to know a lot about what she does—who her friends are and where they work. You were real interested in my job, and you didn't mind telling people about it or using it to scare Natasha."

He told me, "Now, look here," all loud. But he couldn't think of anything to say after that. I could tell he was freaking out at that point. Not scared of me, because he's a big guy, but he didn't want me to run back to Natasha and tell her what I knew.

But the thing was, I wanted him to be afraid for real. Afraid of me and what I could do to him.

Why? Well, because. Look at everything he'd done to Natasha. Not just to her, but to me and Haley, too. He made us scared. He made us feel like shit.

I mean, none of us are perfect, right? We're just normal chicks, doing what we have to for our kids and trying not to go crazy while we're at it. Right? And here comes this fool with his lawyer and his detective and who knows what all else, writing all these papers talking about what's wrong with us. Why, so he can show them to some fat-ass judge who's probably just as messed up as everybody else? You know, we have lawyers come into the Dollhouse all the time. Probably judges, too. Who the hell knows? My point is, who the hell cares? I don't care what people do in their private lives, and I try to mind my own business. But then here comes this ass-hole Mike, all pissed off because his wife got sick of his shit and left him, and he decides he's going to make life hard for her and mess with her friends. And it just pissed me off, you know? And I was like, hell, no. I'm putting a stop to this shit right now.

So I went off on him. I went all ghetto on him, right there in the parking garage. I told him, "All I'm saying, Mike, is that you should think about what you've been doing to Natasha and how it makes her feel. And then think about how you'd feel if I talked about you the way you've been talking about me. What if I told everybody how you hired a heroin-addict hooker from our club and the only reason you don't have AIDS right now is 'cause you couldn't even get your dick up?"

He was looking at me with real big eyes then. Like a dog about to get beat. He said, "You're just bullshitting me. You don't work at the Cabaret. I've never seen you there."

I said, "I've worked at a lot of places. I'll work anywhere, as long as I can make enough money to take care of my kids. Did you know that the owner of your favorite strip club is my cousin? Did you know that he has surveillance cameras running in there all the time? Hey, Mike, how would your new girlfriend—what's her name? Pissy? Missy?—how would she feel if she knew how much you liked my cousin's Cabaret?"

He didn't say a damn thing then. He just looked at me. I could smell the sweat coming off of him.

I told him, "You better drop this stupid-ass lawsuit, if you don't want me to say anything. You better leave Natasha alone."

He wouldn't look me in the face anymore after that. He just said, "Why are you doing this?"

I snapped my fingers in front of his face so he'd look back at me, so he'd be sure to understand what I was going to say. I told him, "Because Natasha doesn't deserve the shit you've been putting her through. She's been a real good friend to me and my kids, even though I'm what I am. You don't want your kids around a stripper? Fine. I don't have to be around them anymore. But you know Natasha's a damned good mother to those kids, and the only reason you're trying to take them away is so you can hurt her."

He didn't say anything to that, but I felt like I got my point across.

I told him one last time, "I swear to God, if you so much as fuck with Natasha *one* more time, I'll give her the video of you leaving the club with that hooker. Don't think I won't." And then I took off.

No, I went back upstairs to Geronima's apartment, to get my kids and put them to bed.

Yeah, Natasha was still there. She came up to me before I left and started trying to thank me for being there and whatever. I just told her it was no big deal, and we left.

Because I couldn't stay. I was real tired all of a sudden. Even though it wasn't my kids who'd been missing, the whole thing still freaked me out, and I kept thinking about how I'd feel if it was Angelica or Monique or Junior who was gone. Just thinking about it made me feel sick and tired, the whole time. So after all that I just wanted to be at home with them for a while. You know?

SO THAT'S IT. That was how it all went down.

I know that Mike listened to me, that he quit trying to get the kids from Natasha, because Alex told Angelica that he goes to his dad's an extra day during the week now, on Wednesday nights. But he said he liked going, and his mom was okay with it, and she didn't have to go to court. So after that I figured you weren't involved in her case anymore. And I knew that she liked coming here, and that you were helping her a lot. Because she told Geronima, and Geronima told me. So I figured I'd call you myself. Because, like I said, you already knew half my story, so all I'd have to do is tell you the rest and see what you could do for me.

Yeah, I think so. I mean, just telling you everything helps. It helps me figure things out.

Haley? Yeah, I heard from her about a week ago. I didn't even tell you that part, did I? She ended up leaving her husband after all. She took off to Portland, right after New Year's.

Yeah, they're getting a legal separation, for real now. She has a lawyer handling the whole deal for her.

Well, that's the thing. She didn't take Jared with her. She left him with his dad.

Yeah. I was pretty surprised, too. Well, no, not really. She left me this long-ass voice mail about it. She said she realized that she got married too young and never had a chance to live her own life and blah, blah, blah. And that she wouldn't have figured it out without me and Natasha being there and helping her see it. And I was like, oh, great—blame me for you taking off and leaving your kid.

No. I don't know. I mean, I feel sad as hell for him. But then again, his dad's rich. He'll be all right. Haley said he got a new puppy for Christmas and he didn't even notice her leave. I think she was trying to play it off—make herself feel better. But I don't know. Maybe it's a good thing for her to be by herself for a while. Get all that stuff out of her system, and then maybe she'll come back.

Hey, maybe she can come back and start coming to see you. Since you already know half her problems anyway, right?

Yeah, I'd hang out with her. She's probably a little different now, after everything. I could probably have a drink with her and listen to her talk about her life and whatever. Because she'd have to tell the truth now, right?

See, it's funny that you're saying that, because that's what I wanted to talk about this time.

I mean...how do I say this? That's what I need, too. Someone to talk to, who I can be real with and who can understand what I'm going through.

Yeah, good one. You're funny. No, you've never been a stripper. Or if you were, you never told me. Right? Yeah. Ha. No, this is different, because you're, like, a professional. You have to listen to me, just like I have to listen to the guys at my work and go along with what they're saying. It's your job. But I'm talking about someone who hangs out with me because they want to, not because I'm paying them.

Yeah, right. A friend. That's what I mean. Stupid, huh? I'm sitting here telling you I want to have friends, and I can't even think of the word for it.

Yeah, the girls at work are my friends, kind of. But...shit. I'm just going to come out and say it.

I miss hanging out with Natasha. You know? She was really cool, and I liked talking to her. She made me feel like...I don't know. Like I could be a better person, you know? A better mom. Somebody my kids will actually be happy to have for a mom someday.

What's that?

Shit. I don't know. That's a good question.

Shit. That's a hard question.

I don't know. Why *would* she want to be friends with me at this point? After all the drama she went through, just for knowing somebody like me? You're right. I'm just some asshole. People like her don't hang out with people like me.

What? Oh. I thought you were, like, being sarcastic, saying, "Why would *she* want to be friends with *you*?" But you're asking me seriously, for real.

Okay, but it's still a hard question. I don't know. Man.

You're like the teachers we used to have in school. The ones who wouldn't believe I was too stupid to do algebra. You're a tough old lady, you know that?

Ha. Yeah, you're right. I'm a tough young lady, too.

Hey, maybe that's something, right? I'm tough. Not in the ghetto way, but in the good way. Like, I work hard and survive through stuff. And I stand up for my friends, if they need me to. I have their backs, you know? What's the word for that—the right word?

Right. *Loyalty.* I'm a loyal friend to people when I care about them. That's all I can think of.

Hmm? Yeah, I make people laugh. That's true. Does that count? It does? Okay. I'm a loyal friend, and I have a good sense of humor. I know how to have a good time. What else? Um...I'm a good bartender? Good to have at parties?

Yeah, I don't know either.

Okay. You're right. I'm going to work on that. Yeah, I'll make a list and bring it next time. See, you are just like a teacher.

Seriously, though, Susan. I'm just going to come out and ask you. You still talk to Natasha. I know she comes to see you, because I saw her car here two weeks ago. Can you please just ask her for me?

You know. Ask her...if she wants to hang out with me again. To be my friend.

No, I know. But I can't be tough here. Look, I'm going to admit it: I'm scared.

No, because I got the new phone, remember? So if she has called, then I don't know about it.

Yeah. I still see her around, in the halls. She doesn't look so stressed out anymore. She looks happier.

No, she never sees me. I make sure she doesn't.

I don't know. What if I say hi but she just ignores me? Or I try to talk to her but she doesn't want to talk to me, so she tries to make some excuse, and then it's just embarrassing and I have to hide from her for real or move someplace else?

Yeah, I know. That is pretty immature. You're right.

Okay. Yeah, you're right. I just need to do it. I *am* going to do it. I'll call her tonight.

But come on, Susan. Help me out here. You've been talking to her. Does she ever say anything about wanting to hang out with me again? Would she even want to? Seriously. She's who she is, and I'm who I am. Yes, I'm loyal and tough and funny or whatever. But let's face it. I'm a stripper, and I'm not going to stop being a stripper, because I need the money. Having that money helps me take care of my kids better than I ever did before, and that's more important than what anybody thinks of me.

So what do *you* think? Am I just crazy here? I *am* a good person, right?

If you were her, would you be my friend?

Natasha

THE BEST PERK of becoming a paralegal, besides the money, of course, is moving from that desk in the middle of everything to a desk in the middle of my own cube. Now I can have personal phone conversations without worrying about everyone and his brother listening in.

Too bad it's mostly Mike I'm having the personal conversations with. But I simply pretend he's a client. It's easier that way.

"So this month your extra weekend with Alex will fall on Valentine's Day, and then next month we'll tack a few days onto the end of spring break," I tell him.

"That's right," he says.

"I'm putting that in the e-mail, then. You can just hit Reply to confirm, and then I'll add it to the calendar."

He says okay, and I hit Send on what I've already composed. The e-mails and shared calendar were the best idea Susan gave us. They don't totally save me from hearing Mike's annoying voice, but they do cut down on the arguing.

"You know," he says, "I've had to spend a lot of money on new furniture for the apartment, for the kids. Last week I got them their own TV. It's a thirty-two-inch, because they said the one you have for them is too small."

This is the kind of statement that Mike makes when he

wants to feel appreciated. And I don't have to let it upset me, even if he's hoping it will. I know that now. So I just say, "I'm sure the kids are enjoying it." I don't say that new TVs aren't my priority right now. I don't remark that he should have asked Missy for an extra TV when she threw him out. Because that's none of my business, and I have other things on which to focus. Susan taught me that.

I can't help but wonder sometimes if meeting Susan a year ago might have kept us from divorcing in the first place.

"Natasha? Did you hear me? I said maybe you should quit going on dates with strange men and spend more time teaching the kids to pick up after themselves."

But then I realize it would have been *even better* if I'd met her ten years ago and she'd kept me from marrying Mike in the first place. And then I'd use the time machine and the turkey baster to have Alex and Lucia on my own.

"I sent the e-mail, Mike. Good-bye."

But *then* I think that instead of wasting time fantasizing about what might have been, I should take what I've learned from Susan—about stress relief, about self-acceptance—and apply it to my life going forward. There's no use wanting to change the past. Besides, Alex does seem to be benefiting from the extra time with his dad, as much as it kills me to admit it. And I've been enjoying the extra time with Lucia, teaching her to play volleyball, teaching her to sew Mr. Beary's arm back in place herself.

It's five o'clock. Time to go home before Alex starts calling my cell, wondering what's taking me so long. Or maybe he's happy to have the extra hour to play his video games, before we have to pack them for the move.

"MOMMY, CAN WE go swimming tomorrow?" That's the first thing Lucia says when I come through the door.

"Remember we talked about this, baby? It's too cold to swim in February."

Undeterred, she follows up with, "Can we go to the new playground, then?"

I say, "Maybe. If we unpack everything before dark, I guess."

Alex looks up from his game and scoffs. "I'm not going to the playground until I unpack all my stuff and get my room set up just the way I like it."

I run a hand through his hair on the way to my bedroom. There, I take off my work shoes and put them into the box labeled MOM: CLOSET.

I look around the room, full of pyramids and towers of similarly labeled boxes. This is my last night in this bedroom. I didn't think I was going to miss living here, but I'm starting to feel little pangs in my chest. Seeing the apartment so bare reminds me of the day we moved in, and it feels like it was a million years ago.

The phone rings. It's Hector. I say, "Hey."

He says, "So are we still on for nine A.M. tomorrow?"

I say, "Yes. Nine A.M. sharp."

He says, "You know, Natasha, I'm glad we're actually dating now, because I really like you. But..."

"But what?" I can't believe he's starting a conversation about our relationship right now.

He says, "You do like me, too, right? I mean, you aren't just using me for my truck? And because of my upper-body strength?"

I say, "I don't know. Why don't you buy me dinner after I'm done moving, and then I'll decide."

He laughs. "All right. I'll see you tomorrow."

I LEFT MY BRIEFCASE in the Blazer. If I don't get it now, it'll be lost among all the moving boxes tomorrow and I won't be able to find it on Monday.

"You guys, I'll be right back. I have to run out to the car real fast."

They look up from their homework. "Okay," Lucia says.

In the parking garage, I watch a silver sedan pull in to a space two rows away. I haven't seen this car before. Is it a new neighbor or someone just visiting?

It's Sara. She got a new car. She climbs out of the driver's seat, and I wonder if I should turn away—pretend not to see her.

No. Why should I turn away?

We're leaving tomorrow. This is the last time I'll ever see her. Unless...

She looks up and sees me standing there. I don't turn away.

I smile. I wave. I walk in her direction.

Alex

MY BIG TOE'S been hurting. When I tell Mom, she'll probably say it's time for new shoes. This time I'm getting Wolverine. He's better than Venom. I've only read half the comic books that Dad gave me about him, but I already know he's my new favorite. I'll tell Dad today, when he picks me up, and we can go to the shoe store. Maybe we can get some cleats for soccer, too, like he's been saying.

I'm glad Dad doesn't live with Missy anymore. Not because I hated her and not because I'm a little baby who thinks Dad and Mom might get married again, like Lucia does. But Shepherd got on my nerves. He cried too much, and we couldn't get him to do tricks, like Baby Junior does.

It's almost time for recess. I can see third grade going past the windows. There's Angelica. I won't wave, but I'll nod my head like this. Okay, she saw me.

Oh, no. I drank too much juice at lunch.

"Alex, what are you doing? Sit down." Ms. Hubacek talks loud. Everybody turns to see me standing by my desk.

"I have to go to the bathroom," I say.

She says, "No, sir. You need to sit down and wait until recess."

But I'm not going to sit down and wait. I can't. "I'm sorry, Ms. Hubacek. I'll be right back."

When I get to the door, I hear Devonique go, "Ooh!" Some of the other kids laugh, but Ms. Hubacek doesn't say anything else.

Walking down the hall by myself makes me feel bigger. I guess it's because I've been growing.

Author's Note

When I write a book, I use music to create and maintain certain moods throughout the story. This story called for a playlist full of minor chords and melodies that alternated between melancholy and optimistic. These are the songs I played over and over while writing this book and that I'll associate with it from now on.

First Draft

1. Cut Copy: "Future"
2. Dabrye: *Two/Three Instrumentals*
3. Digitalism: "Pogo"
4. Menomena: "E. is Stable"
5. Morrissey: "Suedehead" and "Tomorrow"
6. Nick Drake: *Pink Moon*
7. Radiohead: "Weird Fishes/Arpeggi"
8. The Presets: "A New Sky"
9. The Smiths: "Hand in Glove" and "This Charming Man"
10. Tito Puente: "El Cayuco"
11. Vampire Weekend: "Cousins"
12. Yeah Yeah Yeahs: "Zero" and "Heads Will Roll"

Revision

1. Corinne Bailey Rae: "Trouble Sleeping"
2. Fred Everything: "Here I Am (featuring Lisa Shaw)"
3. Dwele: "A.N.G.E.L. (Reprise)"
4. Kaskade: "Move for Me (Kaskade Vs. Deadmau5)"
5. Little Dragon: "Scribbled Paper" and "Constant Surprises"
6. Revl9n: "Walking Machine"
7. Rod Stewart: "Every Picture Tells a Story"
8. Rye Rye: "Hardcore Girls"
9. Santana: "Transcendance"
10. Spoon: "Don't You Evah"
11. Thieves Like Us: "Desire"

Acknowledgments

Thanks to Jenny Bent, Selina McLemore, Kallie Shimek, and Maureen Sugden for making this book happen.

Thanks to Ashley MacLean and Little Bit MacLean for providing safe harbor while I wrote the first draft.

Thanks to Samantha Kelly, Carmen Abrego, Marina Tristan, and Ashley Hess for arranging my career around the writing of this book. Thanks to Inprint, Houston Arts Alliance, and Nuestra Palabra for supporting that career in general.

Thanks to Brie McCain and Tina Clayton for being the kind of readers every author wishes for. They show up at all my readings in Houston, they always bring friends, and they show my books to coworkers, relatives, and strangers on the street.

If it were legal to polygamously marry a team of library staff, I would book a caterer for my marriage to Jennifer Schwartz, Sandra Fernandez, Sarah Borders, and Allen Westrick. We'd do it buffet style, with hot wings, on the fourth floor of the downtown Houston Public Library. Then, after our wedding, I'd cheat on them with all the other librarians who worked with me this year.

Thanks most of all to Mr. Dat V. Lam for being the best spouse-of-an-author an author could ask for, and for helping maintain a household in which people are allowed/encouraged/obliged to do art.

Thanks to Jacob, Austin, and Luke for giving my life focus.

Thanks to Starbuck and Toby for keeping me company, without fail, while I wrote.

Reading Group Guide

1. In the book Natasha talks about feeling alienated from her friends after making the choice to become a young mother and again after making the choice to leave her husband. Is this something that commonly happens to women today? How do pregnancy and divorce affect friendships?

2. In the book Sara makes controversial career decisions based on her need for money. Did she make the right decision? She also criticizes Haley for leaving a financially attractive situation. How important is money when it comes to raising children? How much should parents sacrifice in order to secure the optimal amount of money?

3. How did you feel about Natasha, Haley, and Sara as the story went on? What were some of the mothers' strengths and weaknesses as parents? As friends? As women?

4. How would a judge, a social worker, or some other court official feel about these women? Would they

think that any of them deserve to have their children taken away?

5. What would Natasha, Haley, or Sara say are the pros and cons of being a single mother?

6. What does Geronima have to offer the young single mothers? What are/were her flaws as a mother?

7. How do the characters in this book differentiate themselves from their own mothers?

8. Alex frequently imagines himself as a superhero. How does this help him? Or does it? Does he impart any of these benefits to Angelica within their friendship?

9. What kind of people do you imagine the children of these single mothers will grow up to be? What will they learn from their mothers (or despite them)?

10. There is a motif of judgment in this story. What are some of the different ways in which mothers are judged?

About the Author

This is my third novel but my sixth book. Before this I wrote:

- *Lone Star Legend* (novel)
- *Houston, We Have a Problema* (novel)
- *Sunflowers* (kids' book)
- *Growing Up with Tamales* (other kids' book—this one won an award)
- *To the Last Man I Slept with and All the Jerks Just Like Him* (edgy small-press short-prose collection)

Actually, I've written way more than that, but those are the books I've managed to sell. Besides that I did a lot of writing for various websites back in the day. And, you know, I could tell you about all the rejected manuscripts and the poetry chapbooks and such, but let's leave a little for our next meeting, all right?

I was born in balmy inner-city Houston in 1971 and spent a couple of years at the University of Texas at Austin. After that I had a few kids, and then after that I started up with the book selling.

When I'm not writing books for you and hoping you're enjoying them, I'm hanging out with my kids and my husband or my cats. I also like to read books by other people, and sometimes I knit or make jewelry or play video games.

If you ever get curious and want to find out more about my life or see if/when I'm coming to your town, feel free to visit GwendolynZepeda.com, which is the latest incarnation of the website I've been writing since 1997.

Cheers.

Now available in print and as an e-book from Grand Central Publishing

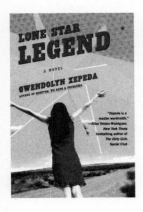

An aspiring young journalist stumbles across a story that gives new meaning to the word "legendary."

"Zepeda is a master wordsmith."
—Alisa Valdes-Rodriguez, *New York Times* bestselling author

"Fresh and smart"

—*Booklist*

A young woman is looking for advice in all the wrong places in this laugh-out-loud debut novel.

"Zepeda…presents a debut about the everyday struggle to find one's way but adds unusual and alluring touches, namely the vibrant Houston setting and the novel's emphasis on Tex-Mex culture, art, and folklore."

—*Booklist*

If you enjoyed *Better with You Here*, then you're sure to love these moving novels as well.

Now available from Grand Central Publishing in print and as e-books

A young man travels from California to Colombia in search of his birth mother.

"[A] poignant tale of truths hidden and laid bare."
—*Booklist* on *Tell Me Something True*

A professional woman's life is turned upside down when she receives an unlikely inheritance: three young children.

"Julia Amante understands the ties that bind all families regardless of culture and nationality."
—Jill Marie Landis, *New York Times* bestselling author

From the sunny shores of 1940s Puerto Rico to the snowy streets of 1950s Chicago, two young lovers wrestle with the marriage they've rushed into.

"A richly told tale of obsessive love… deeply sensual and mysterious."
—Cristina Garcia, award-winning author of *Dreaming in Cuban*

PUBLIC LIBRARY, SUMMIT, N.J.

JUL — 2012

SUMMIT FREE PUBLIC LIBRARY

3 9

FREE PUBLIC LIBRARY, SUMMIT, N.J.

JUL -- 2012